The Galilean Secret
by Evan Howard

"A very imaginative story that will touch the hearts of many, many readers."

—Joseph Girzone, author of *Joshua*

". . . a finely crafted novel with a message of hope."

—Harvey Cox, Harvard University and author of *The Future of Faith*

"*The Galilean Secret* offers an inspiring message that transcends religion."

—Deepak Chopra, author of *Jesus*

"[*The Galilean Secret*] will give you new eyes with which to read the old story!"

—Richard Rohr, author of *The Naked Now*

". . . a search for Jesus' deepest and as yet unrealized truth that will bring peace and love to all who can truly understand its worth."

—*Publishers Weekly*

"Thought-provoking and riveting . . . a tale of truth and treachery that will stay with you long after the final page is turned."

—**Jon Land, author of *The Seven Sins* and *Strong Enough to Die***

"Compelling reading! Evan Howard . . . takes the reader into profound areas of wisdom and healing regarding love and loving relationships."

—**Dr. Margaret Paul, author of *Do I Have To Give Up Me To Be Loved By You?***

"A narrative rooted in vivid characterizations of human longings and the perennial search for the sacred."

—**Janet Cooper Nelson, Brown University Chaplain**

TAKE BACK THE MORNING

EVAN HOWARD

Wilcox
Publishing Group

www.WilcoxPublishingGroup.com

Copyright © 2014 by Evan Howard

ISBN: 978-0-578-13532-8

WILCOX PUBLISHING GROUP
PAWTUCKET, RHODE ISLAND

www.WilcoxPublishingGroup.com
www.evanhowardauthor.com

All rights reserved. No part of this publication may be reproduced, stored in a retrieval system or transmitted, in any form, or by any means, electronic, mechanical, recorded, photocopied, or otherwise, without the prior written permission of both the copyright owner and the above publisher of this book, except by a reviewer who may quote brief passages in a review.

The scanning, uploading, and distribution of this book via the Internet or via any other means without the permission of the publisher is illegal and punishable by law. Please purchase only authorized electronic editions and do not participate in or encourage electronic piracy of copyrightable materials. Your support of the author's rights is appreciated.

This book is a work of fiction. Names, characters, places and incidents are products of the author's imagination. Any resemblance to actual events or persons, living or dead, is purely coincidental.

Cover photo credits: Face of woman, iStockphoto © Seprimoris; New York city, iStockphoto © inigofotografia; cloud images, iStockphoto © IgorKirillov, iStockphoto © Remedios, iStockphoto © silverjohn. Photo manipulation by RD Studio.

Book design by DesignforBooks.com

Printed in the United States of America

*To my wife, Carol,
and our sons, Evanjohn and Peter*

CONTENTS

1. The Graveyard Shift   1
2. A Haunted Man   9
3. A Fight for Survival   19
4. An Unsuspecting Wife   25
5. Where Am I?   33
6. The Mystery Deepens   43
7. The Shrewdest Deception   49
8. Confusion Overload   55
9. Another Answer Demanded   61
10. From Terror to Desperation   69
11. The Other Side of Darkness   75
12. An Apartment on Wayland   83
13. What Really Happened?   93
14. A Refuge or a Trap?   99
15. Into the Turmoil   109
16. The First Challenge of a Transformed Life: Accepted Acceptance   117
17. The Most Perplexing Maze   129
18. The Second Challenge: Healed Emotions   137
19. The Third Challenge: Awakened Intimacy   147

20. Into the Night   155
21. What to Do Next?   159
22. Desperate for Information   167
23. The Baby in the Balance   175
24. The Hardest Work of All   179
25. The Precipice of Risk   185
26. The Fourth Challenge: Reimagined Abundance   193
27. Following the Evidence   203
28. Checkpoint of Decision   213
29. The Galerie Van Gogh   219
30. Opening the Trunk   223
31. The Fifth Challenge: Liberated Service   229
32. At the Salisbury Hotel   237
33. An Encounter at the Museum   247
34. A Suspicious Delivery   253
35. The Secret Agent's Brother   259
36. Trying to Figure It All Out   267
37. The Sixth Challenge: Inspired Creativity   277
38. Breaking and Entering   285
39. What Does It Mean to Love?   293
40. An Excruciating Investigation   303
41. Terminal Memories   313
42. Another Subway Station   317
43. A Mansion in the Hamptons   327
44. The Long Ride Home   333
45. Chapel of Refuge   337
46. Countdown to Catastrophe   345

47. The Seventh Challenge: Transformed Faith 351
48. The Greatest Challenge 365
Questions for Group Study & Personal Reflection 379
Acknowledgments 383
About the Author 387
Share the Message 389

1

The Graveyard Shift

April 2, 1996
New York City
1:37 a.m.

The dreaded moment struck without warning.

It unfolded in slow motion as if in a dream. For forty-three-year-old Franklin Scott, the dream was a nightmare. Everything went silent, as it always had whenever the nightmare had disturbed his sleep during his twelve years as a subway motorman. This time the terror was real. The E train approached the well-lit World Trade Center stop as a man fell from the platform. Franklin grabbed the brake handle and slammed it forward. *No! Dear God, please, no!*

The man landed on the tracks. Franklin's heart leaped into his throat. For an instant, he observed the scene rather than experienced it. In less than a week, he would be wed. His glamorous bride, Katherine—with whom he'd shared several glasses of chardonnay before the graveyard shift—would meet him at the altar. He imagined kissing her and taking her arm before they faced the minister to recite their vows. He needed this job to support the marriage; he *had* to stop his four-hundred-ton train.

Help, God. Please help me! The sudden jolt from the brakes threw him against the windshield, twisting his wrist as he fought to keep hold of the handle. The train screeched beneath him. Sparks rained across the tracks. He clenched his jaw so tightly he nearly dislocated it. Passengers screamed. Loudspeakers buzzed. He feared the train would jackknife and careen off the tracks. Instead it shuddered as it hit the man.

The train ground to a stop.

This can't be happening. The words echoed in Franklin's mind. He righted himself and radioed the command center with the 12-9 code for "man under." He requested that the electricity to the third rail be shut off, that police and paramedics be rushed to the scene.

Ordinarily he would wait in the cab, but if the man died and Franklin failed a Breathalyzer test, he would go to jail. He couldn't stop shaking, and his heart felt as if it would rupture in his chest. He didn't know if he could save the man, but he had to try.

He made an announcement over the PA system to calm the few passengers on board. As soon as he received confirmation that the electricity was off, he climbed down onto the tracks with a flashlight.

He shined the beam under the first car, assaulted by the smell of grease and oil. Nothing.

He rushed to the second car and continued to search. Nothing.

Blood as red as the fire raging in his mind streaked the tracks in front of the third car. Halfway down, he found the motionless body of an athletic man lying on his stomach between the tracks. His head was gashed and bleeding, his white skin a contrast to Franklin's dark African-American complexion. Both of the man's arms and one of his legs appeared dislocated or broken and had been contorted in freakish directions. His navy blue blazer and gray wool slacks were disheveled and ripped.

The mangled body filled Franklin with terror and revulsion. He thought again of his upcoming wedding. Katherine was his passion, an unexpected gift after his disastrous first marriage. They'd survived a seven-year battle with his ex-wife for custody of his young son and daughter. The wedding was supposed to celebrate their long-awaited joy. Would it even happen now?

Franklin steeled himself against the panic in his stomach and climbed under the car. He knelt next to the man in the narrow, cube-like space. The stench of urine made him cough, scaring off a family of rats. The darkness molested him. His ragged breaths were his only defense against the tightening noose of claustrophobia. He fought dizziness and nausea as he groped for the man's wrist. There was no pulse.

He coughed out an anguished sob and released the wrist, his eyes a blur of tears. When he turned to leave, an object glinted in his flashlight's beam. Franklin dried his eyes on the shoulders of his MTA uniform then picked up the object. It was a badge. It had the head and wings of an eagle on top and a five-pointed star at the center. The lettering read *U.S. Secret Service*, and at the bottom were the words *Special Agent*.

The blood drained from his cheeks. Who was this man? How had he ended up crushed by a train? Franklin's chances of a happy future slipped away along with his dream of a joyful wedding and an exotic honeymoon. He was powerless to stop it. The glare of the beam against the badge stung his watery eyes. He cupped the badge in a sweaty palm and turned away.

"Scott? Franklin Scott?"

"Where are you, Scott?"

The shouts came from two voices, one husky and the other higher pitched, that echoed through the dark tunnel. Franklin crawled out from under the car. Two flashlight beams bounced toward him followed by at least a dozen more.

"Over here!" he called. "Beside the third car."

He trudged toward two NYPD cops. A contingent of paramedics carrying a stretcher, a body board, and first aid equipment caught up. They were soon joined by uniformed patrol officers from the MTA and plainclothes detectives in suits and overcoats.

The paramedics climbed under the train and confirmed that the man was dead. After the scene had been photographed, they loaded the body onto a stretcher and headed out of the tunnel. The transit authority officers relieved Franklin of duty, and a substitute motorman boarded the train. A cop and a detective led Franklin through a door in the tunnel wall, up some dirty cement stairs, and onto the E train's island platform.

"I'm Detective Joel Wilson." The man in plain clothes stuck out a hand. He was balding, clean-shaven, and, like Franklin, of medium build. "We're going to need a statement from you."

Franklin returned the firm handshake. The taller, dark-haired cop introduced himself as Sergeant Fernandez. He recorded Franklin's name and other essentials on a form attached to a clipboard. "Okay, now tell us exactly what happened," he said.

Franklin stepped to the far end of the platform where it met the tiled wall. He motioned with both hands. "My train was approaching when a body fell from right here."

"How far away was your car?"

"About a hundred feet."

Fernandez wrote on the clipboard. "What did you do?"

"Applied the brakes immediately."

"It was too late?"

"Yes." Franklin's throat tightened, but he forced himself to describe how he'd taken all the necessary safety precautions and had tried to help the man.

"Okay, that covers the basics." Fernandez eyed Wilson. "Do you have further questions?"

Wilson nodded. "Could you tell if the man fell or jumped?"

Franklin thought back to what he'd seen. He was tempted to say the man had jumped because then he wouldn't be blamed. Many of the ninety-odd subway deaths that happened each year were suicides, and the motormen weren't held responsible. But he couldn't be sure. "It happened so fast. I really can't say which it was."

"When you got out of your cab, did you see anyone on the platform?"

Franklin hesitated as he tried to remember. He'd been so focused on reaching the man he'd paid no attention to the platform. But the implications of the question sent his mind reeling. He didn't worry that there might have been witnesses but rather that the man might have been pushed. A murder would require a more complicated investigation than an accident or suicide . . . especially the murder of a federal agent.

Franklin couldn't be sure that the man hadn't been pushed, but the possibility of becoming entangled in an FBI investigation terrified him. He needed to *sound* sure.

"No," he said with conviction. "The platform was empty. It often is at this hour."

"You're absolutely sure?" Wilson narrowed his eyes as his gravelly voice modulated from intense to demanding.

Franklin tightened his grip on the badge until its edges dug into his skin. The man's body hadn't been completely vertical as it could have been if he'd jumped. Instead he'd leaned forward, perhaps even tried to keep himself upright, which could have been the case whether he'd fallen or been pushed.

Franklin gnawed his lip as he struggled with whether to show Wilson and Fernandez the badge. Beads of sweat broke out on his forehead and upper lip. Which course of action would be most likely to keep him out of trouble? They were going to find out who that guy was anyway, he reasoned. He might as well give them the badge. "I found this next to his body on the tracks."

Wilson examined the badge before showing it to Fernandez. "The Secret Service has an outpost in Seven World Trade Center. My guess is that this agent worked there. The suicide of a Secret Service agent would be a big story and bring shame to the entire organization. But the murder of an agent would be a federal crime. It could even be part of a larger plot against the President of the United States or other government officials."

He gave Franklin a withering glare. "Think hard. Are you *sure* no one else was on the platform?"

Franklin let the question simmer. He glanced at the white beams running across the ceiling and the gray steel pillars along the edge of the platform. One of the pillars held a sign that read *World Trade Center*, but the letters appeared blurry. He thought again of the chardonnay and knew he couldn't allow himself to take a Breathalyzer test. The horror of the accident looped through his mind—the shadowy movement of the man's body, the bucking of the train, the splattered blood and pulverized bones. He just wanted this situation to go away.

"Yes," he said sharply. "I'm sure the platform was deserted."

Even as he spoke, he knew he wasn't sure and never could be.

2

A HAUNTED MAN

WEDNESDAY, APRIL 30, 2003
8:06 A.M.

Justin Connelly's turmoil over whether to turn himself in churned faster than the waves on Block Island Sound. He clung to his seat under threatening skies as the twenty-four-foot sloop cut through the choppy seas off Newport, Rhode Island. He'd learned from his father never to trust the ocean, but he had confidence in sturdy, clear-eyed Ken Spalding, the New England sailing veteran at the helm. He also trusted Ken's girlfriend, Sharon Jenkins, an attractive, thirty-six-year-old brunette who'd crewed *Serendipity* on many previous outings.

But his adrenaline had been surging ever since they'd climbed on board. It happened whenever he was around good people. They activated his impulse to go to the police because he longed to be like these people, and he feared he couldn't be good again . . . unless he cleared his conscience.

Ken eyed him and steered toward Block Island ten miles away. "You must be bad luck. The weather was great until you got on board."

"As I recall, it was your idea to bring me along."

Sharon took a sip of her Sam Adams. "I'm surprised you asked him in the first place. He didn't have ancestors on the *Mayflower*. We New Englanders usually don't speak to such people, let alone invite them sailing."

She laughed, but her searching gaze sliced into Justin. He nervously fingered the keyring in the pocket of his jeans. The polo shirt, light jacket, and topsiders wore well on his frame, which was a bit taller than medium height and toned from regular visits to the gym. His fair complexion and sandy hair reflected his Irish heritage, but his large brown eyes appeared more Middle Eastern. Whenever people asked which ancestor he had to thank for such a distinctive trait, he pleaded ignorance then joked that the inheritance was fitting: the black sheep of the family had the darkest eyes.

Now, with Sharon's gaze seeming to probe for secrets he could never share, he found no humor in his flippant replies. The gusting wind chafed his face, so he decided to add a layer of sunscreen. When he withdrew the small plastic tube from his pocket, his keys fell onto the deck. The antique wooden pendant he carried on the ring caught Sharon's eye.

"Cool," she said. "Does it have some significance?"

"Yeah, it helps me keep track of my keys." He scooped up the reddish-brown pendant. "It brings me luck, like a rabbit's foot. I guess you could say I'm superstitious."

He stuffed the keys back into his pocket, determined not to show his anxiety about the four-inch-long oval engraved with peculiar images. He carried the pendant everywhere but at all costs avoided talking about how he'd come by it.

Sharon gave him a wry smile. "Don't you trust the captain and his first mate?"

Justin shook his head and applied the sunscreen. "I need all the luck I can get."

"That's what you'll say when baseball season heats up." Ken motioned for everyone to duck as he came about. "I usually don't let Yankee fans on my boat, but I made an exception for you. I wanted to give you a taste of *real* sailing, not the boring imitation you learned in New Jersey."

Justin cringed inside and his pulse quickened. He stuffed the sunscreen into his pocket, determined not to continue this line of conversation; it could only end in acrimony. Worse, it would force him to say too much about his past. What he'd done was wrong, and he couldn't talk about it . . . ever, to anyone. Even if he explained the extenuating circumstances, no one would empathize with him. Except maybe God. And ever since Justin's life had become an uninterrupted nightmare, God seemed totally absent . . . if he existed at all.

"Believe me," Justin said, hoping to sound convincing, "storms on the Jersey shore can get pretty fierce. And I've weathered quite a few. I sailed a lot through college, but I haven't been on a boat in several years. That's why I was looking forward to this outing."

The smell of salt reminded him of his youth. He'd never been in trouble and hated his deception, but he didn't have a choice. No one would forgive his treacheries. Going to the police would land him in prison. He couldn't turn himself in, yet he yearned to be delivered from his burden of guilt. Loneliness and fear were the cost of remaining free.

Eager to turn the conversation away from himself, he pointed at the iron-gray water. "The swells are really kicking up."

Ken handed Sharon the tiller then went below. When he returned, he held three yellow rain slickers and as many inflatable life vests. After donning a slicker and a vest, he retook the tiller and tossed the others to Justin and Sharon.

Justin adjusted his vest just as a wave hit the boat, dousing everyone. The cold water matched the temperature of his heart. He'd told Ken and Sharon his well-rehearsed story: that he'd grown up in New Jersey, lived most recently in Albany, and relocated to Providence to be close to the ocean and start his own accounting business.

When Sharon had commented that his athletic build and brown-eyed good looks made him a desirable bachelor, he hadn't protested. Most of what she believed about him was a lie, beginning with the name she and Ken knew him by— Rainer Ferguson, his Rhode Island alias.

Sharon straightened her slicker beneath her life vest and pointed back at the Point Judith Lighthouse. "It's always rougher on the open ocean, but don't worry. We've sailed to Block Island many times and never had a problem."

A gust of spray lashed his face. He hoped she was right, but the experiences of his youth told him differently. The ocean could lull overconfident sailors into complacency then attack with sudden, raging fury, especially on the moody Atlantic.

Sharon rolled her empty Sam Adams bottle between her hands. "I've been meaning to tell you about my friend Diane. She went through a divorce a couple years ago and hasn't found the right guy yet. Would you be interested in taking her out?"

He felt as if a drawstring had tightened around his stomach. From the time Ken and Sharon had befriended him at the

Eastside Athletic Club in Providence, he feared they would try to get too close. He'd told them very little about himself and kept their conversations focused on mutual interests such as their love of the ocean and working out. When Ken had invited him to sail from Newport to Block Island, Justin had accepted only reluctantly, out of loneliness and a desire not to appear rude. Now Sharon was treading on the minefield of his relationships with women. He needed to discourage her.

"Honestly," he said, "I've never had much luck with blind dates."

She put her empty bottle in the cooler as it started to rain. "How 'bout if I introduce you two in a less threatening way?"

His stomach tightened further, and he knew the angry sea wasn't causing the queasiness. Talking about women reminded him of his wife. Nostalgia gripped his chest as he remembered Tori and the life he'd known before all the trouble had started. If only he could have that life back . . .

His heart felt numb, as if it had stopped beating out of sheer exhaustion. Images of fun times with Tori flooded his mind followed by their last year of anguish.

"The four of us could go out to dinner," Ken said. "Or we could just get together for coffee."

Justin swallowed. He recommitted himself to keeping his real name, along with his past transgressions, secret. If Ken and Sharon knew why he'd moved to Rhode Island or the story behind the pendant, he doubted they would invite him sailing again, let alone arrange a blind date. Determined not to raise their suspicions, he said, "Tell me about your friend."

Sharon closed the cooler and smiled. "She's a bit shorter than you and has dark eyes and nice features. She teaches third grade and loves clam bakes, Rhode Island beaches, and the Red Sox."

As attractive as the woman sounded, the thought of dating her or anyone else sent shivers through him. Coming to Providence had been his opportunity to start over as a bachelor. Women had created upheaval in the past and were a major reason for his despair. The prospect of dating again was terrifying, but he couldn't let his true feelings slip.

"She sounds fun. Except she's a Red Sox fan and I was born in Yankee pinstripes. She'd never want to go out with me." He fingered his hood and hoped the darkening sky and thickening rain would save him from discussing the matter further.

"We're getting wet," he told Ken, "and I don't like the looks of those waves."

Ken warned him and Sharon to duck again then came about. "We should be okay. Remember, this is America's Cup territory. You've got to be ready for a little adventure."

When the Point Judith Lighthouse was no longer visible behind them, a thunderclap and several lightning flashes confirmed Justin's fear: adventure had turned to danger. The angry sky unleashed a torrential downpour, and the wind gusted viciously and churned up eight-foot waves. *Serendipity* leaned and swayed as she climbed each crest before slamming down the other side. The three of them were soon drenched. The howling wind made it hard for them to communicate.

"This is more adventure than I bargained for!" His voice went hoarse as he yelled.

Sharon wiped a dripping strand of hair from her eyes. "Shouldn't we turn back?"

Ken used his body to hold the tiller straight and cupped his hands to his mouth. "It's too dangerous to come about. Besides, if we run—" A torrent of rain cut him off. He wiped at his face and yelled louder. "We'll be in the storm longer and could get rolled from behind. We need to take down the sails and ride it out."

The sloop heeled dangerously as Justin crept toward the bow. He helped Sharon untie the halyard that secured the jib and fought to keep his balance above the raging, frothy sea. The wind clawed and bit at him with the singular goal of sweeping him overboard. But they finally won the battle to lower the jib and crawled back toward the mast.

Although secured by the mainsheet, the boom shook and swung on a three-foot path, as much as the sheet would allow. It threatened to knock out anyone who crossed its path. Sharon yanked on the sheet to secure the boom just as a ten-foot wave washed over the boat. Justin clung to the mast with one hand and grabbed her with the other. A massive wall of water pummeled them. Only through the full exertion of his strength was he able to keep them from being swept overboard. He wiped water out of his eyes and let down the mainsail as Sharon steadied the boom.

"Hold on while we lie ahull!" Ken fought to stabilize the boat. He started the outboard engine and began to steer *Serendipity* parallel to the waves. Another wave washed over the boat, and water cascaded across the deck.

Terror paralyzed Justin. For the second time in his life, he thought he was going to die. The white heat of shame seared his cheeks as he remembered the first time. His mind flashed images of the people he'd hurt. *Never again*, he told himself.

"Call in a mayday!" Ken's booming order sent him careening toward the hatch.

"Where's the radio?"

"On the shelf toward the bow, on the port side."

Justin shoved the hatch open against the vicious wind. He lurched down the stairs, ducked into the cramped cabin, and groped in the dark. His fingers ran over blankets, seat cushions, life vests, and buoys. The sloop pitched viciously and slammed him against the sink on the starboard side. He bit his tongue and tasted blood.

Another wave smashed his head against the fiberglass shelves on the port side. He began to lose consciousness and collapsed onto the deck. The water that had seeped in kept him from passing out. An intense longing swept over him in the wet and dark and cold, a sensation more powerful than anything he'd ever felt. He longed for harbor . . . Newport, Block Island, Point Judith, it didn't matter which.

Even more, he longed for the harbor of a woman's arms, the woman he doubted he would ever see again—his wife, Tori. But she was farther from him than ever. Far away and forever gone. An image of her lovely face appeared in his mind. He lifted his head. Then he saw a faint red dot of light on the shelf toward the bow.

The radio.

He stood, careened across the slippery deck, and ran a hand over the instruments on the shelf. Where were the receiver and the on switch? He had to find them fast and locate channel sixteen, the one used for emergencies. They were running out of time.

His fingers stumbled onto a coiled cord. He followed it up to the mike, switched on the receiver, found channel sixteen, and yelled, "Mayday! Mayday! We're three miles south of Point Judith and taking on water. Mayday! Mayday!"

3

A Fight for Survival

Waves thrashed *Serendipity's* hull, rain pelted her deck, booms of thunder reverberated through her frame. The dank, salty air in the cabin carried the stench of death. Justin's head throbbed from having hit the shelves. His ears ached from the changes in air pressure. His legs shook from the strain of holding himself upright.

He dropped the microphone and considered staying below. Staggering guilt and debilitating shame had stalked him ever since he'd run away. Going down with the ship would be an honorable way to die.

Before he could embrace the idea, a chill colder than the water penetrated his spine, making him stiffen. The thought of his life coming to such a dismal end wracked his heart with regret. He couldn't let it happen. Not as long as he could still think and breathe. Not as long as Ken and Sharon needed his help.

The rampaging sloop threw him toward the bow. Fighting to keep his balance, he reached beside the receiver and grabbed the brick-shaped Emergency Position Indicating Radio Beacon. He activated the EPIRB to signal the location of the boat then staggered toward the stairs.

Sharon yelled something that was drowned out by the clang of the rigging, the screech of the wind, the roar of the surf. Her intensity reminded him of how Tori had yelled at him on their last morning together. Now he realized he'd deserved her rage. He'd never known a more intelligent, fun, caring, or gorgeous woman.

Nor had he ever experienced greater oneness than they'd shared in the early years of their marriage. A gust of yearning more powerful than the shrieking wind blew through him. If only he'd appreciated the treasure he'd had in her, he would have guarded their love more vigilantly.

He dragged himself up the stairs then battled through the hatch and closed it behind him, buffeted by wind and spray. The rain, driven horizontally, stung his face. Lightning flashed from cloud to cloud and struck the water in the distance. The cooler broke loose and flew overboard. Sharon clung to the lifeline that ringed the boat and vomited into the sea. Justin turned away and swallowed to keep from doing the same.

His eyes found Ken's. "How can I help?"

Ken motioned for him to sit down. "Stay low, Rainer. Keep your weight balanced against Sharon's."

One eight-foot wave after another crashed over the sloop. Ken strained at the handle of the outboard motor to keep the boat from pitching out of control. Justin had doubted whether lying ahull—taking the sails down and propelling *Serendipity* parallel to the waves—would work given the storm's severity. He also doubted that challenging the mountainous waves head-on or trying to outrun the weather would have worked either.

Just then the sloop stopped. A wave hit the bow and spun it to starboard. Another hit the stern and spun it back to port. Ken gave the engine full throttle.

No response.

He yanked on the starter cord.

Nothing.

He yanked again.

A sputter of smoke.

Justin offered to help, but Ken waved him away and yanked several more times. The engine remained dead. He swore and pounded a fist on the throttle.

With no engine pushing the boat forward, it was at the mercy of the churning currents, the relentless wind, the towering waves. *Serendipity* pitched wildly first in one direction then the other.

Justin prayed that the Coast Guard had heard his distress call. The thought was still in his mind when a wave larger than any he'd ever seen, at least twelve feet tall, broke and crashed against *Serendipity's* port side.

He had no time to think or move. He braced himself against the wave but could do nothing to lessen its crushing impact. His body somersaulted backward into the sea.

He went down and down, propelled by the power of the wave and the weight of his slicker and wet clothes and shoes. Water swirled in his nose. Pressure built in his ears. He felt smothered, lightheaded. Submerged in inky darkness, he fought the temptation to panic. He slipped off his topsiders and pulled the cord that inflated his life vest.

The buoyancy pulled him upward. Desperate for air, he kicked and stroked. He broke the surface, drew a breath, and got a mouthful of water from a surging wave. He spit and coughed, searching for Ken and Sharon. The capsized sloop bobbed on its side, its hull half submerged. Ken swam toward it. Since Justin had closed the hatch, he was confident the boat wouldn't sink and followed Ken's lead.

Then he saw Sharon. She was motionless with her face in the water. A wave between him and the boat crested and broke over her. He swam through another breaking wave, grabbed her hair from behind, and lifted her face out of the water. She was bleeding from a gash on her forehead. She appeared pale and wasn't breathing. He placed one hand on her stomach while supporting her back with the other and pushed.

She vomited seawater and remained motionless. He kicked to elevate himself and rehearsed the skills he'd learned while working as a lifeguard. He breathed into her mouth. She vomited again. He kept kicking and administered as much mouth-to-mouth resuscitation as he could manage. His legs and arms felt as if they were filled with concrete. Still she didn't breathe. Terror stabbed at his heart. "Please breathe. I won't let you die!"

Only the howling wind heard his lament. He kept giving her mouth-to-mouth on the trough side of each wave, fighting to keep her afloat. Her body was limp. He couldn't let her die. He gulped the salty air and breathed into her lungs. Finally her arms moved. She belched and wretched and opened her eyes.

"Oh God . . . oh God . . ." Her eyes went wide when she recognized him. "What happened? Please help me. Please . . ."

"I will. I promise. You'll be all right." He wrapped an arm around her chest and scissor-kicked toward *Serendipity* with his head half in the water. The sloop drifted aimlessly two boat-lengths away. The waves clawed at him, and the wind whipped water into his eyes and mouth, but finally he reached the bobbing hull.

Ken had climbed onto the keel and was splayed across the hull gripping the edge of the deck. Justin grabbed the keel, which was still partially submerged. He held the keel and kicked to push Sharon up as Ken hoisted her from above. His legs cramped. His arms were leaden. Sharon let out a gasp as he shoved her onto the hull.

"You've got to stay with the boat!" he yelled above the screeching wind. "It's your only hope."

She nodded weakly and struggled to hold on. Just as Ken maneuvered her onto the hull, Justin heard a squawking, whirling noise. He glimpsed the lights of a Coast Guard helicopter. A wave hit him from behind and smacked his head against the keel. A murky haze descended. He opened his mouth and water poured into his lungs.

He began to sink. His head ached as if it had been crushed in a vice. The last sound he heard was the whirring cacophony of helicopter rotors above the shrieking wind. He strained to kick, but cramps gnarled his legs. He felt himself sinking deeper and blacking out.

No more light.

No more strength.

Must have air . . . now! . . . Can't wait any longer . . .

His lungs spasmed and inhaled more water. *Help me, God! Please help me! Please . . .*

He tried to scream but couldn't. He was drowning . . . too long without air . . . too pummeled by the waves to save himself.

A massive steel door opened in front of him. Suction pulled his spiritual essence out of his convulsing body. He didn't want to leave. He fought the relentless force but soon grew exhausted. A deafening *whoosh* pierced his ears as his soul left his lifeless body and flew through the door.

Terror ripped through his gut. *Where am I? What's happening to me?* He thrashed and kicked but couldn't stop flying. He remained aware but inhabited a new spiritual body, translucent in essence. Darkness enveloped him. He lost all sense of where he was until he splashed into a frigid, raging river. Foaming rapids swept him along in powerful currents. He stole frantic breaths as he bobbed and swirled downstream. "Help me! Please, anyone . . . help!"

4

An Unsuspecting Wife

Staten Island, New York
Wednesday, April 30, 2003
10:07 a.m.

Tori Connelly should have known better than to discuss men with her mother. On a brisk, overcast morning she had taken her one-year-old son, Justin Jr., and her mom on an invigorating walk along the tidal flats in Great Kills Park. Back at the car, when Tori couldn't escape, her mother asked, "How serious are you about Paul Spardello?"

"I've been seeing a lot of him. Let's just leave it at that." She started the Chevy Impala, eager to stop at the bank then get ready for work.

Her mother ran a brush through her shoulder-length salt-and-pepper hair. "I'm just trying to be supportive."

Tori yanked the wheel as she merged into the light traffic on Buffalo Avenue. "You need to give Paul and me time to decide what's best for us."

She checked her rearview mirror and noticed a lime green motorcycle following closely. Her breath caught in her throat. She told herself to calm down, that the driver in the black modular helmet was just in a hurry.

"You didn't answer my question," her mother said.

Out of the corner of her eye, Tori noticed her mom's furrowed brow. From childhood on, people had told her she was her mother's mirror image—wide-set chocolaty eyes, a pleasing but slightly angular nose, full lips, and a bright smile. Nowadays her mother looked more stern than attractive. Tori pressed on the accelerator and gained speed as a light rain began to fall. "He asked me to marry him."

"I hope you said yes."

"I said I needed time to think about it."

"Whatever for?" Her mother's exasperation rang through every word.

"His divorce isn't final yet. I can't make any decisions until that happens. Besides, Sadie can be a handful. I'm not sure I'm ready for the whole stepmom routine."

Tori checked the rearview mirror again. The motorcycle was gone. She drove through the intersection of Nelson Avenue and Amboy Road at a steady speed.

"It's not just that . . ." Her neck stiffened, but she forced herself to go on. "Sometimes the relationship feels . . . I don't know, painful. I catch myself wishing he hadn't been Justin's best friend. Being reminded of Justin makes me sad."

"I would think Paul could understand those feelings better than anyone."

The rain had turned to drizzle. A memory of Justin's tousle-haired good looks and seductive smile gnawed at her. A hollowed-out ache staggered her heart, as it always did when she thought of him. Their four-year marriage seemed like a blur—a fairy-tale romance that had fizzled into mutual despair in the last year as he'd grown critical, irritable, withdrawn.

She adjusted the rearview mirror so she could see the baby in the backseat then looked away when her eyes misted.

"Wouldn't Justin want you to be happy?" Her mother tossed the brush into her purse and snapped the top shut. "Who would he rather have you marry, anyway?"

"Like I said, it can be a double-edged sword."

"You'll never find a better man. I worry about you and the baby being alone. The stories you cover can be dangerous."

"Give me credit for going back to work, for starting to date again. Coming this far with Paul feels like a real accomplishment."

"Then say yes. There aren't many men like him. If you let him get away, you'll regret it the rest of your life."

Tori met her searching eyes. "I love Paul, I really do. But the relationship is different from my marriage. I had so much passion for Justin. With Paul, I feel admiration and respect."

"There's nothing wrong with that. Passion fades."

Her mother's practical bent was exasperating. Relationships were complicated. They often defied logic. "If Justin had died in some other way, maybe it would be easier to get over him. As it is, he still has a big piece of my heart."

Her mother looked out the window. Finally she said, "I just don't want you to miss an opportunity you may never get again."

She had a point. Tori loved Paul, just not with the overwhelming, weak-at-the-knees feeling Justin had evoked. Perhaps common interests and shared goals would make a better foundation for marriage. It was all too much to think about.

The rain had stopped. She avoided eye contact with her mom and switched on the radio. A male newscaster said,

"There was high drama on the stormy seas off Rhode Island this morning. A man by the name of Rainer Ferguson saved his friend's life during a sailing accident and is now in a coma after nearly drowning. Authorities have been unable to locate Mr. Ferguson's next of kin, but his friends say he has New Jersey roots."

Interesting story, Tori thought. Maybe she'd ask her editor at *The New York Herald* if she could investigate it further. The story made her think of the times Justin had taken her sailing off Staten Island. She'd loved the sun and the surf and picnicking with him at the tiller, his hair windblown, his face tan. The first time they'd made love on the boat came back to her . . . the smell of sunscreen, the lap of the waves against the hull, the glimmer of the stars out the cabin window. The mystical aura of the night had turned their sighs into music, their kisses into fine wine. Her heart yearned for that kind of romance again.

She glanced into the rearview mirror and saw the motorcycle.

Her spine went rigid.

She slowed in the hope that the broad-shouldered driver would grow frustrated and pass them. But when she braked, so did he.

"Don't turn around, Mama. I think we're being followed."

"How do you know?"

"The same motorcycle was behind us after we left the park. The driver turned off, so I thought nothing of it. Now he's back."

The baby started to cry as her mother's face grew pale. They were only half a mile from the Patriot Savings Bank on

Richmond Avenue. She decided to keep driving. If the sleek motorcycle was still tailing them when they arrived at the bank, she would continue on to the police station.

As she approached the building, she slowed again. This time the driver swerved and sped past. She couldn't see his face because the helmet's shield was tinted, but she caught a glimpse of the insignia on the motorcycle—Kawasaki ZX-12R.

Her mother turned to calm the baby and let out an audible sigh. "If you're being followed, it's probably because of some investigation you're involved in. What is it this time?"

"You know I can't discuss it."

"If you're going to put me in danger, I deserve to know."

Tori settled back into her seat. "Let's not overreact. I'm being selective about my assignments. Reporting is a calling. I have to do it."

She parked in the long rectangular lot behind the bank and turned off the engine. She grabbed her leather purse, threw the strap over a shoulder, and hurried alongside the building toward the front entrance. The ATM was in the foyer. Through the glass doors that led into the lobby, she noticed a brawny, redheaded security guard keeping watch inside. She endorsed her check, sealed it into an envelope, and made her deposit as other customers came and went.

Everything appeared normal with the usual bustle and rising energy of a spring morning in Staten Island. It was still windy and overcast. She hurried out the door, eager to get home and change before catching the ferry to Manhattan. She rounded the corner and rummaged in her purse. When she found the car keys, she looked up, and her knees went weak.

The lime green motorcycle was parked on the street.

Before she could move, the driver came around the back of the bank still wearing his helmet. He lunged and snatched her purse. A flash of terror numbed her arms and legs. The purse and the keys flew out of her hands, but the strap caught her wrist. She latched on and pulled against the man's strength.

"Give me the pendant!" He swore in a guttural voice.

"What are you talking about?"

She fought him, determined to keep her purse. It contained her most cherished keepsake, the engraved locket Justin had given her on their first wedding anniversary. She tightened her grip, but the man shoved her. Her arm hit the pavement, and a jolt of pain shot through it. He yanked the purse loose and dashed for the Kawasaki. The roar of the engine pierced her ears and was followed by the squeal of tires. She grew disoriented and struggled to stand. By the time she did, the man had sped away.

"Are you all right?" The brawny security guard sprinted from the front of the bank.

She picked up her keys and inhaled to steady her voice. "I'm okay, but my purse is gone."

"I saw the guy flee. I'm calling 911." The guard withdrew a cell phone from the pocket of his slacks.

Her mother came running. "What happened?"

"The driver of the motorcycle snatched my purse." Tori gasped as emotion gathered in her throat over the lost locket.

Her mother hugged her. "Who is this guy? Why would he pick you?"

"I wish I knew."

Tori felt as if the ground were buckling beneath her. She pulled away, bent over, sucked in air. She dredged her memory for any investigation she'd conducted that involved a pendant. Nothing surfaced. The assailant's demand had been bizarre. She hadn't written about a pendant, didn't even own one that was worth anything except in sentimental value. A siren wailed in the distance. Not since the day Justin had died had she felt so vulnerable.

"May I use your phone?" she asked the guard.

Her mother squeezed her arm. "Who are you calling?"

"Paul."

Tori punched in his number.

5

WHERE AM I?

*J*ustin felt ready to vomit and couldn't grasp what was happening. He fought the rapids, writhing and flaying. "Oh God, oh God, save me!" He gulped breaths between cries. His chest spasmed with terror. "Someone please help me!" The roaring, churning rapids drowned him out. He vaguely remembered slamming his head on the keel of the sailboat, swallowing too much water, being pulled through a massive door.

His body was different now. His head still throbbed, and he felt the frigid coldness of the river that swept him along, but his flesh and bones had been transformed into a mysterious translucent substance. *Is this some kind of dream? When will I wake up? How can I get back home?* His confusion dizzied him. He didn't know where he was, how he'd gotten there, how much longer he could survive. Exhausted, he surrendered to the current. It forced him down and sent him somersaulting beneath the rapids as if he were a ragdoll.

He swallowed water and began to choke. He was suffocating . . . trying to breathe . . . growing increasingly claustrophobic. He was sure he was drowning, but instead of dying, he descended deeper and deeper into panic. The descent continued into what felt like madness, utter insanity. Just as his soul began to implode into itself, an eruption from below catapulted him up. He broke the surface retching and vomiting.

The current slowed enough for him to gasp for breath. He coughed and spit as he managed to swim to shore and climb out. He collapsed on the sandy bank and fought to catch his breath in the searing cold. Panic wrenched his gut as his eyes failed to adjust to the thick darkness. He felt as if he were blind. A tide of loneliness more desperate than any he'd ever known washed through him—loneliness for friendship, for love.

For Tori.

The feeling was like the gnawing, grinding alienation he'd known during moments of despair, but its intensity kept increasing, as if his heart were drifting farther and farther from human contact.

All his memories of love and relationship vanished. He longed to weep but couldn't. *Why do I feel so unbearably sad? Why does the sadness keep getting worse?* The longing and confusion filled his chest with mounting pressure. His heart felt as if it had been crushed. The ache spread and intensified as the darkness mauled him. The anguish made him shriek in terror. He shrieked and shrieked until his ears hurt and his throat grew hoarse, but no one heard.

The air had grown so cold it felt torrid. The hot coldness burned through him like a chemical fire. He gagged on the rancid, sulfur-like stench. Desperate for relief, he ran down a grassy ridge and along a dirt path until he came to a cavern wider and longer than the sea.

His mouth went dry and his eyes stung. Multitudes of translucent bodies like his were trapped inside the cavern.

Their weeping and shrieking pierced his ears. As they tried to crawl out, they fought each other, but the cliffs were too steep and high. No one could escape.

Where am I? Who are these beings? How can I get out of this place? The questions assaulted him like rapid gunfire. Paralyzing dread settled in as he pondered the unthinkable: could this be hell? He stepped back from the rim, horrified by the scene while also mesmerized by it.

He wanted to follow the river upstream back to *Serendipity*, but an enormous birdlike creature with six feathered wings blocked his way. The creature was radiant. Light shone through its body, giving it an ethereal aura.

"You cannot go back that way," the creature said in a deep, resonant voice.

Justin stepped to the right as terror drove him forward. "You can't stop me."

The creature extended a wing and knocked him down. "I already have."

He got up and tried to shove the creature aside. "Who are you?"

"I am a messenger sent to you from the Holy One who speaks on the sacred mountain. It lies on the forbidden side beyond the dark forest at the northern boundary of this place. Only those who trust in him and his message gain their freedom."

"I don't care about any sacred mountain. I just want out of this place."

Beyond and above the river, he could see the ocean and the storm off Block Island. A Coast Guard diver entered the water and lifted Justin's lifeless body into a rescue basket. The basket rose into the fuselage as the helicopter flew toward the mainland.

The creature held his shoulders. "I know you want to go back. Everyone who comes here does."

Justin struggled to break free. "Where am I?"

"This is the cavern of eternal—"

A cry from inside the cavern drowned out the messenger's voice. "Food . . . food . . . please!"

Another cry shriller than the last arose. "First bring me water! I'm thirsty."

Justin stopped struggling. "Can't anyone bring them food or water?"

"Plenty of both are available," the messenger said as it relaxed its wings, "but the souls are starving and thirsty because they refuse to share. They also suffer from the unbearable loneliness you feel. Even surrounded by other souls, they're incapable of love. They care only about themselves, which makes their loneliness torturous and inescapable. Do you recognize anyone?"

Justin stared at the multitudes. "How can I? They have no faces."

The creature pointed at a group huddled on a wide ledge halfway up the cavern wall. Their charred bodies broiled in flames as dozens of naked women danced around them. "Do you see that group on the ledge?"

"Yes."

"They were the hijackers of September 11th, 2001. They murdered their victims with fire and now suffer the consequences. The glamorous women are the seventy-two virgins for whom they lusted. The men's burning desire will never be satisfied. Their fate could be yours if you don't learn from your misdeeds and make amends."

Justin broke away and climbed onto the dirt path that led to the river. "I've seen enough. I have to get out of this place."

"You can't. Your hurtful actions along with your ignorance have condemned you to be here. The only way out is to receive forgiveness and a second chance from the Holy One. Only you can decide if you are ready to seek him."

Above the roar of the rapids, Justin heard what sounded like the yelping of dogs. "What's that?"

"The three-headed dogs lead the demons of death. The dogs follow the scent of lust, greed, vengeance, guilt . . . of all destructive thoughts. The only way to escape is to think about purity, truth, beauty, love, or other noble qualities. Focus on the ways you helped people during your time on earth. If you fail, the demons of death will cast you into the cavern of despair. Those souls have rejected the love of the Holy One. Your only hope is to let his love transform you."

The yelping grew closer. "Please just let me go home."

"I am not allowed to do that. Only the Holy One can set the captives free."

"What must I do?" Justin left the path and ran into the dark forest that lay beside it.

The creature kept pace with him. "The forbidden side lies beyond this forest. You must pass through the forest and come to the gate that leads to the sacred mountain. The keeper of the gate will determine whether you are worthy to enter."

"How can I be worthy?"

"The deepest desire of your heart must be to love and be loved by the Holy One." The creature stopped him with a wing. "Go due north and do not stop until you reach the gate. Your pendant holds the secret to your survival. In the past, you doubted its power, but you were wrong. The power can be used for tremendous good or horrific evil."

Justin shoved his hand into his pocket and fingered the engravings. Candace had believed that the pendant possessed special powers, but he'd always mocked the idea. He saw the pendant as nothing more than her good luck charm—one that he'd kept to remind him of his terrible indiscretions and his commitment to build a new life. He hadn't tried to use the pendant's powers because to him the idea that it had any was ludicrous. "Do you really expect me to believe that?"

"If you don't believe it, you'll be at the mercy of the dogs. The demons want the pendant so they can enslave and torture the souls here. As long as you point it at them while thinking noble thoughts, they cower in its presence. If they catch you, the pendant is your only hope of escaping. Do you promise to follow these instructions?"

"As you said, I have no other choice."

Justin fled into the dark forest as the yelping grew louder. He imagined dozens of long, salivating tongues and nail-sharp teeth yearning to seize him and drag him back to the cavern of despair.

He wove through thickets of towering pines and cedars. The underbrush rustled and popped beneath his bare feet. The thighs and calves of his mysterious translucent body burned, his lungs pled for air, his heart begged for rest.

When he heard rushing water, he headed toward the sound. If he waded through the river, he could throw the dogs off his scent and possibly outrun them. The yelping was no more than a quarter mile behind him as he reached the river. He waded up to his waist in the icy water and began to swim. The current was swift, but he kicked and stroked until he reached the opposite bank fifty yards away. Climbing up, he caught his breath then kept running north. Gratitude for the opportunity to reach the mountain filled his thoughts. He no longer heard the dogs.

After a mile of hard running, he approached a wide bend in the river where the water grew peaceful. He paused to rest and stared at the glassy surface. To his surprise, he saw not only his own reflection but that of a exquisitely sculpted feminine face. He turned and nearly stumbled into a voluptuous woman. She had full rosy lips, long white hair, and eyes the color of sapphires. "Who are you?" he asked.

"I am the woman who inhabits men's dreams. Come, swim with me."

She took off her long white dress. Justin stood slack-jawed as she dove naked into the river. A powerful surge of desire swept through him weakening his knees. His first impulse was to dive in after her, but before he could move, he remembered the messenger's warning. Lustful thoughts would draw the dogs. He focused his attention on the sacred mountain.

"I have to go."

After a few steps, he almost collided with a tall, rawboned man who ran out of the forest. The naked man stood on the bank gazing at the woman. "I've been following you. May I join you?"

The woman waved for him to come closer. He dove in. Justin quickened his pace, and when he approached the tree line, he glanced back. The man embraced the woman, but when his lips met hers, his body melted and disappeared into a mist. Astonished, Justin went back.

"What happened to him?"

The woman smiled and swam toward the riverbank. "I'm a Spirit woman assigned to see which men are more possessed by lust than by yearning for the Holy One. That man has been transported to the cavern of eternal despair."

A tremor of relief passed through him as he realized how close he'd come to destruction. He headed north at a steady pace as the air grew now frigid, now sizzling hot. The sacred mountain was several miles away. He studied its majestic slopes and pondered his desire to see and hear the Holy One.

He barely noticed a pile of leaves in his path. As he barged through, his foot hit something solid like a tree trunk. He tripped and landed hard on the ground. Pain radiated up his leg.

A deep voice said, "Watch where you're going, you clumsy fool!"

A hunchbacked man with broad shoulders and a round, pockmarked face charged him. Justin sprang to his feet and braced to fight the gnarled, hulking creature.

"Hold on! I didn't see you lying there."

"That's 'cause you weren't watching, you miserable wretch."

The hunchback threw a punch then followed with two more. One of the punches landed on Justin's chest, knocking him down. He leaped up and assumed a boxer's stance as a surge of anger welled up in his gut. "All right. If you want a fight, you've got one."

The hunchback stepped back and laughed. "I knew you'd lose your temper and want revenge. Now you've signaled your location to the dogs. I won't have to punish you for disturbing the peace of the forest. They'll do it for me."

"Who are you?"

"Who wants to know?"

"Justin Connelly. I'm trying to make it to the sacred mountain."

"You can't go there. It's on the forbidden side. But there's no chance of your gettin' there anyway. The dogs'll smell your vengeful thoughts and track you down like a wounded rabbit." He let out a belly laugh. "What a fool!"

Justin took off running, cut back to the river, and followed it toward the mountain. He sloshed through the swampy shallows to throw the dogs off his scent. Meditating on his efforts to rescue Sharon Jenkins turned his thoughts away from his former life and his scathing guilt. He ran for more than two miles with the swampy odor clinging to him. When he caught a glimpse of what lay ahead, he stopped in stunned disbelief.

6

THE MYSTERY DEEPENS

MANHATTAN, NEW YORK
WEDNESDAY, APRIL 30, 2003
12:16 P.M.

Tori headed for her editor's glassed-in office. The clusters of desks and snarls of computer screens in the newsroom of *The New York Herald* made the auditorium-like space a challenging obstacle course. A shiver ran through her whenever she thought of having her purse snatched. Thankfully Paul had come through for her again when she'd needed comfort. He offered her stability and companionship, but the question of whether these were enough to sustain a marriage gnawed at her. The closer she got to her meeting with Grant Richards, the colder the shiver grew until it matched the air outside. She wished she'd worn something heavier than her double-knit gray slacks and black sweater.

The images flashing on the enormous flat-screen TV at the front of the room drew her attention. A fine-boned anchorwoman with long auburn hair reported a new Middle East peace initiative called the Roadmap. Tori kept going through the bustle of activity. She'd entered the newsroom hoping its familiar coffee smells and harried chatter would help her regain her equilibrium. Now that she was here, she needed something more. Only her boss could provide it.

She found his office empty and glanced around. Her gaze darted to a neatly coiffed sportscaster on the TV who was reading the baseball scores: the Red Sox had beaten the Yankees at Fenway. Then a slender man with the worst comb-over in Manhattan besides that of former mayor Rudy Guliani emerged from another office. Grant Richards approached holding a rolled up newspaper.

"You wanted to see me?" he asked.

"Yes. Something has come up."

She followed him into his cramped office and sat in the wooden chair across from his metal desk. He pointed the remote at the TV and lowered the volume. "I also have something to discuss with you, but go ahead."

She drew a quick breath. "My purse was snatched this morning."

"What!" He came around the desk, his thin face draped with concern. "Where?"

"In the parking lot of the Patriot Savings Bank a few blocks from my house."

"Are you all right?"

"I am now, but it gave me quite a scare."

He leaned against the desk and hugged the newspaper. "What happened?"

She told him about the guy on the motorcycle, about her attempt to save her purse.

"You fought him?" Grant sounded incredulous. "Not a good idea. Did you get his plate number?"

"Everything happened too fast." The memory of the man slamming her down brought back the chills. She rubbed her arms. "All I could tell the police was the make of the motorcycle, and that the guy had the trim, muscular physique of an athlete." She locked eyes with Grant. "But here's what's really strange. He was sure I had a pendant of some kind in my purse."

"A pendant?" He sat on the edge of the desk. "What's that about?"

"I'm mystified. That's why I had to talk with you. I'd like some time to investigate the incident."

"Why? You reported it to the police, didn't you?"

She'd expected him to oppose the idea and had come prepared. "Yes, but the police have failed me in the past. Remember the threats I've gotten because of my articles? My laptop has been stolen from my car. My home was burglarized. The cops didn't produce a single suspect in those cases."

He examined the rolled-up newspaper through the square lenses of his thick-framed glasses. "You know the detectives are overwhelmed. They don't have time to investigate small crimes thoroughly."

She slapped the armrest. "That's my point. I'm afraid they won't even try to catch this guy, and he'll come after me again when he doesn't find the pendant in my purse."

"Look, I know you're concerned, and so am I but . . ." He slid around to the other side of the desk and unfurled the paper. "This is a good lead-in to an assignment I want to discuss with you. Even the *Post* is eating our lunch on the Iraq War. We've got to expand our coverage. I'm going to need your help."

"I've been helping for more than a month, ever since the war started." She stared at the coffee mug full of pens on his cluttered desk and thought of the endless hours she'd spent earning her journalism degree. She couldn't afford to alienate her boss. Neither could she sleep at night if the attacker who thought she had some valuable pendant stayed at large. "What more do you want me to do?"

"We need some captivating human interest stories. People want to know about the soldiers from New York and New Jersey—what they're facing in Iraq, how their families are coping. We also need more features about the fallen."

She felt herself tense. Writing about tragic deaths had become excruciating for her since September 11th. Features about bereaved wives were especially painful. She found herself gripped by the longing to have Justin back, if only for a moment. She would gladly give her life to have him kiss and hold her one last time.

As always, Grant was obsessed with the paper. He would only agree to her request if she wrote more about the soldiers and their families. "I'm ready to take on any of those assignments. You can add to them an interesting story I heard on the radio this morning. A guy from New Jersey saved his friend from drowning in Rhode Island and ended up in a coma. All I ask is that you also let me see if I can find out anything about the purse snatcher."

Grant whacked the newspaper with an open palm. "Don't you realize what's at stake here? Your job could be on the line . . . and mine too."

She stood and gripped the edge of the desk. "I'm more concerned about my life." She leaned forward to within inches of his reddening face. "I can do both. Trust me."

He stepped back and grew reflective. "I'm concerned about you, I really am, but . . ."

She caught a glimpse of the TV in the newsroom as the camera zoomed in on a photograph of a man who looked eerily familiar. He reminded her of Justin. She turned and stared at the smaller TV behind her. "Quick, Grant. Turn up the volume."

The anchorwoman said, "In an extraordinary development, the man in the photograph, known as Rainer Ferguson, was knocked unconscious while rescuing a woman during a sailing accident off the Rhode Island shore. He was feared drowned, but the Coast Guard plucked him from the water and airlifted him to Rhode Island Hospital, where he remains in a coma.

"Hospital personnel discovered that he had been living in Providence for twenty months under a false identity. A check of the man's fingerprints revealed that his real name is Justin Connelly. He has been missing since September 11th, 2001. He worked in the North Tower of the World Trade Center and was presumed dead. Connelly, who had been hailed as a hero for rescuing a woman at sea, could now wake up to a court summons for falsifying government documents."

Tori sank to her knees. Her cry echoed off the glass walls of the office as her stomach was assaulted by nausea. "This can't be happening! My . . . husband . . . on TV . . . alive?"

7

THE SHREWDEST DECEPTION

A wave of confusion washed over Justin as he gazed at a luxury resort community. Then confusion turned to relief. Maybe he wasn't in hell. Perhaps this was really heaven. But why would he be there? He'd done great evil in his life. If anyone deserved to be in hell, he did.

Perhaps the gorgeous woman and the angry hunchback had been placed in his path as tests. The sacred mountain lay less than a mile ahead, but with the resort in front of him and no yelping dogs nearby, he longed to stop and rest.

He approached the wrought iron gates wide-eyed with amazement. Inside, golden streets were lined with gleaming palatial mansions. Behind them several hundred people picnicked on the lawn, their bodies translucent like his. A tingle rippled through his body as he pondered staying there forever. A smiling man who shone with glorious light startled him.

"I've been waiting for you." The man had a thick mane of golden hair and a face so luminous he appeared divine. He held out a hand.

"How do you know me?" Justin squinted as he shook the man's hand, suspicious that the light was too dazzling to be real.

"I know everyone in this place, but for you I have a special offer. I invite you to join our luxurious community." Dazzling Light blew on him. The swampy odor of the dark forest dissipated and was replaced with the freshness of spring. "You smell so clean. Let me show you around."

Justin shook his head and began to walk away. "No, I—"

Dazzling Light guided him through the gates. Justin's conscience told him he should resist, but he convinced himself he wouldn't stay long.

"One of these mansions can be yours," Dazzling Light said. "Simply give me your pendant and abandon your quest for the sacred mountain."

Justin arched an eyebrow. Maybe he was wrong about the pendant only being a good luck charm. The residents of this place obviously believed it was something more, but he didn't know what. "My pendant? Why would you want it?"

"You won't need it anymore. Here everyone is too busy enjoying their luxuries to threaten you."

A vision of the glittering resort and all its amenities besieged his mind. He imagined himself being richer than anyone on Wall Street. The temptation felt like a whirlwind roaring through him. Only his business instinct never to buy on impulse saved him. "I need to tour one of the mansions before I decide," he said.

"Sorry. You can't go near the mansions without first surrendering the pendant."

Justin bolted up the walk to the nearest mansion. He started to ring the doorbell but stopped when from inside the home he heard the same moaning and shrieking that had filled the cavern of despair. Now he understood. The people in the resort suffered as much as those in the cavern. They hid their anguish behind stately pillars, whitewashed walls, and five-car garages.

Dazzling Light pushed his hand away from the doorbell. "Don't worry about the sounds you hear. The family performs dramas for the community; their rehearsals can be rather theatrical."

Before Justin could challenge the lie, Dazzling Light grabbed his arm and led him to the spacious lawn that bordered the back of the mansions. He clapped to get the attention of the picnicking crowd. "Let's have a warm welcome for Justin Connelly."

The people leaped up and gave him a standing ovation.

"These people adore you." Dazzling Light guided him to the center of the lawn. "Let's hear it again for our new friend."

The crowd showered him with another raucous ovation.

"With this kind of support, you could easily become president of the community. Think of the power and adulation you would enjoy. Just give me the pendant."

Justin studied the cheering crowd as his entire body tingled with their adoration. The temptation to surrender the pendant sent ecstasy from the soles of his feet to the crown of his head. He'd never received such exultant praise, yet now he couldn't imagine living without it. He reached into his pocket and fingered the pendant. In doing so, he remembered who he was—a being who craved love above all things.

The ecstasy that had enlivened his body vanished and was replaced by that desperate loneliness. He withdrew his hand, realizing that the ecstasy had been a form of lust. The experience had revealed more about the pendant—that it did possess mysterious power and that he could use it for a good purpose. He shot Dazzling Light an angry stare as the yelping of the dogs grew louder. "I won't let you trick me into surrendering the pendant," he said.

He sprinted into the forest barely ahead of the dogs. The sacred mountain loomed to the north half a mile away. He ran until his legs were exhausted then knelt behind a tall round stone. Peeking out, he glimpsed the lead dog and its ghoulish master but managed to stay hidden. He stopped breathing and meditated on thoughts of love and goodness. A three-headed dog passed the stone, followed by a hooded translucent skeleton holding the leash. The skeleton struggled to control the powerful animal, whose panting breath stank like manure. Several other dogs approached. Their yelps erupted in the evening air when they saw Justin.

"We got him!" A faceless hooded demon reached for him.

Justin dodged while waving the pendant. He didn't fully understand its powers but had no other way to defend himself. "As long as I have this, you'll never take me to the cavern."

The demon dove at him but missed. "Don't play games. You're coming with us. We'll receive a fine reward for capturing you."

Justin kept threatening with the pendant and marveled at how it warded off the demons. "I have something better for you. Come with me to freedom."

"Our elders told us you would try to trick us!"

The demon seized his arm and wrestled him in the direction of the cavern. Justin broke loose and pointed the pendant at him as he ran backwards toward the sacred mountain.

The three-headed dogs pursued, nipping at his shins, but as long as he held up the pendant, they couldn't hurt him.

He kept running backward despite his throbbing head and aching legs. As he neared the tall, steel-barred gate, one of the dogs knocked him down. The pendant slipped out of his hand and several demons restrained him. He kicked and fought and screamed in terror. One of the demons cackled.

"I hope you like the cavern of despair," he said. "You'll be there a long time."

8

CONFUSION OVERLOAD

STATEN ISLAND, NEW YORK
WEDNESDAY, APRIL 30, 2003
3:34 P.M.

A day that had begun with an invigorating walk on the beach had turned into an uphill marathon for Tori. She unlocked the front door of her three-story townhouse on Arden Avenue with the grainy headshot of Justin still vivid in her mind. The news report seemed unreal, as did everything else in her life. She massaged her temples hoping to calm her thoughts but without success. Hearing the news about Justin was like having the Staten Island Ferry crush her against the pilings. The experience had pulverized her heart and left her aching from every pore.

She stepped inside and pushed the door closed with her back. The dull thud emphasized the barrier between the inside and outside of the townhouse, just like the news had closed a door between the ordered life she'd known that morning and the confusion she was now in.

This day had sucked her back into the panic of September 11th—the unanswered calls to Justin's cell phone, the plumes of soot and ash darkening the sky, the unbearable silence in the house, the ache of terror and loss settling into her gut.

She leaned on the door and closed her eyes, but nothing made sense. The Justin Connelly she'd married wasn't capable of such deception. Their marriage hadn't been perfect, but she couldn't imagine him running away and living a secret life for nearly two years. There must be more to the story. A lot more.

Pondering the mystery and thinking of him lying in a coma intensified her need to rush to Providence, but she had to wait for Paul, a New York City fireman currently working the graveyard shift. When she'd called and told him about Justin, the phone had gone silent.

"Paul . . . Paul . . . Are you okay?" she'd asked.

"No, definitely not okay. I've taken some strange calls in my career. This one's bizarre."

"More bizarre than any story I've ever covered. I need your support. Will you come to Providence with me?"

There was a pause then a strained sigh. "What you're asking . . . it puts me in an impossible position. I want to be supportive of you but, honestly, if Justin weren't in a coma right now, I'd be tempted to put him in one."

"But he *is* in a coma . . . after saving a woman's life. I have no choice but to go to him."

"I won't let you go alone."

Finally he'd promised to meet her that afternoon and drive with her in the morning. Her mother had also reacted with disbelief and anger, but after holding Tori for a long time, she'd agreed to keep baby Justin.

Tori slipped off her pumps in the living room, soothed by the earth tones of the contemporary furnishings and décor, then bounded up the stairs. Some men might have tried to convince her not to go, to pressure her into accepting the marriage proposal, to forget about the louse of a husband who'd run away. Not Paul.

Her foot missed a stair. She broke her fall with her hands, wondering what would happen to their relationship if Justin woke from his coma. She glanced at her watch. She had to shower before Paul arrived. In her bedroom, she pulled a pair of jeans from the dresser. As she closed the drawer, she heard rustling behind her. She turned and went blind with terror.

A broad-shouldered figure in a black ski mask rushed from the closet holding a nylon rope. "No way are you going to Providence."

She recognized the voice as that of the purse snatcher. She dodged and fled the room, screaming and slamming the door on him. She dashed down the stairs as his raspy voice echoed in her ears. Her skin felt as if it were on fire. She yelled, "I already called the cops! They're on their way!"

His feet pounded behind her. "Cooperate or you'll be dead before they get here."

She reached the front door, turned the knob, and pulled, but the man slammed the door from behind and locked the deadbolt. She broke free and ran through the living room, shoving an overstuffed divan into his path.

A crazed look burned in his dark eyes. A feeling of violation spiraled up from Tori's gut and made her choke. She slipped on the parquet floor in the kitchen, crashed into the table, and pushed off it to keep running. The man bore down and shoved the table aside with a screech. She lurched toward the back door and in one motion unlocked and yanked it open. As she stepped outside, the man seized her ankle and tripped her.

He dragged her back inside. She lunged to her feet and swung. Her fist connected with his nose. He cursed and landed a backhanded blow on her chin, knocking her to the floor again. *Oh God, oh God, oh God* . . . he could kill her.

A feeling of abandonment pierced her heart. She wasn't ready to die—to make her son an orphan, to give up Paul, to lose everything she'd worked for as a journalist. She kicked at his groin, thrusting heel-first.

He keeled over. She broke for the back door again. He recovered and snagged the sleeve of her sweater. As it stretched, she spun and thrust a knee into his gut. He belched and latched on to her throat with gloved hands. She felt the wind go out of her. He scooted a high-backed chair over and forced her onto it. "We've got some business to attend to," he said.

He withdrew a roll of duct tape from the pocket of his jeans and taped her mouth shut. Then he tied her to the chair with the rope. "You're going to give me what I came for." He shook the stiletto knife in front of her face. "Any screaming and you're a dead woman."

She nodded.

He stripped off the tape and stuck it on the tabletop. "Your husband had a plan when he fled to Providence, didn't he? And you're in on it, aren't you?"

"In on what?"

"The pendant. Where is it?"

"I have no idea what you're talking about."

He gripped the back of her neck. "Don't lie to me."

The closeness of the blade made her shudder. Sweat poured down her neck.

"I'm not leaving until you tell me your husband's plan." He brought the knife under her throat. "He's been in touch with you, hasn't he?"

"No . . . no, he hasn't. I thought he was dead until today. I haven't heard from him in nearly two years."

"I don't believe you. You've been in on the plot from the beginning. Where is the pendant?"

"There's a jewelry box in my dresser upstairs, second drawer from the top. The pendants I own aren't expensive. Take them. Just let me go . . . please let me go."

The man squeezed her neck harder. "You know which pendant I want. It's made of burnished wood and has engravings on it. Tell me where it is or you'll die."

Tori struggled against the pain, her breathing labored. "I don't own a wooden pendant. Why would I want one?"

"You're a lousy liar." He pointed the knife at her heart. "For the last time . . ."

He brought the knife to her throat again. Under her breath, Tori desperately prayed, *Please, God, don't let him kill me. Who'll take care of my son?*

9

Another Answer Demanded

"You aren't taking him anywhere!" an assertive female voice yelled.

Justin turned and saw a sturdy woman. Her eyes were pools of glimmering amethyst. A sigh of relief gushed out followed by a breath of hope. With her help, he might yet escape the vicious demons and three-headed dogs. The woman brandished a pendant slightly longer than his.

"No one defies the keeper of the gate." She threatened his ruthless attackers with her pendant. "I command you to let him go. Leave this place and never return!"

Some of the demons tried to challenge her, but like a warrior in battle, she used the gleaming pendant to drive them back. They retreated into the forest. She offered Justin a hand. He took it, gasping for breath. "Where did you get that pendant?" he asked.

She narrowed her enchanting eyes. "I cannot reveal the secret. I can only tell you that it came from the same source from which yours was fashioned."

Frustration welled up inside him. "After all I've been through, I deserve to know."

"You're not ready for this knowledge. I can only say that the search for perfect love is the greatest challenge any soul faces. Everything must be risked in the quest. Are you sure you want to continue?"

Justin glanced back at the dark forest and ahead at the towering mountain. His eyes darted between them until they hurt. "I have no other choice."

"Then prove that you're worth saving. You have to embrace your entire life, your past, present, and future; the good, the bad—everything. Otherwise you'll never get back home."

"I'm ready to do that."

She pulled him toward the gate. "You must answer one question before I can let you in. What is the deepest desire of your heart?"

The question riveted his attention. He remembered what the six-winged creature had told him. Before he'd traversed the dark forest, he would have spoken the answer just because he knew it. But having survived the temptations, something had changed inside him. Not only did he want out of this gruesome place but he also longed for peace. The creature had said that only the Holy One could grant that peace and free him for the journey home. He pressed his face against the gate and marveled at the feeling. More than anything he'd ever wanted before, he longed to scale the sacred mountain.

He caught the woman's flashing eyes and expressed his true feelings. "The deepest desire of my heart is to love, and be loved by, the Holy One."

She opened the gate. "Pick up your pendant and come inside."

He scooped the pendant into one hand and followed her through the gate.

"Go in peace," she said and started him up the mountain.

The path was strewn with jagged rocks and overgrown with roots and weeds. Justin had to leap from stone to stone. Gradually he ascended until he entered the mist-shrouded region at the tree line. Whenever he glanced back, dizziness seized him and he clung to the stones to keep from falling. Although the temperature dropped, he began to sweat under the strain. The steeper the path grew, the more he needed the low-hanging branches to keep his balance and pull himself upward.

After about a mile, he was exhausted and relieved to reach a clearing. A large group of souls with translucent bodies had gathered there. The face of a tall, broad-shouldered man in front shone like the midday sun. His shoulder-length hair was as white as snow. His eyes were like flames. He wore a long robe with a golden sash across his chest. Next to him, a stream flowed down the mountain. When the man spoke, his voice was like the rushing waters.

"The Spirit of the Lord is upon me," he said, "because he has anointed me to proclaim freedom for the prisoners. Come to me, all who are weary and are carrying heavy burdens, and I will give you rest."

Pins and needles of joy rippled across Justin's shoulders. Hearing the Holy One's words made his bones ache for freedom from guilt and shame. The loneliness, misery, and despair he'd felt in this place reminded him of feelings he'd experienced on earth, but here they penetrated every fiber of his being. He shuddered in terror that he might never escape.

"How can we be set free?" a heavyset elderly woman asked with a trembling voice.

The Holy One said, "I am the resurrection and the life. Those who believe in me, even though they die, yet will they live, and everyone who lives and believes in me will never die. Do you believe this?"

"I believe." The woman made her way forward.

The Holy One surveyed the vast gathering of souls. "This is my commandment, that you love one another as I have loved you. No one has greater love than this, to lay down one's life for one's friends. Are you willing to do this?"

"With all my heart," the woman said.

A long-haired man in the middle of the gathering followed her. "I, too, believe and promise to love."

Soon many more souls came forward. The Holy One said, "Blessed are your eyes, for they see, and your ears, for they hear. Truly I tell you, many prophets and kings longed to see what you see, but did not see it, and to hear what you hear, but did not hear it." Then he blessed the souls and sent them up the mountain.

Justin joined the line and bumped a man with a disfigured face.

"What's your hurry?" the man asked as they walked along together.

"I don't want to be left here. Where are these souls going?"

The disfigured man smiled so brightly his entire body appeared radiant. "The Eternal City lies on the other side of the mountain beyond the crystal sea. These souls have been set free. They are going to the City to live in glory forever."

Justin's energy soared, and a powerful ecstasy swept through him. The Holy One stretched out his arms to reveal jagged wounds on his palms. A ring of scars circled his forehead and a bleeding gash marred his side. Justin recognized the glorious face of Jesus Christ crucified and risen. In that moment, a love more powerful than anything he'd ever known flowed through him. All the bitter memories of his sins and failures melted away. He felt forgiven and whole, joyful and at peace.

Jesus met his eyes. "Do not be afraid. I am the first and the last, and the living one. I was dead, and see, I am alive forever and ever; and I have the keys of Death and of Hades."

"Please let me go to the Eternal City. I want—"

Jesus put a finger on Justin's lips. "What you want has no meaning in this place. You neglected my mercy for much of your life. Now it's all that can save you."

Justin dropped to one knee. "Now I realize how many mistakes I made . . . how I wasted my life. Please forgive me and let me have another chance. I'll do anything to go to the Eternal City."

"I have other plans for you." He laid a hand on Justin's head. "You must return to earth and make amends for the hurt you caused. Now that you have seen what awaits those who do evil, you must warn people to do good and teach them to love me and one another."

"No, please, I—" Justin tried to stand but couldn't. "Life on earth is too painful. The Eternal City . . . I really want—"

"You're not ready yet. You haven't learned the lessons of your pain and shared them to help me heal the world." Jesus lifted him up. "That is the work I have for you to do. To everyone who conquers, I give permission to eat from the tree of life in the paradise of God. If you conquer, you will be clothed in white robes, and I will not blot your name out of the book of life." Jesus embraced him. "Go . . . and remember I am with you always to the end of the age."

A burning sensation washed over Justin's body. Suddenly he was flying again and a blinding light drew him to its center. A wide door opened. He heard a deafening *whoosh*, and the light enveloped him. He opened his eyes then blinked them closed against the sting.

A man's voice said, "Look, he's waking up. I saw him open his eyes."

Someone grabbed his hand. "Can you hear me, Rainer . . . I mean, Justin?"

When he heard his real name and recognized Ken Spalding's voice, terror surged through him. If Ken knew, so must the authorities. But that's not what concerned him most. One woman could hurt him more than the police . . . a woman who wasn't his wife.

He'd tried to control it all, to manage and subdue it, and it had taken him to the depths of abandonment and despair. Now he needed the courage to face life again and to discover the secrets of the pendant's power. Only by doing so could he help to heal the world. He hesitated a moment then blinked and squeezed the hand.

"He's back with us!" Excitement rang in Ken's voice.

Justin tried to speak but choked. Although he was breathing, he felt as if he was getting too much air. He blinked again and held his eyes open despite the blinding light. Medical equipment beeped and whirred all around. He was in what appeared to be a hospital's intensive care unit. Ken Spalding and Sharon Jenkins stood at his bedside along with a petite brunette nurse. A taller nurse and a thin, balding doctor were also present. He realized he had a breathing tube in his throat.

Sharon rubbed his other hand. "You made it, Justin. You're going to be all right. And because of you, so am I."

"Welcome back, Justin." The petite nurse helped the doctor remove the breathing tube.

Justin squeezed the hands that held his and tried to smile at the radiant faces. As the tube came out, tears trickled from the corners of his eyes.

10

FROM TERROR TO DESPERATION

WEDNESDAY, APRIL 30, 2003
3:52 P.M.

Tori's palms were clammy, and she felt faint as she jerked away from the knife. Who was this man in the ski mask? Why had he broken in and threatened to kill her? She berated herself for not having asked Paul to meet her as soon as she got home.

Major events from her past flashed through her mind. She had tried to be a good person and wasn't afraid to die, but she desperately wanted to live. Stalling for time, she said, "This wooden pendant with the engravings . . . why is it so valuable?"

The intruder began to draw the knife against her neck. The chime of the doorbell stopped him. He cupped one hand over her mouth, set the knife on the table, and sealed her mouth with duct tape before picking up the knife again.

The doorbell rang several more times, accompanied by knocking. "Tori, it's Paul. Are you all right?"

His urgency made the intruder freeze. The man glanced around nervously. Paul yelled again. After a moment of indecision, the intruder ran out the rear entrance locking the door behind him. The rumble of his footsteps on the stairs disappeared as she fought to free herself.

When she didn't answer the front door, Paul stopped ringing and knocking. Soon she heard footsteps coming up the back staircase. He knocked on the door then kicked it. The lock held. He kicked the door again. And again. The kicking grew more frantic and determined. Finally there was a loud crack, and the door slammed into the stove. Paul dashed in, removed the duct tape, and untied her. "Who did this to you?"

"A guy in a ski mask. He'd broken in and was hiding in my bedroom closet."

A lump formed in her throat at Paul's touch. His habit of shaving every other day and wearing his thick black hair dry and windblown gave him a roughhewn attractiveness. At thirty-seven, he had an approachable manner and an authenticity that inspired trust. With his athletic build, square jaw, and wide, disarming smile, he got his share of attention at the Staten Island beaches. Still, his strong nose and the sadness in the tilt of his dark eyes made him too unconventionally handsome for the cover of *GQ*.

"If you hadn't come, I—"

He pressed a finger to her lips. "I'm here now and I won't leave."

For a moment, the expression reminded her of Justin. The similarity comforted her, but it was also unsettling. She wanted to love Paul for who he was, not for the qualities he shared with her wayward husband. Most of the time, comparisons weren't a problem because the two men were different in many ways. On occasion, though, the resemblances were uncanny.

He removed the last rope and fished his cell phone out of his khakis. She straightened her clothes and rubbed her arms while he reported the break-in and attack. "The police are on their way," he said.

She stood and reached out to him. "I recognized the intruder's voice. I think he was the same guy who snatched my purse. He was sure Justin had concocted some sort of scheme and that I'm in on it."

"What kind of scheme?"

"All I know is that it involves a pendant—an oval one made of wood with engravings on it. The guy thought I knew where this pendant is, and he was determined to keep me from going to Providence."

Paul scowled and crossed his arms on his chest. "If Justin's really involved in some kind of scheme, he didn't only deceive you, he nearly got you killed."

She slapped the table, stinging her fingers. The spontaneous release of fury shocked her; Justin hadn't ever provoked such an outburst. Her hallowed memories turned into murky suspicions. The sting radiated up her arms and across her shoulders. "It sounds as if he's in some kind of trouble, and it involves this pendant."

"If he wakes from the coma, he'll be in worse trouble with me . . . and with the law. A man can't fake his death then just show up two years later without suffering the consequences."

Tori grabbed a paper towel from the dispenser, wet it, and sat down at the table. "I've covered enough murder cases to know the power of rage. I have to control mine or it'll destroy me." She caught a glimpse of a photo of her holding baby Justin. It hung on the refrigerator in a small Plexiglas frame amid various bills hanging from magnet clips. She stood, grabbed the photo, and stashed it in a drawer.

"Why did you do that?"

"I can't look at it right now." She blinked back tears. "Idealizing Justin got me through my pregnancy, the birth of my son, and the struggles of being a single mom. Now the ideal has been shattered."

She turned away, choosing not to share an even deeper anguish: her memories of the sympathy she'd received as a pregnant 9/11 widow. She wondered what people would think of her now. Would they accuse her of scamming the victims' fund? Of concocting some bizarre plot with her husband? Of being the wife of the coward who faked his death to flee his bad marriage?

A rush of shame intensified her rage and had her dabbing hot tears from her eyes. She turned away and lowered her voice. "I've had enough drama for one day. After the police leave, I need some downtime at my mom's house. The trip to Providence will have to wait until I recover."

She borrowed his cell phone and called her mom. Tori didn't want to alarm her, so she told her she was too tired to leave that afternoon. Thankfully her mother was willing to babysit the next day and saw the wisdom of having them stay at her house that night. As Tori ended the call, Paul took her hand.

"I'm going to insist that the police keep an eye on your mom's house."

She smiled. His hand felt strong, the grip firm but gentle. Her pulse quickened, radiating warmth through her. He drew her closer.

"What you need is a bodyguard." He cupped her hand in both of his. "I would volunteer, but with Justin back in the picture . . . well, I'm not sure where I stand with you."

She gazed into his vulnerable wide-set eyes, confused about how to respond. She, too, wondered how Justin's reemergence would affect all three of them. She dabbed at her lip then fired the crumpled paper towel at the wastebasket beside the door. She missed.

"It's all too much to think about," she said. "I need some time to work things through."

Paul scooped up the paper towel and flung it into the trash. "Whatever happens, my friendship with Justin is over."

"Are you sure you can handle seeing him? Maybe you shouldn't—"

He waved a hand of protest. "No way are you going alone."

"My mother would be relieved to hear you say that. She's worried I'll let you get away."

"Maybe she should be. I can't—"

He met her gaze and held it for a moment before finishing.

"I can't wait forever."

She reflected on his words and stared deeper into his eyes. Their glistening richness, the color of fresh-brewed coffee, invited her to explore what lay within. She stood up, gripping his hand. "If you offered to hold me until the police get here, I wouldn't say no."

She saw determination in his eyes as he gathered her into his arms. His air of self-assurance challenged her to take the further risk—to trust him. And to trust herself. Her mother was right. There weren't many men like Paul Spardello. She drew a thoughtful breath. Right now, the trust didn't have to be forever. Just for today. For this moment. She pressed her cheek against his firm chest, exhaled slowly, and surrendered to his embrace. But as she tightened her arms around him, she lamented that she didn't feel more passion for the man who'd rescued her.

11

The Other
Side of Darkness

Providence, Rhode Island
Friday, May 2, 2003
10:13 a.m.

*J*ustin forged ahead of Nurse Fernanda Cordeiro, a slender woman with salt-and-pepper hair who spoke with a Portuguese accent. She was accompanying him on one of his walks in the hospital corridor to regain his strength. The coma lingered in his mind as powerfully as the storm that had almost killed him. His near-death experience had infused terror into every nerve of his body. Now he wondered whether it had been real or had been caused by the medications he'd been given to prevent his brain from swelling after the concussion.

The question haunted him, but he had no answer. He decided to focus on what he knew for sure. To breathe again, to see daylight and hear Ken and Sharon's voices had brought him from a horrific ending to a new beginning. But the act of waking seemed long ago now. After two days in the hospital, he'd had enough of institutional food, bed rest, and nurses and therapists poking and exercising him. He had to get out of there—now.

Still, he was glad for one thing: the hospital protected him from the reporters who kept calling for interviews. They wanted to know why he'd run away, how he'd managed to live a secret life, what it was like to wake up after six hours in a coma. The police had called too, asking about his phony driver's license and Social Security card.

He needed to deal with his legal problems and plan how to use the pendant. He also worried that Tori had seen him on TV and would come looking for him. Or worse, that Candace Donahue would. The thought made him grimace. A breath became a wheeze. He would eventually have to face both women, but he wanted to do it his own way, on his own timetable. He wasn't ready yet.

"Has the doctor signed my discharge papers?" he asked.

"The doctor hasn't been in yet." Fernanda seized his arm to slow him down. "But it's still early."

"When do you expect him?"

"I never know. I'll look into it but only if you're a model patient the rest of the day."

"No promises but I'll try."

He sped up, uncomfortable being away from his room for long. He'd hidden the pendant under his mattress and didn't want anyone tampering with it. A rush of adrenaline jolted him as he thought of the burnished oval. He wondered if it really possessed miraculous power as the six-winged creature had claimed.

Under his breath, he cursed the TV news anchor who'd broadcast his photo. In seconds she'd made him a public figure—the Rhode Island hero who turned out to be a September 11th runaway. His cheeks grew hot as he stewed in the implications of his notoriety. He and Fernanda approached the elevators. His semiprivate room was only a short walk away.

"Maybe I should go home right now." He rushed to press the call button.

"You haven't been discharged," Fernanda said as she caught up. "You're not authorized to leave."

He pressed the button harder. "I've been waiting since yesterday."

She pulled him back. "Would you discharge yourself against medical advice?"

"The doctor said I'm fine. He just needs to sign the papers."

"I advise you to wait. Insurance companies don't pay for 'against medical advice' discharges."

He allowed her to lead him down the corridor. "May I ask you a question?" she said.

"What?"

"Why did you choose Providence?"

He was tempted to say something flippant, but making light of his heartfelt reasons would feel like a betrayal. Instead he tried the truth.

"Providence is close to New York, but its laid-back mindset is a world away. I love the ocean, and I thought I'd have the best chance to start over in a state known for welcoming rogues and . . ."

He trailed off as a stunning raven-haired woman entered his room. Her finely carved profile looked like that of Candace

Donahue, the founder and CEO of Donahue Financial Management and his former boss. He felt the coma coming back.

"You look pale." Fernanda nudged him from behind. "You better go lie down."

He wanted to flee, but if the woman was Candace, she might find the pendant. He trudged ahead. When he and Fernanda entered the room, the woman had her back to them. She was rummaging in the drawer of his nightstand.

"May I help you?" Fernanda said.

The woman closed the drawer and turned around. Justin gasped . . . it was Candace. He felt as if he were back on *Serendipity's* roiling deck. He grabbed Fernanda's arm.

"I'm here to visit Justin," Candace said. "We're old friends."

"Maybe he'll listen to you." Fernanda tapped her arm free and turned to leave. "Tell him he can't go home until he's been properly discharged."

Justin felt as if he'd wandered into a land of illusions and gotten lost. Candace's emerald green eyes were mesmerizing. She still had the figure of a model or Hollywood actress, the same exotic cheekbones and full, sensuous lips.

"Hello, Justin." She gave him a hug and a kiss on the cheek.

He grabbed the tray table for support. She was wearing the small gold locket he'd given her. He'd had it inscribed with the words *To Candace, my lover and friend, from Justin.* Disbelief and dread attacked every organ in his body. He wanted a normal life; Candace would deny him that forever. The feeling reminded him of drowning, as if water even now poured into his lungs and dragged him into the darkness and terror of hell. The panic of his near-death experience assailed him. He tightened his grip on the table until his fingers ached and went numb.

Candace backed away from him. "You look as dazed as I was when I heard you'd been found. When I saw your photo on TV, I nearly fainted."

He couldn't stop blinking. "It wasn't my idea to broadcast that photo." He moved the tray-table aside and massaged his fingers as he sat on the edge of the bed.

"Nor was it mine to be separated from you on September 11th." She carressed the locket. "All I remember is running down the stairs with you. I thought you died when the North Tower came down."

His heart beat so fast he could barely speak. "I saw you die in a fireman's arms."

The horror of that September morning returned: the plane crashing into the offices above them, the massive explosion and screeching of steel against steel, the stairwells of the North Tower trembling and swaying as they labored down ninety floors. Once they'd reached the plaza, sirens blared, people ran in all directions, torrents of concrete and steel, soot and ash rained down. The last time he'd seen her swan-like neck it had been bent and limp, cradled in a fireman's arms.

"Debris hit you on the plaza and knocked you out," he said. "I carried you to a rescue truck and handed you to a fireman. He told me you were gone. There was nothing I could do."

"So you just left me?"

"The fireman was holding you when the tower began to crumble. We all ran for our lives."

A spark of rage glinted in her eyes. "You could've stayed with us."

"I lost you in a fog of debris. I thought you were dead."

"You *thought*?"

He didn't answer right away, shocked speechless by the bizarre experience of seeing the Queen of Wall Street again. She wore an immaculately pressed peach blouse, black linen slacks and stylish spiked heels. It was her trademark look, a cross between glamorous and professional. But her startling beauty and net worth of billions now seemed ugly and cheap. He swallowed to keep from gagging. "I was sure. The fireman said you were dead. I believed him."

"All I remember is waking up in the hospital," Candace said. "I had a bad concussion and wondered what happened to you. It took me several months to recover from the internal injuries."

"I did all I could. I tried—"

She waved him off. "What happened to the pendant?"

"It got torn off your neck when you were hit. I picked it up."

"And then you left for Providence?"

"Yes."

"Where is it now?" She opened the nightstand drawer again and pulled out two books of crossword puzzles and some pens and scratch pads. She glared at him. "You've hidden it here somewhere, haven't you!"

"It's in a safe place. You'll never find it."

She stepped around him and opened a tall closet near the door. "I want it back."

He restrained a shiver as he thought of the pendant under the mattress. "You're not going to get it."

She intensified her glare then rifled through the pockets of his jeans and shirt. "I won't leave without that pendant." She raised her voice and moved toward him jutting out her chin. "Now where is it?"

He said nothing.

She moved her chin to within inches of his and lowered her voice. "We both know what we were doing in the weeks before the towers came down. I'm willing to rehire you but only if you stop this nonsense and return my pendant to me."

Justin got up and moved to the head of the bed. "I'm not returning to the firm. A lot has happened. My days as a stockbroker are over. I'm also going back to my wife."

Candace formed a fist around the locket. "Let me remind you who you're dealing with. No one walks away from Candace Donahue until I say. That's how I run my business, and there was more than business between us."

Justin felt as if scalding water had been poured into his veins. She could use the locket to blackmail him. He remembered their after-work dalliances and the hotel rooms they'd shared on business trips. He couldn't do it anymore, no matter the cost.

"I don't owe you anything," he said, "and I have enough dirt on you to take you down if I need to. I hope you'll see the wisdom of our going our separate ways."

Candace's face reddened. She opened the bathroom door adjacent to the bed and looked around frantically. He got up and closed the door. "This visit is over."

"No, it's not. Not until I say it is."

She pushed against him as she grew even redder. When she couldn't budge the bathroom door, she headed for the closet again. As she reached for the door, he slammed one hand against it. "Nurse, call security!"

Candace tugged at the knob, but he wrapped his arms around her and pulled her toward the hall. Fernanda rushed in with a shocked expression. She helped Justin restrain Candace and called security. When the burly guard arrived, he took her by the arms and immobilized her.

"That's enough, ma'am," he said. "Either leave with me or I'll call the police."

The guard pulled her into the corridor and hauled her away. Justin watched them disappear around a corner as Fernanda hurried to the nurses' station. He grabbed the pendant from under the mattress and got into bed.

A few minutes later, Fernanda returned. "I spoke with your doctor. He'll be in this afternoon to discharge you."

"Does that mean I was a model patient?" Justin fingered the pendant under the covers.

"That's not even funny."

12

An Apartment on Wayland

Providence, Rhode Island
Friday, May 2, 2003
5:16 p.m.

Tori sensed Paul's tension as he parked his Mustang in front of Justin's apartment. After calling Rhode Island Hospital and learning that Justin had been released earlier that day, they'd done an Internet search on Rainer Ferguson. They discovered he lived at 457 Wayland Avenue on the upscale East Side.

Since hearing that he was alive, Tori hadn't been able to stop her mind from racing. The soft leather of the Mustang's bucket seat, warm from the four-hour drive from Staten Island, contrasted sharply with the chill between her and Paul.

She'd thought he would comfort and support her. His presence meant he was trying, but their conversation had been rancorous. He and Justin had played high school basketball together and worked as lifeguards on New York beaches during the summers. They'd kissed girls behind the bathhouse at Coney Island, played in a rock band together, and been best men at each other's weddings. Paul was also struggling with his emotions . . . and with a similar need to confront Justin.

"You're not going in without me." He pulled on his door handle.

Tori held his arm. "No, I need to do this alone."

"Then why did you ask me to come along? I'm not your chauffeur."

She found his stormy eyes. "This is impossible for both of us. I just need you to respect my wishes."

"What about my wishes? I deserve an explanation too. And he deserves to face the pain he's caused!"

"You'll get your chance. Right now it would just complicate things." She squeezed his arm. "Please, Paul. It's already so hard. Don't make it worse."

He closed his door. "Justin was your husband . . . he *is* your husband. How do you expect me to react?"

She drew her hand away. "I'd like nothing more than to drive back to Staten Island and forget all this, but I can't. I need to know why Justin ran away."

She opened her door and started to get out. Paul came around from the other side and held her arms. "One of us has to tell him about our relationship—that we're a couple now. He needs to know he no longer has a wife or a best friend. If you can't do it, I will."

"You're too furious to be rational."

"Who wouldn't be furious in this situation?"

She pulled herself away. "If you can't support me, you might as well go home."

"Maybe I will." He spun away from her.

"Paul, no!" She ran after him and grabbed his arm. "Please just calm down and let me get this over with. Then you can say what you need to say and we can leave."

He hesitated a moment, his eyes piercing hers. Then he threw up his hands and returned to the driver's side. He slid behind the wheel and rolled down the window of the passenger's door. "Have it your way. I'll go grab a bite to eat. Call me when you're done."

She hurried up the sidewalk to the tired-looking two-family home and rang the doorbell marked *Rainer Ferguson*. The neighborhood was quiet and residential with lots of older brick and wooden colonials as well as capes, bungalows, and an occasional ranch. The shock of Justin's twenty-month deception made her wonder what other secrets lurked behind the well-groomed hedges, towering maples, and dappled flowers that bordered the neatly trimmed lawns.

No one answered, but a TV blared the news inside. Someone was home. She rang the bell again and rapped on the door several times. The volume on the TV lowered and footsteps approached. After a pause, the deadbolt clicked, the knob squeaked, the door opened. An unshaven man with large brown eyes and disheveled sandy hair stood behind it.

Justin.

Tori stared at the husband she hadn't seen in almost two years. The sight of him brought an acrid taste to the back of her throat, as if she'd witnessed a terrible accident on the expressway. The experience was surreal and played in her mind like a scene from some macabre movie. Yet part of her was relieved he was alive. At a level she could barely fathom, let alone admit to, she longed to embrace him and never let go.

Justin stepped toward her. "Tori, I—"

She put up both hands. "Don't even try to explain. I'm not much for soap operas, especially when I'm cast in a supporting role without being consulted. I just needed to see if you're really alive and find out what's been going on for the past twenty months."

He ran a hand across his forehead. "All I can say is how very sorry I am."

"How could—" She shook her head and swallowed to dislodge the constriction in her throat. "If you only knew . . ." She paused and gulped a breath, restraining herself from hitting him. Her voice rose as she spit out the words. "How many tears I've cried for you . . . how many sleepless nights I've had. You should realize how paltry and inadequate 'I'm sorry' sounds."

He spoke haltingly, his breathing labored. "Look, I'm trying to apologize. That's all I can do because I have no excuses. This can't be a soap opera because the feelings I'm expressing are real. You have every right to hate me. To divorce me. All I can say is there's more to what happened than you've heard. So much more."

"There are also more stars than anyone can count. And some explanations for how they got there are ludicrous."

"At least let me try."

He waved for her to come inside. She hesitated, fighting the urge either to kick him or flee and forget he existed. Neither would give her any answers. She swallowed hard and walked in.

The odor of fried fish hung in the air. The cramped, boxlike living room looked worse than that of a tenant in the throes of moving. Books and CDs had been pulled from the shelves and scattered across the floor. Army green cushions from a threadbare couch lay at odd angles in front of it. A card table, a lamp, and two aluminum chairs had been overturned. She started to back away. He gestured toward the mess.

"This is all part of my explanation, but if you want to hear it, I've got to talk fast."

"You've always been a fast-talker. This time, I doubt it'll help."

"It may not, but please listen. The police just left, and I doubt they'll catch the thugs who did this. In fact, the thugs may come back."

She gave him a piercing glare. "This is crazy. You show up on TV after I thought you were dead, and then I track you down and find your apartment trashed, and you tell me that whoever did it might come back?" She shook her head.

He rubbed his temples. "I deserve your anger, but if you can't get beyond it, how can we have any kind of relationship?"

"I just can't deal with any more lies."

He closed and locked the door. "Neither can I."

The possibility that he could somehow stop the questions haunting her mind made her want to hear more. "So how is this mess here related to the mess you've made of our lives?"

He exhaled a deep breath. "I ran away because I'd been helping Candace Donahue conduct an insider trading scheme. I was terrified of getting caught. Our marriage had also been through a horrendous year. I saw an opportunity for a new start for both of us."

"Now you've gone from soap operas to class B movies. That line wouldn't be allowed in either." She restrained herself from yelling. "You ran away for only one reason, to save your hide, and for only one person. Yourself."

"Like I said, I . . ." He trailed off and stared at the floor.

Tori needed to sit down. She tossed a cushion onto the couch and fell into it as the words *insider trading scheme* echoed in her thoughts and tears stung her eyes. From the time she'd met Justin at NYU, she'd known he wanted to make lots of money. Now he was painting himself as a man who'd been corrupted in the process. She realized this nightmare had been foreshadowed during their marriage. The problems she'd either ignored or denied now threatened to suffocate her soul.

She berated herself for thinking his drive to succeed had been admirable. It had really been a dangerous obsession, and she'd turned a blind eye to it. How could she have been so naïve? The answer filled her with shame. Maybe she'd liked the idea of marrying rich . . . of being rich herself. Thus she'd compromised her integrity and chosen not to confront him. She needed to speak quickly in order to stop turning her anger inward in self-condemnation.

"I didn't think you were capable of such deception." She got up and straddled the arm of the couch. "And I don't get the connection between the insider trading and your trashed apartment."

His face grew flushed. "Candace made her billions on Wall Street with the help of a mysterious pendant. That's what the thugs were searching for in my apartment."

"A pendant!" She raised her voice without considering who might be listening. "Some guy on a motorcycle snatched my purse looking for a pendant. Then a man wearing a ski mask held me at knifepoint in my home. He accused me of being in on your scheme, but I'd never heard of it. He might have slit my throat if Paul hadn't arrived and scared him off."

Justin rubbed his palms over his eyes and forehead. "It's all my fault. Candace visited me at the hospital. Apparently her informants told her I was alive. I suspect she hadn't sent her henchmen after you earlier because she thought the pendant had been buried in the rubble of the World Trade Center. When she heard I was alive, she probably decided to intensify her search in a desperate attempt to recover it. I'm so very sorry."

Tori turned away. She noticed that the vinyl top of the overturned card table had a jagged tear in it. The table reminded her of her life—upside down and cut wide open. Rage poured out of her as from an open wound. She glared at him. "It's like you've become a different person. I don't even know you anymore."

Justin's upper lip trembled. "If you'll let me explain, you'll see that I'm a better person. I've learned from my mistakes." He reached into his pocket and withdrew the pendant. "The man was after this. I took it from Candace on September 11th, and she'll do anything to get it back—even kill. I suspect that her men trashed my apartment."

Tori stepped toward the door. "Do you really expect me to believe all this? What power could a scratched-up old pendant have?"

"It apparently gives a kind of charisma and clairvoyance to whoever possesses it. At first I didn't believe it, but I'm no longer the complete skeptic I once was."

A phone in the back of the apartment rang. He waved for her to follow and led her through a small dining room into a messy efficiency kitchen. He let the phone ring until the machine picked up. The caller didn't leave a message.

"I didn't answer because it could be Candace's men checking to see if I'm home." He went to the back door and made sure it was locked. "You mentioned Paul. How is he?"

She eyed the greasy frying pan. "Paul is well. We've been seeing a lot of each other. He dropped me off and wants to talk with you later."

"You've been dating Paul?" His voice went soft.

"Yes, for nine months. You didn't expect me to stop living, did you?"

"No, but the thought of you dating my best friend . . . I just didn't expect it."

The phone rang again. He grabbed her hand. "We've got to get out of here." He broke into a run, pulling her along. "My car's on the street."

She rushed with him out the front door. As he locked the deadbolt, a lime green motorcycle approached from the south. Its rider wore a black modular helmet. A wave of horror washed over her, and she pulled at Justin's hand.

"The driver of that motorcycle is the guy who held me at knifepoint!"

A silver BMW pulled in front of the house from the other direction. A woman at the wheel, two men with her. Tori dashed back inside. Justin caught up and led her through the house and out the back door.

"Where are we going?" She glanced back at the street. The motorcycle rider was conferring with the people in the BMW.

"I don't know." Justin guided her across the lawn. "We have to find a place to hide until we lose them."

She heard the roar of an engine and glanced back. The motorcycle was entering the yard. She and Justin ran between two garages as the motorcycle sped after them. A row of free-standing shrubs bordered the next yard. They shoved aside the branches and kept moving. The shrubs slowed the motorcycle.

She dodged a swing set and raced across a wide patch of grass with Justin. They crossed a patio and a driveway. They came to a tall wooden fence, opened the gate, and entered a yard that had an in-ground swimming pool. They hid behind a shed, catching their breath. She heard the motorcycle on a nearby side street.

"I recognized the driver of the BMW." Justin kept his voice low. "It's Candace. Now do you believe my story?"

Tori ignored the question. His theories about a miraculous pendant were too bizarre. "Who are the guys with her?"

"I've never seen them before. I suspect she hired them from some private security firm to help track me down."

The revving of the motorcycle drew closer. She followed Justin to the front of the house. They hid behind an enormous maple tree. Her anger and confusion were as all-encompassing as its bark. From there they could see the street that paralleled Wayland Avenue.

The BMW passed by heading north. It stopped, and the two men, both well-toned and wearing navy blue slacks and purple golf shirts, got out. They split up on foot.

Tori gave Justin a distressed look. He motioned for her to stay down and guided her south. They dashed across lawns and threaded between cars parked in driveways. When she glanced back, her blood turned frigid. The motorcycle was half a block behind them. The driver tucked his chin against the handlebars and gunned the engine.

Justin steered her through a backyard garden. The motorcycle left the street and bore down. They swerved around a doghouse and leaped over a waist-high stone wall. The motorcycle had to stop. The driver yelled curses as they left him behind.

They doubled back to Wayland Avenue heading south on the sidewalk. After a couple blocks they came to a cathedral-like gold stone church at the corner of Lloyd Avenue—the Community Church of Providence. The back door was open. A sign announced that an Alcoholics Anonymous meeting was going on downstairs. Tori pulled Justin inside. The motorcycle roared by on Wayland Avenue. Then she heard the engine downshift and the tires squeal.

13

WHAT REALLY HAPPENED?

Paul Spardello hated lies, but when he'd dropped Tori at Justin's apartment, he hadn't told her where he was really going. He couldn't wait at a restaurant or eat anything, not with his stomach churning over her meeting with her prodigal husband.

He needed to know what had happened to the Justin Connelly he'd grown up with. How had his smartest-kid-in-the-class, most-likely-to-succeed friend become a runaway coward and fraud? A middle-aged couple walking their dog near Justin's apartment had directed him to the Rockefeller Library at Brown University.

After the guard had granted him a guest pass, Paul approached the thirty-something woman at the circulation desk. "I need to do some Internet research, and I don't have much time. May I use a computer?"

The librarian gave him a rueful smile. "If you're brave enough to enter Red Sox Nation in a Yankees sweatshirt, you must be desperate for help." She asked a slender Asian woman to cover the checkout requests and stepped around the desk.

He followed her through the wide, corridor-like lobby. The polished terrazzo floor and the "I Believe" quote from John D. Rockefeller, Jr. embossed on the marble wall complemented the neatly shelved books behind the circulation desk. Paul's life was anything but neat. Nothing fit anymore. A New England nor'easter howled inside him, lashing his confidence with vicious wind and rain.

The librarian led him into a large room illuminated by floor-to-ceiling windows. More than a dozen rows of shelves and at least fifty computer terminals sat in a section marked *Reference*. She paused inside the glass double doors. "My name is Darlene. May I ask what you're researching? Perhaps I can help."

He stared at the tightly woven red carpet. After the flippant comment she'd made about his sweatshirt, her politeness surprised him. She reminded him of the women who flirted with him on the Staten Island Ferry as he commuted to and from the firehouse in Manhattan. They saw that he didn't wear a wedding band and assumed he was fair game. He usually told them he had a girlfriend. Now he didn't know if that was still true.

"I'm trying to find information about a man who was in the news this week" he said. "He fled the World Trade Center on September 11th and lived a secret life in Providence."

Darlene peered at him through designer glasses. "You mean he faked his death and got away with it?"

"Yes, for almost two years."

"Was he trying to cash in on a life insurance policy or something?"

"That's what I'm trying to find out."

She gave a cynical laugh. "He came to the right place. This state's nickname is 'Rogue's Island.' He probably felt right at home."

"He may have, but it all ended a couple days ago."

She led him to the first row of computers. "Do you know this guy?"

"I might." He wiped his moist forehead on the shoulder of his sweatshirt.

"Here's our terminal for guests. Let's get you logged in." She sat in the swivel chair and typed in the password. When the computer booted, she stood and let him sit. "You've got me curious. Do you mind if I see what you find?"

"Be my guest."

He brought up Google and typed *Justin Connelly, sailing accident, Rhode Island*. More than ten entries appeared. He clicked on an article from the state's major newspaper, the *Providence Journal*, and navigated to the headline *Hero in Boating Accident Is 9/11 Runaway*. With Darlene looking on, he brought up the article and began to read. She finished first.

"What a story," she said. "The woman Justin Connelly saved calls him a hero. Without him, she would've drowned."

Paul gave her a dismissive stare. "A flawed hero, in my opinion." The article tore at his insides. It described the man he thought he'd known, the man who'd worked with him as a lifeguard and risked his welfare for others. It made no sense that his noble friend had used the worst attack on American soil as an opportunity to desert his wife and live on the lam for twenty months.

"So you do know him. You must be concerned." She pointed at the screen. "The article says he ingested lots of water. When the Coast Guard lifted him into the helicopter, they put him on a respirator, but he was still comatose when they arrived at Rhode Island Hospital. The emergency room doctors stimulated his heart and intubated him, but he stayed in the coma for six hours."

"That must've been one heck of a storm." Paul placed his elbows on either side of the keyboard and cupped his chin in his hands. "It's all quite shocking."

"If the story you told me is true, he must've woken up to a heap of trouble."

Paul barely heard her comment. His fury at Justin had set his pulse hammering in his ears. The pressure in his chest had grown so intense that all forty-four inches of it ached. She couldn't possibly fathom how Justin's reemergence had changed Paul's life. He and Tori had both been close to Justin and that had given them a powerful bond. Paul had believed he was honoring his friend by loving his widow and caring for her. Now his friend could become his rival in love. Even if he didn't, Justin would surely complicate Paul's relationship with Tori. How could he not? She and Justin had a son together . . . . His throat felt as if razor-sharp claws were scratching its tissues.

"Where's the restroom?"

She pointed toward the lobby. "At the bottom of the stairs."

He retraced his steps and found the stairway across from the circulation desk. On the way down the curved wooden spiral, he wondered why Tori hadn't called yet. She'd been with Justin for more than an hour.

Paul splashed cold water on his face as imaginary snippets of her conversation with her vagabond husband looped through his mind. His haggard reflection startled him. Dark circles around his eyes made him appear a decade older. He soaked a paper towel in hot water and dabbed the puffy circles. His cell phone vibrated. He answered as he left the men's room. The voice belonged to his lawyer, Stephen Constantino.

"If you're standing, you might want to sit down," Stephen said. "I got a call from your wife's attorney today. She's having second thoughts about the divorce and wants to meet with you and a mediator."

"What?" Paul stopped as if he'd hit a wall. "Did her lawyer say what brought on this sudden revelation?"

"No, but I've had other cases like yours, and I'm not surprised. You're both good people, there was no affair, you have a child together . . . you both have a lot to lose."

"So now you're my therapist as well as my lawyer?"

"I'm just saying I've seen it before. The court date approaches and the woman realizes what it will be like to be alone, to be a single mom. It's like she climbs onto the high dive and walks to the end of the board then looks down and sees it's higher than she thought. Linda might not have the nerve to jump."

Paul gripped the bannister at the bottom of the stairs. First Justin reappeared, upsetting his relationship with Tori; now Linda might want to reconcile? He glanced up. The ceiling tiles appeared out of focus and bright enough to blind him. He thought about Tori and wondered what their relationship was really about. Had they built it on love or on the need they'd both had for comfort in grief? He wouldn't be asking the question if Justin hadn't returned. Now Linda's proposal had forced the issue and raised the possibility that his divorce wasn't as inevitable as he'd believed for the past year. Contrasted with the brightness of the ceiling, the murkiness in his mind appeared as dark as midnight. "Do you have any advice?"

"Are you willing to meet with her?"

Paul fumbled for an answer. He wondered if Linda had heard the news about Justin, wondered if it had factored into her decision to suggest a meeting. It didn't matter. To consider reconciling was too much to process right now.

"Tell her lawyer I need some time to think about it," he said. "I'll call you when I get home. I'm in Rhode Island."

"Rhode Island? What are you doing there?"

"You wouldn't believe it if I told you."

14

A Refuge
or a Trap?

*J*ustin ran into the church fellowship hall and waved for Tori to follow. The auditorium-like space was empty and appeared to be a good place to hide. But when he spotted rooms on the mezzanine that encircled the hall, he decided one of them would be safer. He sprinted for the back stairs with Tori at his side.

"Shouldn't we call the police?" She brushed against him as they bounded up the wide staircase.

At her touch, powerful energy shot through him. He took the stairs two at a time. "I can't. I'll tell you why later."

He paused at the top as their footsteps echoed off the high ceiling and plaster walls. For a moment, the reverberating sound reminded him of the stampede-like rumble of people climbing down the stairs of the North Tower. A stab of grief cut through him. He was determined to make amends for his cowardice and to honor the memory of those who'd died.

They would have to hide in the church until dark then escape into the shadows. He sprinted to the far end of the mezzanine, thinking the last room would be the safest.

"I can't believe what a mess you've created," she said. "You could get us killed!"

The door was locked. He backpedaled to the second-to-the-last room. "I told you how sorry I am. Everything's going to be different, I promise."

"Your bizarre explanation only makes it worse."

He turned the knob—locked. His dreams of reconciliation mocked him as he rushed to the door in the middle of the mezzanine. When he stopped, Tori's momentum pushed her into him. He longed to hold her, but she recoiled, and another ember of hope died inside him.

He jiggled the knob—locked. They approached the two doors nearest the stairs at the back of the building, and he tried the closest knob. To his relief, the door opened. He pulled her into what looked like a children's classroom. Several short-legged tables and small chairs stood in the middle, and windows lined two sides. He locked the hollow wooden door. Tori's intense eyes scanned the spacious room. "If he finds us here, we'll be trapped."

"We have nowhere else to go." Justin went to a window to see if they could climb down, but the second floor was too high. He faced her and kept his voice low. "I may not have another chance to explain why I ran away. When Candace told me the pendant had helped her get inside information that made her billions, I thought it was a joke."

Tori glared at him and spoke in a stage whisper. "Why didn't you report the insider trading?"

"Because I helped with it. I would've gone to jail with her. I still may."

She narrowed her eyes. "Don't expect sympathy from me."

"I'm not asking for any. But I want you to know the whole story of the sailing accident. I was unconscious for about six hours and had a horrifying near-death experience." He paused, his expression grave. "Tori, I went to hell."

"And you took me with you."

Her words burned his conscience like acid but didn't dampen his feelings for her. He drew a ragged breath, staggered by the implications of what he was about to say. "I met Jesus there, and he gave me a second chance. Now I have to use the pendant to share the spiritual secrets I learned."

"You met Jesus in hell?" She gave a muffled laugh. "Now I know you're lying. If anyone's in heaven, it's Jesus. And how could a pendant help you to share spiritual secrets?"

Her skepticism fed his own doubts about whether his near-death experience was real or a drug-induced hallucination. "Apparently it gives extraordinary powers of persuasion to whoever possesses it. I need to find out more, and I could use your investigative skills."

"Don't count on it."

A lacerating ache gnawed at his heart. He was startled by the resilience, even the brazenness, of his desire for her, yet he wasn't ready to tell her about his relationship with Candace. Tori was the only woman who could help heal his shame. If she knew the truth, she would surely let him drown in it. Even a saint would. He focused on her anxious face.

"I still love you."

She pushed him away. "How dare you talk about love to me? If you were sincere, you would've at least called me in the past two years! You didn't even have the decency to divorce me before you left. Instead you had me grieving as if you were a fallen martyr. I even accepted money from a special fund. You've made me look like a fool. Even a thief!"

Justin stared at the chipping paint on a house across the street. He'd stayed away from the media so as not to be reminded of his treachery. Now he fought to keep her words from chipping away the last of his sanity. "Did you quit working?"

"No."

"Why not?"

She said nothing for a moment as she inhaled deeply. "Because I invested the money for your son's education."

"My son?" Justin's knees went weak.

"Yes. I was pregnant on September 11th. Justin Jr. will be a year old next month."

Justin grabbed the windowsill as blood drained from his face. The shock exploded in his mind. Him, a father? "I . . . I don't know what to say."

"I do. It'll be a long time before you see him—if ever."

Justin fought to keep his voice from breaking. He concentrated on not saying anything he would later regret. "He's my son. Of course I want to see him."

"He may be your son, but you ended our marriage when you abandoned us." Her tone intensified. "You have no rights."

The thud of footsteps on the back stairs sent her words echoing through his mind. He pressed a finger to his lips as his pulse pounded. The footsteps reached the mezzanine. The door to the adjoining room shook and rattled. The rattling was followed by a kicking sound then a bang. Justin feared that the motorcycle driver had broken through the flimsy door.

The footsteps drew closer. He and Tori stayed back so their shoes wouldn't be seen through the thin gap at the bottom of the door. He wondered how he'd ended up in a church with his aggrieved wife hiding from an obsessed man. The question sent turmoil cascading through him. Tori gave him a terrified glance. There was a shuffle outside the door.

The knob shook.

"If you're in there, Connelly, you know what I want. Give it up!"

Justin remained still. He recognized the intense, raspy voice as that of Quentin Rathbun, Candace's brilliant but devious senior stock analyst. The sour taste of bile flooded his mouth as he remembered the unlimited cash, the lavish parties, the cocaine highs of their years together. Rathbun's military background and his passion for bodybuilding and extreme sports qualified him to do Candace's bidding with terrifying precision and brutality. And his obsession with her motivated his vendettas against any man who competed with him for her affections.

Justin had fled both Candace's possessiveness and Rathbun's jealousy while he'd still had a life. Now he was in danger of losing that life to his handsome former mentor, a man who'd once been an up-and-coming Wall Street professional but whom Candace had apparently turned into a ruthless thug.

Rathbun kicked the door. Justin pressed a shoulder against it, strengthened by fear and determination. Tori did the same.

Rathbun rammed the door. Justin pushed harder.

He heard running in the hall followed by a thundering crash.

The door jarred open.

Rathbun shoved his way in. His straight black hair was matted from the helmet, and his wide-set brown eyes were fiery. Justin assumed a wrestler's stance. "Tori, call the cops!"

Rathbun knocked her down then lunged at him. "You'll go to jail with me."

Justin dodged him. "I didn't realize you moonlighted as a thug. You should stick to reading spreadsheets, arranging conference calls."

Rathbun threw a punch that grazed his cheek. "At least I'm not a thief who steals from an unconscious woman."

Justin retreated to a spot near the windows and raised his fists. "All this time, I thought you were a genius. Now I know Candace was making you look good. But she's lost her edge, and you've lost your bonuses. No wonder you're desperate."

Rathbun kicked him in the stomach. "You're in no position to moralize. Just hand over the pendant."

Justin struggled up and threw him off. "You'll have to take it from me."

Rathbun pulled a knife from an ankle holster and dove. Blood welled from Justin's shoulder.

"Stop it!" Tori tried to step between them but backed off as they clashed then separated. "Both of you. Please, it's not worth it!"

Justin kept one eye on the six-inch blade and the other on Rathbun's body. He had to disarm him. That meant grabbing his hand and wrestling the weapon free. If he missed and left himself vulnerable, he would be stabbed. He waited for

Rathbun's lunge and sidestepped but missed the knife hand. He stayed on the balls of his feet and refused to give ground.

"I used to respect you." He faked a dive at Rathbun's legs. "I wanted to learn from you."

The knife came at him again. This time he latched on to Rathbun's wrist, first with one hand then the other. He pushed down and twisted. "Now I think you're pathetic."

The knife fell free, but Rathbun tackled him and slammed Justin's head against the floor. Lights flashed in his brain. He felt as if a needle had pierced his nerve center to inject agony and dizziness. Rathbun rifled the pocket of Justin's jeans and scooped out the pendant.

"I don't care what you think," he said. "I have what I came for."

He punched Justin in the mouth, picked up the knife, and cocked his arm to stab him. Tori dove and knocked him away. Justin rolled over and prevented him from attacking her.

"What's going on in here?" A slender, gray-haired man in a muscle shirt stood in the doorway. He was accompanied by a stocky, bald-headed man.

Justin sucked in air and pointed at Rathbun. "He robbed me."

Rathbun wielded the knife and stepped toward the men. "No I didn't. I took what was mine."

The gray-haired man stepped back and told his friend, "Call 911!"

As the friend fumbled for his cell phone, the gray-haired man said, "I'm the head of the A.A. group, and I'm responsible for the building. No one's going to rob anyone. What did he take?"

"My wooden pendant. It's very valuable."

The man held out a palm. "Let's have the pendant."

Rathbun threatened with the knife. "No way."

Justin sprang up, grabbed the knife hand, and yanked. He wrestled Rathbun to the floor until he dropped the weapon. Justin seized his other hand, pried the fingers loose, and took the pendant. The gray-haired man and his companion leaped in to restrain Rathbun, but he swung vicious fists. Driving them back, he ran for the door. He was met there by several more men from the A.A. group.

"You're not going anywhere," one of them said.

Rathbun fought his way through and fled down the stairs. Justin and Tori chased him with the others but encountered two security guards outside. Candace was waiting in the BMW.

They let Rathbun through and fought everyone else back. Justin slammed the door to protect the pendant. The motorcycle's engine roared to life, and tires squealed. The gray-haired man stayed inside. He reached the police dispatcher and reported the incident. Justin pulled Tori aside.

"I suspect that Rathbun hired those guards to help recover the pendant but didn't tell them anything about it. I hope the cops nail him." He showed her the pendant. "There's an event in Providence tonight called WaterFire. Thousands of people gather downtown to see the burning cauldrons on the rivers. I want to test the pendant there. If it doesn't give me the powers of spiritual clarity and persuasion, you can go home and forget I ever mentioned it. But if something extraordinary happens, wouldn't you want to know how and why?"

She looked away. A blaring siren grew closer. He awaited her response, knowing his proposal sounded farfetched. He wasn't even sure he believed in the pendant, but he had to give it a chance. He led her outside as a squad car entered the lot.

"I need to call Paul and tell him what's happening." She raised her voice to be heard over the siren. "I don't want to make the same mistakes with him that I made with you."

15

INTO THE TURMOIL

Seeing the squad car in the church parking lot made Paul wish he'd resisted that second beer. The taste of the spearmint gum he was chewing to cover the alcohol on his breath was fading. He pulled the Mustang into the single-row lot behind the church and parked at the end.

When he'd dropped Tori off at Justin's apartment, he'd expected the night to progress without major complications. But seeing *Providence Police* on the side of the cruiser reminded him how many times he'd gone on a call thinking it was routine only to have an elderly woman's fainting spell turn into a stroke or have a hidden accelerant escalate a one-alarm fire to three alarms.

Tori's call had had a similar effect. He'd been watching the Brown University students on Thayer Street from his table at the Shanghai Restaurant and had been ready to order another beer. He'd left the moment she told him that Justin's former mentor at Donahue Financial, Quentin Rathbun, had attacked them.

Paul's adrenaline hadn't stopped surging since. He got out of the Mustang and searched for an inner bedrock as solid as the towering stone church. Facing the greatest romantic challenge of his life, he hit quicksand instead. Tori needed him, but he wasn't ready to see her with Justin, and he doubted he ever would be. The narrow parking lot, dwarfed by the cathedral-like edifice, made him feel claustrophobic.

He approached Tori and Justin. They and a group of rumpled men had gathered around a barrel-chested African-American cop. A slender, gray-haired man wearing a muscle shirt with a New England Patriots emblem said, "The church allows our A.A. group to meet here for free, but if there's trouble, they might kick us out."

He pointed an accusing finger at Tori and Justin, both of whom looked sweaty and disheveled. "These two entered without permission and endangered everybody. I should charge them with trespassing."

Paul felt his jaw clench. The sight of Justin gagged him as if he'd swallowed rancid food. He had an urge to attack him, but he caught a glimpse of his large brown eyes, as enchanting as ever, and remembered how they'd often had fun and laughed together. Crushing grief left him motionless as the man commanded the group's attention.

"Whether you press charges is up to you," the cop said. He wrote on a form on his clipboard. "According to their story, they had no alternative."

The A.A. leader smirked. "They could've chosen some other hiding place."

"In these situations, there's a lot of second-guessing. My concern is that we catch the guy with the knife."

The A.A. leader thought for a moment. "All right, I won't press charges, but they ain't comin' back inside."

"I'll make sure of that. We're almost done here."

"Good." The man and his two friends went inside leaving the door hooked open.

The cop noticed Paul. "May I help you, sir?"

Tori came over and gave Paul a hug. "He's with us, officer."

The cop opened the door of his cruiser and threw his clipboard on the seat. "Good, because you can't stay here." He regarded Justin with concern. "I wouldn't go back to your apartment either. Can you get a room for a couple nights?"

Tori pointed at the Mustang. "We'll figure it out as we go."

"All right." The officer got into his car and rolled down his window. "A bulletin has gone out on this guy Rathbun. Cops all over the city will be looking for him." The officer pulled out of the lot.

Paul could restrain himself no more. He flew at Justin and seized the collar of his khaki shirt. "I've seen people do some cowardly things in a crisis, but using a national tragedy to fake your death is as low as it gets. Now you've returned and almost gotten Tori killed." He pulled the collar so tight it choked him. "You're lucky she's okay because there's no telling what I'd do to you if she weren't."

Justin coughed and struggled to break free. "You're right . . . it was stupid . . . and cowardly but—"

Tori wedged in between them. "Paul, stop it!"

He kept choking him, unable to control his rage. She launched her shoulder into him and drove with her legs. "I said stop!"

He slammed Justin to the pavement. He appeared to have lost weight. The weeks and months since September 11th fell away in the ache of the moment and in scathing memories beyond naming. Paul sucked in air and looked away. His moist, burning eyes gazed unseeing at the leafy trees bordering the lot. Justin stood and approached him with a hand extended.

Paul searched out Tori's rich brown eyes and saw that they were unsettled. He drew back and said, "Now you know Justin's okay. Let's start home before it gets too late."

Tori tightened her lips. "No. I told him I would stay."

"Stay here? But I thought—"

"He has something to show us."

Paul shot him an intimidating look. "I've seen enough already."

"I thought you were my friend." Justin withdrew his hand.

"I'd emphasize *were*." Paul shook his head dismissively, losing the battle against the disgust festering inside him. "You gave up our friendship when you bolted on September 11th."

Justin swung his gaze from him to Tori then back. "I'll tell you the same thing I told her. I'm sorry for what I did. I know I betrayed you, as well as her, but I can't relive the past. All I ask for is a chance to—"

Paul shoved and knocked him down. "You don't deserve any more chances!" He tried to keep his voice steady, but his rising emotions made his words intense. "I lost a lot of buddies in the North Tower. They ran into that burning building to save as many people as they could and didn't come out. You ran in the opposite direction. What kind of man does that?"

The harshness of his response was a surprise. The sight of Justin had aroused passions he hadn't been able to control since that fateful day.

"I've never known you to jump to conclusions without having all the facts." Justin grabbed the trunk of a beat-up Honda Civic and pulled himself up. "You don't have any idea what I was going through on that day."

"And I don't want to know. I can't stand—"

Tori pulled at his arm then glared at both of them. "If you two don't stop this, I'm leaving."

Paul also raised his voice. "I just want him to know that everything has changed, and that he has no one to blame but himself."

He tried to calm down but couldn't quell the resentment in his chest. Even sensing that he was alienating Tori didn't calm his anger. He kept thinking of the buddies he'd lost, the four people he'd risked his life to save, the terror of his own narrow escape.

The A.A. leader appeared at the back door. "I want you guys out of here. Now. Any more arguin' and I'll call that cop back."

Paul started toward the Mustang. "Okay, we're going."

The man left as Justin stared at the blacktop. "I'm well aware of whose fault it is."

Paul tossed his gum into the trashcan beside the door. "There's something else I want you to know. I've asked Tori to marry me."

Justin stared at her as his slack-jawed expression darkened. "Why didn't you tell me?"

She stepped away from both the men. "I told you I've been seeing a lot of Paul. I planned to tell you more but didn't get the chance."

Justin crossed his arms. "Have you given him an answer?"

She glanced at Paul, her eyes flashing confusion. She took a step toward the Mustang. "Not yet, but I do love him."

Justin eyed him incredulously. "We're friends. We should be able to—"

"I told you our friendship is over." He followed Tori and spoke over a shoulder. "I cared for your widow as a true friend would. Feelings developed between us, partly because we were both close to you. You're the one who's caused this pain!"

He caught up to Tori and reached for her hand. "Let's just go home."

She pulled away. "I can't. Justin's told me a lot about the pendant that almost got me killed. I need to find out if it's true."

"What are you talking about?"

Justin withdrew a small oval of burnished wood from his pocket. He held it out for Paul to see along with its braided gold chain. "This."

The sight of the pendant infused him with rage. Tori could've been killed for this worthless trinket! He lunged for the oval, but Justin tightened his fist around it. Paul grabbed his wrist.

"Stop it!" Tori pulled his hand away. "That pendant's a real mystery. We need to give Justin the chance to show us why."

"I don't owe him anything." Paul yanked his hand free.

Justin held up the pendant. "If my former boss is right, this is no ordinary piece of jewelry. Candace Donahue believes it helped her become the richest hedge fund manager on Wall Street."

Paul gave a dismissive laugh. "So this pendant is some kind of high-tech good luck charm? That's absurd."

Justin returned the pendant to his pocket. "That's what I thought too, and you've known me since we were kids. I'm not an irrational person, right?"

"Until today I would've answered no. Now I'm not so sure."

"What happened to me was totally irrational. It took a sailing accident to make me question my skepticism."

Paul crossed his arms on his chest. "I know all about the accident from the Internet."

Justin shook his head. "Your research couldn't possibly describe the hell I went through."

"What do you know about hell?" He nearly spat the words. "I know what hell looks and smells like, what it feels like too. I experienced it on September 11th when the towers came down and incinerated nearly three thousand people, including men from my fire station. They were braver than you'll ever be. You believe what you want about your silly pendant, but don't tell me you know anything about hell!"

Paul took Tori's hand. "I've heard enough. You can stay and listen to this nonsense if you want, but I'm leaving." He opened the driver's door of the Mustang.

Tori held his arm. "I don't want you to go, but if you insist, I'll let you. I need to see for myself whether the pendant is real."

"Tori, this is crazy. I—"

She seized his other arm and shook him. "I mean it, Paul. At least give Justin a chance."

He saw the fire in her eyes and feared he'd lost her. "How?"

Justin held his ground to her right. "I invited her to an event called WaterFire. Thirty-thousand people gather downtown. I'm going to test the pendant by seeing if it gives me a message for the people and if they'll listen to me."

Paul got in the Mustang and rolled down the window. "I can't do it. I need to go."

He started the engine and shifted into reverse. Tori grabbed the door. "If you leave, you're taking your marriage proposal with you. I need to see if Justin's telling the truth. If you can't honor that, how can I be married to you?"

Paul applied the brake as the rumble of the engine cut through him. It was a softer version of the sound his rescue vehicle made on a call. A similar sense of emergency swept through him. He wanted to leave Justin behind forever, but if he drove away, he'd lose Tori. He couldn't do it. "All right. Get in . . . both of you."

Tori took the front seat and Justin the back. Paul pulled out of the lot and headed downtown. As he turned right on Lloyd Avenue, he thought of that third beer and how good it would taste right now.

16

THE FIRST CHALLENGE OF A TRANSFORMED LIFE: ACCEPTED ACCEPTANCE

A WaterFire lighting was supposed to be mystical, not life-threatening. Torchbearers in gondolas on the three rivers of Providence ignited cauldrons of wood accompanied by liturgical, choral, or classical music. The lightings were always safe and peaceful, and that's what the thousands of people gathered in darkness expected.

Justin feared they would witness a brutal attack instead.

Trailed by Tori and Paul, he pushed through the crowd lining the cobblestone walkway above the Woonasquatucket River. He usually enjoyed the city's ornate hotel and apartment facades, Colonial-style mall, and white marble State House, but tonight a burning sensation roiled his chest. Either the smoke from the flaming braziers on the rivers or his anxiety about Rathbun and his men was causing the sensation, he couldn't tell which. He scanned the crowd. When he didn't see any of the thugs, he fastened the gold chain around his neck so that the pendant hung in front.

He passed under a footbridge and imagined the ridicule the crowd would heap on him if they knew the depths of his treachery. His upper lip grew moist. He wiped away the sweat and noticed the brilliant embers shooting up from the Woonasquatucket. He'd been at WaterFire only one other time, in July of 2002. Back then he'd been relieved to be in Providence free of his dalliance with Candace and relatively happy despite his fear of being discovered. Now everything was different. His happiness, like the embers, had glowed and soared only briefly before burning out.

"Can you spare some change?"

A grimy man sitting against a cement pillar reached a hand out to three teenage boys. He wore a dirty red shirt and carpenter's pants held up by ill-fitting suspenders. He had a straggly beard, long, greasy hair, no front teeth. His other hand clutched a bottle concealed in a paper bag. The boys twirled plastic necklaces that glowed green, yellow, and red.

"Get a job, mister." The pudgiest of the three pushed his thick glasses up on his nose and laughed.

"Yeah," another said. He craned his gangly neck, his face dotted with acne. "Don't spend your money on booze. Then you won't have to beg."

Justin saw his opportunity. He approached the boys and gulped a breath. "Don't bully this man. He needs understanding and help."

The boys laughed harder. "Maybe you're a drunk too," the pimply one said.

Justin tried to speak, but his words died in his throat, victims of his questions about whether his near-death experience had been real. He stroked the pendant's rough surface. "Actually, I've done worse than he has." A surge of energy freed up the words. His tongue grew thick. His voice modulated into a tone he hadn't heard before, resonant and compelling. He stepped between the boys and the man. "I was given a second chance, and I'm trying to make the best of it."

He moved onto the plaza in front of Citizens Bank where the Woonasquatucket and Moshassack rivers intersected to form the Providence River. Unfamiliar thoughts rose in his mind—thoughts about inner healing, about God and faith and love.

"I ruined my life." He raised his voice so the cadre of several hundred people nearby could hear. "My choices landed me in hell . . . literally. I met Jesus of Nazareth there, and he sent me back with a hopeful message."

A middle-aged man in a yellow windbreaker stepped from the crowd. "Jesus is in hell?"

The aching loneliness of Justin's brush with death returned to him. He drew several quick breaths to keep the vertigo at bay. "I met him there."

The man covered his ears as if they hurt. "Anyone who's read the Bible knows Jesus is in heaven with God."

The crowd applauded, but Justin held up one hand. "Before today I would've agreed, but I had a horrifying near-death experience that changed my mind. I have a new appreciation for the First Epistle of Peter, that Christ 'went and preached to the spirits in prison.'"

Justin's knees trembled. Then a peculiar peace washed over him and drew his muscles taut. "The Apostles' Creed says, 'he descended into hell.' I met Christ there and received forgiveness and a new beginning."

Tori brushed behind him. Amazement sounded in her whispered words. "I've never heard you talk like this. Where is this coming from?"

"From beyond me. The pendant's inspiring me."

The man in the windbreaker took another step toward him. "Are you saying Jesus gives souls in hell a second chance?"

"I can only say he gave me one, and that I saw him set thousands of prisoners free."

The man gave a sarcastic laugh. "You can't prove any of it."

Justin knew the man was right, that his near-death experience could've been a drug-induced hallucination, but then where were these thoughts coming from? He stood as tall as his six-foot-one frame would allow. "No one can prove what happens after we die. I'm speaking from my experience. I grew up in the church, but I wasn't living as a Christian when I nearly drowned in a sailing accident. I was in a coma for six terrifying hours, and I was shown an extreme version of what I'd already experienced in my darkest times . . . which we all have."

The homeless man struggled to his feet. "Hell is real. I live it every day."

Justin took him by the shoulders. "You shouldn't have to. No one should."

He lifted his grimy face. "Those are the first kind words I've heard in a long time."

Justin stepped back and addressed the crowd before the flaming rivers. "I know what lands us in hell. It's our own stupidity and our failure to love."

The teenage boys made faces, but a Hispanic woman with a baby in a wraparound carrier told them, "You should listen.

He speaks the truth." She turned to Justin. "Why do we have such a hard time finding our way?"

He fingered the pendant, searching for the right words to express the ideas swirling in his mind. "We don't choose hell intentionally but out of ignorance. No one wakes up and says, 'I'm going to make myself miserable today.' We make ourselves miserable while trying our hardest to be happy. The problem is that we seek happiness in self-sabotaging, destructive ways."

"So all we have to do is think correctly and we'll be happy?"

A torrent of unfamiliar ideas poured into Justin's mind. "That's a faulty and dangerous idea. We can't *think* our way to God."

He was surprised to hear himself sound so spiritual. He hadn't attended church in many years. Hot shame crept up his neck; he was aghast that he might be considered a religious fanatic. But the more he resisted speaking, the more impossible it became to hold back the words.

"What we need are welcoming hearts . . . hearts that receive God's love in the present moment, in the midst of our daily challenges as well as our heartbreak."

The homeless man leaped up and pointed at Justin's head. "What's that?" He cowered back and shielded his eyes. "Your head's glowing, man! It's like the sun's shining from your face. If I look at you, I'll . . . I'll go blind. Doesn't anyone else see it?"

The pudgy teenager stepped away from the crowd. "I don't see nothing."

"I do," the Hispanic woman said. "It's a reflection of the fires on the water."

"You're probably right," Justin said. He didn't want anything to sidetrack the crowd. "In hell, I learned the truth. In Christ, God completely and unconditionally accepts us. The harder work is for each of us to accept ourselves."

The pudgy teenager threw his glowing necklace at him. "Why don't you shut up and let us enjoy the night?"

"Yeah," his pimply friend said. "We didn't come here to listen to no street preacher!"

The teenagers pelted him with their necklaces and ran away. Justin refused to leave.

"Let them go," the Hispanic woman said. "The rest of us want to hear more."

Justin cradled the pendant in his palms. The words he'd spoken echoed in his thoughts, making him wonder if he'd become clairvoyant. He felt as if the fires on the rivers were burning in his bones. The only way to relieve the heat was to keep speaking.

"The best gift we can give ourselves," he said, "is to accept our acceptance. The world tells us we aren't handsome, beautiful, smart, or successful enough. We feel inadequate, especially when others hurt or belittle us, or when we compare ourselves to them. We can overcome negative messages and self-defeating attitudes by remembering who we really are—the Lord's beloved. By returning to our true identities, we can reclaim our uniqueness and our infinite worth in God's sight. Our dignity and purpose will outweigh all the negatives."

The homeless man faced the crowd. "When this man speaks, it's like I hear his voice in my heart and I see light all around his head. Somethin' powerful's happenin' here. If you feel it, clap with me."

The applause sounded raucous, like a crowd celebrating a touchdown at a football game. But the man in the yellow windbreaker didn't join in, nor did a small minority of other listeners. Justin glanced at Tori and Paul standing on the plaza. Her expression, formerly hardened with skepticism, had softened into surprise and respect. She went over to the homeless man and clapped with him.

Paul didn't participate. He waited for the applause to die down then faced the crowd. "I grew up with this man and I've never—"

"Religion that isn't rooted in radical acceptance leaves us bitter and depressed." Justin swept a hand over the three rivers. "Judgmental religion beats us down. We struggle to be good but are denied the satisfaction of achieving goodness. Judgmental religion enslaves us to an impossible standard of perfection. We end up feeling inadequate, frustrated, exhausted."

The crowd clapped and cheered even louder. Justin swept a hand over the rivers again.

"Jesus offers the opposite. He tells us we're already acceptable to God based on the free gift of his suffering love. My friends, this is scandalous! It gives us an unlimited number of chances to learn from our mistakes and failures. Think of it. Judgmental religion no longer has any power. Neither does shame or humiliation. If God is for us, nothing can condemn us."

The man in the yellow windbreaker rushed forward. "You're selling snake oil! We should always strive to improve ourselves. The Bible says, 'God helps those who help—'"

"Actually, that phrase isn't in the Bible." Justin stepped in front of the man. "Accepting our acceptance is the best way to improve our lives. Why? Because it silences the lies we tell ourselves—the lie that we don't measure up, that we can't get it right, the lie that we're not worthy of love or happiness. When we believe these lies, we spend our lives trying to earn approval, trying to show by our accomplishments that we deserve honor and respect. The problem is, all of our striving leaves us exhausted. Even when we succeed, we feel empty and joyless."

The homeless man staggered to the front, squinting and shielding his eyes. "It's like I've needed this message my entire life. I've waited so long to hear it."

Justin went on, "Accepting our acceptance changes everything. We stop railing against the mistakes we've made, against the family we were born into, against the tough breaks and raw deals we've received. Instead we start giving thanks for our minds and our appearance, our emotional makeup and our personal histories—everything—as priceless gifts of our humanness. Rather than grow more and more bitter over what we lack, we begin to appreciate how rare and fleeting our lives are, and our negativity turns to wonder. From this liberating perspective, no matter what tragedies we experience or what messes we create, God can make something beautiful of it—even in hell. We only accept others to the degree to which we accept ourselves."

His cheeks began to burn. He hadn't fully experienced the truth of the words he spoke. He believed he'd met Jesus in hell and received forgiveness, but he hadn't completely forgiven himself. His cheeks burned hotter with guilt and shame. He remembered how he'd lied and cheated and done cocaine, and how he'd run away on September 11th to avoid the consequences of his sexual sins.

The best gift we can give ourselves is to accept our acceptance.

He focused on the fires and prayed that his past would be burned up like the wood in the flaming cauldrons. He vowed to live his words and continue to test the pendant. As his cheeks cooled, a well-muscled man parked a lime green motorcycle on the edge of the plaza. The man wore a black helmet.

Rathbun.

Justin pulled Tori and Paul aside. "Rathbun's here. Get the car. I'll meet you in front of the mall."

Tori took Paul's hand and pulled him toward the riverwalk. Justin returned to the middle of the plaza and addressed the crowd. "Take my message to heart and share it in the way you live."

The man in the yellow windbreaker held up a hand. "Wait, I have more questions!"

"I'm sorry. I have to go."

Just then, Rathbun yelled, "Stop that man! He's a thief!"

"Don't listen to him. Judge my message on its merits, not by false accusations."

As Justin backed away, he stuffed the pendant into his pocket. Rathbun pushed toward him. Justin climbed down the stairs to the riverwalk and disappeared into a sea of bodies. He wove his way along the water saying repeatedly, "Emergency. Please let me pass."

He reached the small cobblestone landing from which gondolas were launched and fled up the stairs into the parking lot behind Citizens Bank. He ran past rows of cars toward a cluster of office buildings. Footsteps pounded behind him. A sprawling field lay on the other side of the buildings. From there it would be a short sprint to the mall. He paused beside a minivan to catch his breath. The footsteps bounded up the next row twenty yards behind him. He broke for the grassy hill at the edge of the lot and climbed up. At the top, a hand grabbed the collar of his shirt and yanked him backward.

"Aren't you tired of running?" Rathbun asked.

"Not from you and Candace." Justin swung an arm and threw him off. "If you were smart, you'd run from her too."

"I'm smart enough to know where the money comes from." Rathbun dove at his legs.

Justin sidestepped him. "You're smart but not wise. There's a difference."

He took off toward the train station with Rathbun at his heels. Justin darted up some stairs, crossed a cement plaza, and ran into the field. Thankfully it was dark. He lost Rathbun by hiding in a garden in front of an office building. He waited until he heard no one moving then sprinted along the cinder path out to the street.

He headed for the mall. Tori would be waiting. He'd just reached top speed when a man's head and shoulder slammed into his gut. Justin crashed onto the field as Rathbun reached for the pocket of his jeans. "I want that pendant. Now!"

Justin rolled left, pushed off the ground, and threw him off. "You're even more pathetic than I thought."

Rathbun lunged at him with a knife. Justin grabbed his wrist and twisted the weapon loose. He broke for the mall. Paul's Mustang sat near the main entrance with the driver's window down. Halfway there, Justin saw the BMW come through the intersection on his right. The two security men got out and ran toward him. Paul executed a U-turn, drove the Mustang over the curb, and headed across the field.

"Rathbun's behind you!" He revved the engine. "Jump in!"

The Mustang pulled alongside and continued to move. Justin yanked the back door open and dove in. Paul spun the car around, kicking up a spray of dirt and barely missing Rathbun. He swerved to avoid the security men and accelerated back onto the street.

17

THE MOST PERPLEXING MAZE

The lights of Providence flashed by in a blur. Tori clung to the dashboard as the Mustang wove in and out of traffic. Lights brighter than those shining in the mall or on the streets also flashed in her mind, cautioning her to flee the violence Rathbun had unleashed. She longed to heed the warning, but everything was happening too fast. Her fear made the squeal of the Mustang's tires sound twice as shrill. The realization that she was trapped settled into her gut. The squeal grew deafening.

"Which direction should I go?" Paul yelled. His knuckles were white from gripping the wheel. He glanced back at Justin as he searched for the seat belt. "I'm dropping you off before you get us all killed!"

Tori peered through the rear window. "Rathbun got into the BMW. They're gaining on us!"

"Who's driving?" Paul sped up.

"Candace Donahue, Justin's old boss." Tori gripped her armrest. The Mustang powered through two intersections, passed the Westin Hotel, and wound onto a narrow street that reminded her of an alley. Tires squealed. An engine roared behind them. She glanced back; the BMW was catching up.

"You missed the on-ramp to the expressway," Justin said. "I know how to get to another one."

Tori felt as if they were trapped in a maze of one-way streets. The more perplexing maze was inside. She'd come to Providence looking for answers and gotten sucked into a wild scheme involving a mysterious pendant. If the BMW overtook them, they might all be killed. She searched for Justin's eyes in the darkness. "Where do you want us to take you?"

"I'll get a motel in Seekonk, over the Massachusetts line. Rathbun and Candace won't think to look for me there."

"Which way?" Paul asked.

"We have to get to 195 East."

Paul turned onto a brightly lit street dotted with stores, restaurants, and walk-up office buildings. "Good. After we drop you, Tori and I can go home."

She glanced out the rear window. The BMW was caught in traffic. "They're stuck. If you turn, you can lose them. Hurry!"

Paul ran a red light and took a sharp left into an alley. He gunned the Mustang to the next intersection and bore right onto a narrow street lined with modernized Colonial storefronts. The handful of pedestrians gawked at the speeding car.

"Be careful!" Tori braced her palms on the front console.

Paul accelerated across a cobblestone crosswalk, lost control, and ran over the curb. A loud pop was followed by grinding sounds as the Mustang slammed to a stop. Tori's shoulders chafed against her seat belt. Her airbag deployed and smothered her face. She pushed it away as Justin came around and opened the door. "Are you okay?"

She took his hand and got out. "I think so."

"I popped the front tire." Paul shook his head in disgust.

"The car isn't drivable," Justin said. "We'll have to leave it and get a cab to Seekonk."

Paul shoved him. "No, we won't." He climbed back into the driver's seat and parked the car parallel to the curb.

"It's our only good option."

"No, it's not." He got out and reached for Tori's hand. "She and I can call AAA and wait with the car. *You* can get a cab to Seekonk."

"Rathbun will hurt or kill anyone who stays here. He'll take one or both of you hostage to force me to turn over the pendant."

Exasperation showed on Paul's face. "You don't know what—"

"I know enough to keep us alive." Justin pointed at Grace Church across the street. "The Providence Performing Arts Center is behind this church. Lots of cabs drop people out front."

Paul's expression hardened. "Is there anything you don't run from?"

Tori broke for the nearest side street. "We don't have time to bicker. I'm going for a cab."

She hurried south on Mathewson. It was dimly lit, and her foot hit the curb wrong. A jabbing pain shot up her leg. Although she kept running, she was limping. It staggered her to think that only a few days earlier she'd been quietly raising her son and pondering whether to marry Paul. Now she was on the run with her treacherous husband and fearing for her life.

She considered fleeing into the darkness and leaving him for good, but the complexity of the situation stopped her. Not only was she still attached to him against all logic, but she also blamed herself for not recognizing the signs of his insider trading. She should've been alarmed by his growing obsession with his work, his irritable and erratic behavior, his lavish bonuses. Perhaps she hadn't confronted him because his greed had also infected her. Perhaps only by staying and eventually forgiving him could she heal her shame and her rage at him *and* herself.

When Justin and Paul caught up, she veered into a parking lot and ducked behind a Jeep SUV. The two men knelt on either side of her.

"Are you okay?" Justin struggled to catch his breath.

Tori massaged her ankle. "I'll be fine in a minute."

Paul caught Justin's eye. "Go ahead on your own."

"The decision has already been made. We're staying together."

Paul stiff-armed him. "Go!"

"I won't. You can leave the Mustang on the street overnight."

Tori slid between them and glared at Paul. His displeasure showed in his stony expression. "All right, but I don't know why we're risking our lives to protect some weird pendant."

"I'm starting to believe it's much more than that," Justin said.

Paul sneered at him. "You didn't tell the WaterFire crowd anything I haven't heard on a PBS Telethon. Maybe when you came to Providence you read books by Eastern gurus or attended a megachurch. You sound like you got religion, but you can't prove your words came from a higher source."

Tori knew he could be right, but she wondered about the mystical sensation she'd had while listening to Justin. It was as if she'd heard a voice from another world. His call to accepted acceptance echoed in her thoughts. His emphasis wasn't on believing doctrines or sacred teachings but on surrendering to a love that led to a new life. It sounded irresistible.

"We're stuck in the same dilemma, Paul," she said. "Is the pendant real or fake? We need more evidence."

Paul laid a hand on the Jeep. "I don't need more. I can't think of anyone less qualified to preach about spiritual things."

"You could be wrong. I felt something powerful when he spoke. There's only one way to find out." She struggled to her feet. "Justin, use the pendant to convince him."

He appeared surprised and hesitated. Then he dug the pendant out of his pocket and fastened it around his neck. "You were once my best friend. I'd like to make peace. I don't know the full extent of this pendant's power. But if you'll suspend your disbelief for a moment, maybe the power will surprise you as it surprised me at WaterFire."

Paul stayed kneeling, his gaze trained on the Jeep. Tori wondered what he was thinking and whether Justin's words had reached him. After a few moments, he stood.

"I don't feel anything," Paul said. "You probably made up this whole thing to deflect attention from your outrageous behavior. I'm only humoring you because of Tori. Since the pendant almost got her killed, I should destroy it and put an end to this whole charade!" He reached for the necklace.

"No, Paul." Tori held him back. "You don't feel the pendant's power, but others obviously do. Who knows what harm might come to you if you try to destroy it?"

She put her weight on her ankle. When she felt only slight pain, she headed through the parking lot. She was careful to avoid the main street and the possibility that Candace, Rathbun, and their men would spot them.

"Tori's right," Justin said as he followed. "The pendant is mysterious. According to my near-death experience, whoever possesses it can use it for either great good or terrible evil. I don't know what I believe about my six hours in hell or about the pendant, but failing with you makes me more determined to find out more."

"I always knew you were stubborn," Paul said, "but not gullible."

Tori picked up her pace and led them toward an alley. "The pendant was effective when you spoke to a group, Justin, but not to an individual. I wonder what that means."

"I don't know," he said. "Maybe I'll learn more as I test it further."

She wondered if she could trust him. Her investigative instincts raised warning flags. He hadn't told her about the pendant and her life had been threatened. What else might he be hiding that would make the situation worse? Her crime investigations seemed safe and contained by comparison. "Is there more I should know?" she asked.

"Yes," Justin said as Paul fell in on the other side of Tori. "Candace claimed the pendant helped her convince stockbrokers and the heads of banks and corporations to give her inside information. I always thought of it as a good luck charm. I wondered where she got it, but she never told me."

Tori's curiosity surged. An engraved pendant with extraordinary powers that must be used properly? She had to learn more and hoped she would get the chance. With all the questions swirling in her mind, her greater concern was the ache in her heart. When she'd come to Providence, she'd been sure she loved Paul and only wanted to vent her anger at Justin and find out what had happened. But since hearing him speak, she'd been drawn to the radiance that flowed from him as well as to his passion and insight. These were the qualities that had first attracted her to him.

Her heartbeat accelerated as she acknowledged, inexplicably, that she still cared about him. She also didn't want to hurt Paul. It hadn't been long since he'd held her; she could still feel the warmth of his embrace. But since Justin had been found alive, everything had grown more complicated. She knew Paul cared about her as much as ever, but she wondered if he was even more concerned about her spending time with Justin.

She shared that concern. Part of her wanted to return to Staten Island, to her work at the *Herald*, to her son. But after hearing Justin's powerful message, her resentment had eased somewhat, and her curiosity about the pendant had grown. No matter how much he'd hurt her, she couldn't imagine abandoning him while his life was in danger. If he were killed, she would blame herself. Even worse, her son would never meet his biological father.

The only way to keep her sanity, she decided, was to focus on one task at a time. She and Paul needed to get Justin to Seekonk. Everything would look clearer in the morning.

As they entered the alley, they stumbled into a group of tough, threatening youths. *These are definitely not theatergoers*, she thought. The last thing she needed was more danger.

18

THE SECOND CHALLENGE: HEALED EMOTIONS

The high-school-age boys in jeans, T-shirts, baseball caps, and sneakers didn't see Justin approach. Haunted by the pendant's failure, he considered moving on, but the anguish on the faces of these dozen or so youths made him pause. The air crackled with hostility. A circle was closing around two of the boys. One was a short, well-built Asian in a muscle shirt and carpenter shorts. He had long black hair and multiple tattoos on his arms. The other was a taller, broad-shouldered Hispanic. He wore baggy jeans low on his waist and a Red Sox cap with the brim turned backward.

Tori whispered, "Let's get out of here."

"Yeah." Paul spread his arms to hold them back. "The last thing we need is to get involved in a street fight."

Justin sensed they were right, but he also saw an opportunity to test the pendant further. He was baffled why it hadn't worked on Paul. Perhaps its power only affected groups rather than individuals. Even then, not everyone in a group responded. At WaterFire, the teenagers and the man in the windbreaker had resisted his message.

He'd hoped to use the pendant to win back Tori's love but now doubted it would help. He caught a glimpse of her graceful profile dark against the moonlight, and his eyes began to burn. He longed to convince her that he still loved her and was worth loving. After the pendant's failure, he couldn't rely on it in personal matters. He kept his voice low and pushed against Paul's arm. "I can't let these kids hurt each other."

"Don't try to be a hero."

A gangly Hispanic kid in the crowd yelled, "He's all yours, Ramon. Show him you don't take no crap from nobody."

A big white kid with a jagged scar on his cheek smacked his fist into his palm several times. "He dissed you, Chen. Make him pay."

"Paul's right," Tori said. "We're in enough trouble already. Let it go."

"This is something I have to do. You can leave if you want."

Justin fastened the pendant around his neck as Ramon delivered two brutal punches to Chen's body. Half the group cheered to egg Ramon on. Justin had seen fights before, but the viciousness of the blows created a sick, panicky feeling inside. Such savagery could kill.

Chen broke away then punched Ramon twice in the face. Shouts of "Yeah!" and "Get him, Chen!" rose from the other half of the group. The scar-faced kid raised his voice.

"That'll keep him away from your girl!"

The multiracial character of the group and the violence clashed in Justin's vision. Only the flickering lights in the distance illuminated the darkness. He felt as if he were being sucked into the abyss.

A grimace of rage flashed across Ramon's face. He charged and dove at Chen's legs, but the Asian was too fast. The boys separated before coming back together to exchange blow for blow. Justin pinched the pendant between his thumb and forefinger and shook it. "Stop this madness!"

He pushed into the circle, his temples throbbing. To his surprise, the two fighters and everyone in the crowd turned and stared. He felt like a cop who'd just fired his service revolver into the air. Ramon gave him a shove and swore. "Who are you?"

"Justin Connelly. My friends and I stumbled onto your fight."

Excitement swelled in his chest, reminding him of the feeling he'd had at WaterFire. The same power filled him with determination. He felt the danger, but none of the youths moved. Curiosity fell across their faces.

"Listen to me, all of you." He moved between the two fighters. "I'm here to challenge both of you. If you're as tough as you think, you'll listen. That goes for the rest of you too."

"Who are you, talkin' like this?" The scar-faced kid strutted toward him. He had a large frame, deep-set eyes, and curly blond hair. "Why should we listen?"

"Because I've had the same struggles you have. I let my emotions drive me to ruin. I don't want the same to happen to you."

"You're nobody to us. Who cares what you want?"

Justin saw defiance and rage in his eyes that masked a deeper hurt. "You don't have to care, but if you're smart, you'll hear me out."

The kid shoved him. "You sayin' we're dumb?"

"How you respond will answer your question."

The kid shoved him again. "Get out the way and let these two fight."

Justin stood firm and focused on the words crystallizing in his thoughts. "Any idiot can fight. I challenge you to do something much harder—to feel the pain inside you. To feel your sadness, disappointment, jealousy, heartache. You're fighting in a desperate attempt to stop the pain. You're denying or avoiding your suffering. But denying and avoiding never work. Your pain and the turmoil it creates will destroy you from within. So will your lust and hatred and rage."

The scar-faced kid narrowed his eyes. "You're talkin' smack, man."

Justin's memories of hell sent agonizing jolts of loneliness, grief, and shame through his body. His legs felt rubbery. He pressed the pendant against the bottom of his chin and prayed. To his amazement, his legs stabilized and the fighters dropped their fists. He asked them, "What are your names?"

"Ramon Souza," the Hispanic said.

"I'm Chen Tang," the Asian said.

"What are you fighting about?"

"He talked to my girlfriend," Chen said. "No one messes with my girl."

"I wasn't messin' with her," Ramon said. "I just said 'hi.' I see her in school sometimes, and I think she's nice. I didn't do nothin' wrong."

Justin pressed the pendant against his neck, and the scar-faced kid backed away. "Make peace with one another by first making peace inside yourselves. This is the way of the strong.

It's also the way to success and fulfillment. How we manage our emotions shapes the direction of our lives."

Chen reached around Justin to jab at Ramon. "It was more than 'hi.'"

He shoved Justin aside and crouched down in a fighting stance. Ramon lunged, but when Justin stroked the pendant, he stopped short. Both fighters stared in amazement.

"Fighting," Justin said, "is a sign that you aren't strong enough to control your emotions. Instead they control you. The question is whether you're willing to do the work necessary to walk the path to peace. Are you willing to stand alone and look like a fool to the crowd? If not, you'll wind up on a cross of your own making—jail or even death. You'll waste your potential and never find true happiness."

Chen grabbed his head with both hands. "What are you doin'? It's like you're messin' with my mind 'cause you're startin' to make sense."

Ramon tore off his cap. "Mine too. Why don't you just leave us alone?"

"I care too much about you," he said. "You're fighting to feel powerful. True power comes from within, from healing your damaged emotions. Many people ignore this challenge. They live in misery and make other people miserable too. You don't have to suffer. You can learn to drain your rage of its power."

Ramon picked up his cap and tossed it from hand to hand. "I dunno what you're talking about."

Tori and Paul stood in the circle with shadows from the streetlight behind them. Each shadow triggered a new question in Justin's mind about the validity of his near-death experience, about how the pendant worked, where his words came from, what he would say next. But something in their eyes shone brighter than the shadows—wonder.

He needed to trust the pendant. He touched it; the wood felt slippery. He drew his hand away to find his fingers red with blood. A tremor ran down his spine. What was happening? Where had the blood come from? He didn't know, but he felt even more energized.

"Figure out what's causing your rage. Often a more powerful emotion hides below it . . . fear. We're afraid of losing something precious—respect, acceptance, stature, possessions. But beating up someone won't make us more secure. It only introduces new fears—getting beaten in return, being sued or thrown in jail. The same is true when we use self-defeating ways to handle any negative emotion."

Ramon pointed at the pendant. "Look, man, it's dripping blood! And when you talk, it's like I hear two voices—yours and someone else's in the back of my head. I tried to turn off that second voice but couldn't."

Blood on the pendant? Two voices? Justin wondered if he was creating some kind of strange echo in people's minds. He didn't understand how the pendant worked but sensed that Ramon was opening to his message. He wiped the pendant on his shirt, leaving a streak of red.

"You guys cut each other," he said. "Some of the blood must've gotten on me."

"No way," Ramon said. "You weren't close enough to us."

Justin couldn't argue. He also couldn't explain how blood had gotten on the pendant. The phenomenon intensified his already fervent words.

"Destructive emotions appear when others hurt us or we hurt them. Sometimes they emerge from our darker nature or as a protest against the unfairness of life. We can't control what happens to us or even within us. We can only control how we act."

Chen dropped to one knee with his hands covering his ears. "That two-voice thing . . . it's like I can't stop listenin' even if I try."

"We suffer needlessly," Justin said, "because of ignorance. We think our painful feelings will heal if we change something in our outer world, but what needs to change is within us. The healing we yearn for is spiritual."

That last phrase made him pause. The pendant had inspired him to advocate the same solution at WaterFire, but he hadn't applied it fully in his own life. He longed to stop wallowing in shame and forgive himself. That was the hardest kind of forgiveness. His voice choked with awe as he vowed to keep working at it.

"Our pain is rooted in how we feel about ourselves. If we lash out in hate, chances are we hated ourselves first. If we're overwhelmed by guilt or shame or loneliness or envy, we've become alienated from our true essence, which is love." He felt winded, as if there was so much to say that he couldn't get the words out fast enough.

"Don't stop!" The shout came from a well-muscled African-American kid with dredlocks. He approached Justin shaking his head. "I don't know why, but I need to hear more."

Justin embraced him before continuing. "The spiritual power within us is greater than our wounds. No matter how deeply we've been hurt, God's love goes deeper still. We can soothe our aching emotions by immersing ourselves in that love. I challenge everyone here to find an outlet for your pain. Heal your emotions by allowing yourself to feel and express them in cleansing ways. Go off by yourself and let them flow through you. Share them with someone you love and trust. Let them out through dance or song. Play music. Write poetry or stories. Express yourself as an actor, an athlete, a painter, a sculptor. Direct your pain toward changing the world for the better."

"That echo thing . . ." Chen stood up. "It's moved from my head to my chest. To my heart."

Justin held his arms wide. "Loving ourselves as God does is the way out of hell. It unlocks the prison and sets us free."

Ramon and Chen studied each other, shifting their weight from leg to leg. Ramon turned his cap inside out then right-side in. Justin grabbed each of them by an arm. "We can even learn to forgive. Are you willing to try?"

Resistance and disgust played on their faces, but he held them in his piercing gaze. He stroked the pendant and prayed for them to be released from rage, jealousy, and pride. Their features contorted in pain. *True power comes from within, from healing your damaged emotions.* "Shake hands," he said.

"No way," Chen said. "Not after he dissed me."

"And I'll beat you!"

Justin held Ramon back and reached for the pendant. Again it was slippery. *True power comes from within, from healing your damaged emotions.* He showed them his red fingers. "This blood isn't from either of you. It's from my pendant. It's a sign that it's time for you to stop fighting and make peace."

Chen touched Justin's fingers then jerked back. "This is no joke, man. That's real blood."

Ramon did the same and stared, his mouth agape.

"It's time for you two to become friends." Justin pulled them closer to each other.

After a moment's hesitation, Ramon reached out to Chen. Chen took his hand.

They both appeared shocked. Then they smiled and lifted their joined hands into the air.

Ramon looked at the others. "What're you guys waitin' for?"

After some wary consideration, the boys who had cheered for him began to shake hands with those who had rooted for Chen. Justin felt an infusion of awe. *True power comes from within, from healing your damaged emotions.*

"You did it. If you continue to resolve your inner pain nonviolently, your future will be bright. You'll bring hope to this city and beyond." He turned to Chen. "You mentioned a girl. Where is she?"

"At the pizza shop with the other girls."

Justin walked toward the street and waved for the boys to follow. "Let's go find her. I've got some things I want the girls to hear. If you can make peace inside yourselves, you're ready to fight an even tougher battle."

19

THE THIRD CHALLENGE: AWAKENED INTIMACY

Justin followed the boys to the pizza shop with Tori and Paul, awestruck by the mystery of his persuasive words and the blood. It seemed impossible that an antique pendant could inspire such an unlikely peace, but he had no other explanation. He would investigate the pendant's origins, but the peace was as fragile as the storefront windows; right now he had to keep the inspiration flowing and address the issues that had provoked the fight. With Candace and Rathbun searching for him, he felt safer among these boys than he would have fleeing through the streets.

The group meandered past closed stores and dark office buildings. A stiff wind off the bay reminded Justin of his sailing accident. Terrifying memories of the cavern of despair and the ghoulish demons intensified his desire to redeem himself in Tori's eyes. He also yearned to help these youths avoid the pain he'd experienced. Heartbreak in love caused more suffering than any disease.

Paul pulled even with him. "What's happening with you? I've never heard you talk like you did at WaterFire and in the alley."

"Neither have I," Justin said. "It must be the pendant. If only I knew how it works . . . let alone why."

"The bigger problem is that you haven't applied the words to your own life."

Paul disappeared into the pizza shop. Justin bristled but followed him inside. The shop had a scuffed tile floor and a few artificial plants on a ledge below some greasy windows. A large white billboard that listed the menu hung over a tall counter in front. A center aisle ran between two rows of stationary tables with benches for seats. A group of high-school-age girls sat at several of the tables.

A short man with curly gray hair and olive skin rushed from behind the counter. His apron was stained with tomato paste. He waved his arms in a staccato fashion. "No fighting in my shop! I'll call the cops."

"Don't worry, we're cool," Ramon said.

"These kids are peaceful, sir," Justin said. "And they're going to order lots of pizza. Just give me a minute with them."

"All right." The man returned to his place behind the counter. "But remember what I said."

Part of Justin felt like fleeing. He didn't want to create chaos, and Candace and Rathbun might find him here. Thinking about them made him jittery, but his passion for helping the kids overruled his fear. He approached Chen, who stood beside a table occupied by six girls: two Hispanics, two caucasians, one Asian, and one African-American. "You promised to introduce me to your girlfriend."

Chen pointed to the Asian girl. She had golden skin, black hair, and a pleasing mix of Eastern and Western features. "This is Hi Mae," Chen said.

"So you're the one who caused the controversy," Justin said.

She sipped her Coke. "I didn't mean to. I begged them not to fight, but they wouldn't listen."

"I hope they'll listen now." Justin moved to the front near the counter. Everyone could see him there, and he could watch the door as well as the street. "If the fight had continued, Chen and Ramon—and maybe some of you others—would've been hurt. Instead we have the chance to learn something important. If we understood the relationship between the sexes better, we could save ourselves a lot of misery."

"What's to understand?" Chen said. "Another guy hit on my girl. No way was I going to allow that."

Justin couldn't address his attitude with his own limited knowledge, so he brushed the pendant with the back of his hand. As before, a host of new ideas flooded his mind. He recognized the mistakes he'd made with Tori, and bitter regret filled him. He glanced at her, wishing he'd understood those ideas during their marriage.

"Real love isn't about dominating another person," he said. "It's about appreciating them for who they are and bringing out their best."

Chen straightened and raised his chin. "What makes you an authority on love?"

"My only authority is that I'm learning from my mistakes." Justin diverted his eyes from Tori's. "Most of us are disappointed in love because we expect the other person to make us happy. If we're empty inside, no one can do that." He cringed knowing he was describing the reason his own marriage had failed.

"You don't understand our culture," Chen said. "We Chinese men are very protective of our women. I had to fight Ramon to keep respect."

Justin latched on to the pendant and felt something like a rush of wind flow into him. "Real love has to be offered freely. It can't be forced. Trying to control someone else means we're straining to feel better about ourselves. We'll never find happiness that way. In the best relationships, partners relate to each other out of their fullness rather than their need."

"No real man would've backed down."

"That's the problem." Justin glanced at Tori. Her surprised stare burned into him, scorching his conscience with the shame of his past failures. He refused to dwell on them. Instead he remembered how Jesus had met him in hell, and he tried to believe that the experience and the forgiveness he'd received were real. He kept working at forgiving himself as he said, "Our loneliness comes from alienation within. If we're not intimate with ourselves, we can't get close to another person. We'll expect more from them than they can give."

Hi Mae climbed over the other girls at her table. She stumbled into the center aisle and clutched her chest. "Somethin's burning me!"

Justin rushed to her side. "What's wrong?"

"When you speak, it feels like my heart's on fire."

Chen brought her a cup of water then massaged her back. A redheaded white girl with glasses stood. "I feel it too."

"So do I," said a heavyset African-American girl.

Justin knew he couldn't have caused such a reaction; the pendant must have ignited it. Other strange concepts spun in his thoughts and demanded expression. "The Bible says we've been created in the image of God, male and female. We feel fully alive when we bond with our opposite gender within. That's the way to discover our own genius and ability to love."

"You're losin' me, man." Ramon crossed his arms.

Justin was also perplexed. He groped for words to explain such a complicated concept. The pendant grew hot against his neck. The memory of the September 11th hijackers in hell returned, and he shook with terror. Their suicidal crimes had been motivated by the promise of sex with seventy-two virgins in heaven. What a horrific example, he thought, of the tragedy that results when people aren't whole within. He longed to save Ramon and the rest of the kids from such suffering.

He pulled the pendant away from his skin. With his fingers burning, he began to speak. "Jesus of Nazareth, more than anyone who has ever lived, embraced both the masculine and the feminine in himself. He had an extraordinary ability to relate to men and women. He broke down barriers between them."

"So what?" Ramon flung out a hand. "Why should we care?"

"Jesus models the fullness of God's image in a human being. The first step toward experiencing that fullness is to awaken to it. Then we can be intimate with ourselves and love another person in a healthy way."

The scar-faced white kid stood up at a crowded table, appearing shaken. "I've always wanted that but never found it. I gave up trying."

"At some point, we all know despair. Our hearts are fragile and easily broken. It helps to understand what happens when we fall in love—that the queasiness in the pit of our stomach comes from expecting another person to give us a missing part of ourselves. But no matter how attuned we become to these mysterious dynamics, we'll all get wounded in relationships. Only a God who meets us in the hell of our heartbreak can heal our pain." He stole a glance at Tori. She appeared spellbound.

"We seek true oneness with another person despite all the evidence that we'll never find it. That's because the love that created us is the essence of who we are. Like the God of love, we don't want to be alone. We're willing to risk a relationship, and to believe that we'll survive if we get hurt." Justin searched out Tori's eyes. He locked onto her gaze and said, "Even in the best marriages, love wanes at times. This happens because of the harmful effects of our inner alienation. The rejection and conflict that flow from these effects cause severe pain, and we grow desperate for relief. But contrary to what our unconscious mind tells us, the answer doesn't lie in receiving perfect love from another person. No fallible human being can give us that. The answer lies in the opposite direction. We have to awaken to the fullness of God's image within us. That's how we heal our alienation and experience the inner intimacy we craved from the beginning. Then we can rekindle the spark to burn even brighter."

He stroked the pendant and prayed his message would bring her heart back to him, but skepticism clouded her face. A gust of despair blew through him. Only when he stroked the pendant again did his hope return.

"My head keeps yellin' for you to shut up." Ramon yanked off his cap and ran a hand through his hair. "But my heart wants to hear more."

Hi Mae took a sip of water. "My heart feels the same."

Justin laid a hand on her shoulder. "Love doesn't always make sense. Sometimes our best efforts don't bring us the closeness we desire. We think, 'I can't give any more or try any harder.' The answer is to awaken to the fullness of God's image and to experience that fullness in healing, empowering ways. Inner intimacy helps us to buffer the pain of falling in love and to find hope when our marriages get hard."

The scar-faced kid threw off his jacket. "I'm sweating all over."

Several other youths stood. One said he felt dizzy; another claimed he could hardly breathe. Tori wiped sweat from her brow. Her face was animated with amazement. The pendant was inspiring his words. *The answer is to awaken to the fullness of God's image within us.* He wondered what accounted for the powerful responses. How did this mysterious object work? He needed to know. He took off the pendant, shoved it into his jeans' pocket, and broke for the door, waving for Tori to follow.

20

Into the Night

*T*he pizza shop erupted into chaos. "Don't go, man! Tell us more."

Justin wished he knew what Tori was thinking and whether she had softened toward him. She hesitated as her eyes searched his, but her gaze revealed little; it reflected fascination and curiosity more than warmth. Still she followed him, joined by a cluster of youths. They jammed the aisle, trapping Paul in back.

Justin turned at the door with his mouth burning. "I need to go, but if all of you practice what I've shared, your lives—and the life of this city—will get better."

He led Tori toward the flashing marquee of the Providence Performing Arts Center a block away. The expansive foyer bustled with people. A cop stopped a line of cars and waved a group of pedestrians into the crosswalk. Justin caught up with them, with Tori close behind.

"Where are the taxis?" she asked.

Justin glanced around. There were none at the taxi stand in front of PPAC or on the street. "Our timing couldn't be—"

He fell silent as he spotted a silver BMW in traffic a block away. Three men leaped out and exploded toward them. Justin took Tori's arm and fled up the sidewalk, dodging groups of theater-goers dressed for the evening.

"Rathbun and his men are coming after us!"

A dozen strides brought him alongside the grassy quadrangle of Johnson & Wales University. He tried the wrought iron gate—locked.

He rushed to the vehicle entrance and shook the wide, high bars—locked.

Tori pointed at the gaping space beneath the vehicle gate. "We can slide under."

He dropped to the brick, flipped onto his back, and shimmied into the courtyard. She did the same. He pulled her up and led her to a brick building on the right.

They hid in the dark.

The beam of a flashlight swept the area. "No trespassing!" The voice of a security guard shouted from the far end of the quadrangle. "The university's closed."

Justin broke for the side exit with Tori on his heels. The flashlight bounded toward them, but they eluded the guard, scooted under a second vehicle gate across the quadrangle, and emerged on a narrow street. He scanned the shadowy pavement in search of Rathbun and his men but saw no one.

A sprawling pay-to-park lot lay in front of them. To the left, one block of brick buildings after another stretched down to the Providence River. Heavy traffic flowed in front of the water a quarter mile away.

"There's got to be a taxi among those cars."

Staying close to the buildings, he took Tori's hand and sprinted toward the river. A deafening pop sounded. A bullet whizzed by his ear.

"Stop right there, Connelly!"

Justin kept running with Tori's hand in his. Rathbun's threat echoed off asphalt and brick along with the sound of pounding feet. A city bus had stopped at a red light half a block away. Justin waved and dashed toward the intersection with Tori. They were thirty feet away . . . twenty-five. Rathbun wouldn't shoot at innocent passengers. The bus would take them out of danger. Fifteen feet . . . ten. They had to catch that bus.

The light changed. The engine roared and the bus pulled away. Justin chased after it, but the driver didn't see him. The bus accelerated toward the onramp to I-95.

He pulled Tori into a double-decker parking lot that was open on all sides. A bullet ripped past them and shattered a windshield. They dove behind an SUV then kept running, hiding behind one car after another. Bullets blew out tires and pulverized windows.

Justin's pulse hammered in his ears. He wouldn't mind dying; it would release him from his shame. But he couldn't let Tori die. He ran behind her to shield her from the bullets.

The river was less than a block away across the busy street. They emerged from the garage and darted through the traffic. A grove of shrubs lay just beyond the curb. They dove for cover.

It was too late. Rathbun and his men were only three car lengths away. He pointed a handgun at Justin. "Throw me the pendant, Connelly."

Justin fled onto the riverwalk. Bullets zinged off the bricks and into the water. He leaped over a short wrought iron fence and yanked the pendant out of his pocket. He dangled it over the water and leaned back as his other hand gripped the fence. "Shoot me and you'll never see the pendant again."

Rathbun trained the gun on him from the riverwalk and waved for his men to move closer. "Give it up or die."

"You can't have it." Justin lowered his hand toward the water. "Call your men off and put down the gun or this pendant disappears forever."

"Stetson, Fowler, wait." Rathbun shook the gun. "I'll give you the count of three, Connelly. One . . ." He stepped toward him.

Tori leaped out of the shrubs. "Just give it to him, Justin!"

Rathbun ignored her and took another step. "I mean it, Connelly. Two . . ."

"This pendant has amazing power," he said. "I'd never trust you and Candace with it."

Tori clapped her hands to her cheeks. "Justin, please."

"No!"

She stepped in front of Rathbun. "Then you'll have to shoot me first."

"No!" Justin threw the pendant as far as he could into traffic then jumped the fence and draped his body over Tori.

He braced himself for the bullets.

None came.

He saw Rathbun scoop up the pendant and disappear into the night.

21

WHAT TO DO NEXT?

After staggering through the streets of Providence, Tori approached the crippled Mustang with Justin. She was still shaking from the encounter with Rathbun. When Paul saw her, he dropped his conversation with a grizzle-haired tow truck driver and ran to embrace her. His arms felt familiar but strangely uncomfortable after she'd been with Justin.

"I was so worried." He kissed her forehead. "Are you all right?"

She leaned into the hug. "I'll be fine."

The driver came over wiping his hands on a rag. "I'm in a bit of a hurry, sir."

Paul pulled away and returned to the Mustang's mangled front end. Tori stared at Justin and tried to calm down. "You keep talking about hell. That tour of Providence was like going there."

"I didn't mean for you to see the city like that. It's all my—"

She clamped her hands over her ears and shook her head. "Your fault? You keep admitting it and making it worse."

He ran a hand across the car's trunk. "The damage looks bad. We'll probably need to find a cab."

"No cab can rescue us from your outrageous follies."

"Once you get back to Staten Island, you'll be safe."

"Safe! By what warped definition of the word?" She kept her voice low but passionate. "Rathbun has already broken into my house. How can I ever go back there?"

He laid a hand on her arm. "Maybe you shouldn't."

"I'm certainly not staying here." She pushed his hand away.

"Now that Rathbun and Candace have the pendant, I need your help."

His brazen audacity galled her. "After all you've put me through, I shouldn't speak to you, let alone help you."

"Don't do it for me but for the sake of my message. I saw how closely you listened."

She looked away, unsettled by the thought of further encounters with Rathbun. Her emotions churned, and she started to yell no, but a peculiar intuition stopped her. The aura that had surrounded Justin whenever he wore the pendant drew her to him. His challenges resonated in her heart—accepted acceptance, healed emotions, awakened intimacy.

She was torn between love for Paul and a growing fascination with Justin's message. In spite of her concerns and the danger, she felt the urge to learn more about what had changed him. "How did you get so religious?"

Justin leaned against the car. "I wouldn't call myself religious. All I know is that I encountered Jesus in hell and I'm different now."

"You've always been different."

He laughed. "Not in the way I am now. After I passed out, I felt an awful loneliness that made me scream and cry. It kept growing worse, as if I were plunging into an abyss with no way out. The pendant protected me as I fled to the forbidden side of hell where Jesus preaches. I haven't practiced Christianity for a long time, but after hearing him speak, I experienced deeper forgiveness and peace than I had ever known. If only I could be sure it wasn't all caused by the medications . . ."

Obviously something very powerful had happened to her husband. If she didn't believe that, she would've called him a hypocrite at the pizza shop and left in disgust. Instead she found herself spellbound by his story and the passion with which he told it. She only wished he'd known and lived those insights during their marriage. A desire to learn more spiraled up from an unguarded place inside her. "Do you remember anything else?"

"Yes. The suffering souls. They taught me more about how to stay out of hell than I could've learned any other way." His voice broke but he kept talking. "They also taught me how to live better on earth. It's about growing beyond lust and greed and selfishness."

She couldn't believe this was the same man who'd run away and lived a secret life for nearly two years. A swath of illumination broke through the shadows of hurt and unresolved confusion.

He moved close to her and lowered his voice. "Did you save any of my belongings?"

"A few. Why?"

"I kept a journal when I worked for Candace. She made some odd comments about the pendant when she first got it. I need to know when that was and I remember writing an entry about it. Do you still have the journal?"

Tori thought about the three boxes of keepsakes she'd put aside. She'd discovered the journal while going through his belongings but didn't recall any mention of a pendant. In early 2002, she'd given his clothes away and stored the boxes in the attic. She hadn't opened them since. "Does the journal have a hard cover, brown, with a fancy design?"

"That's the one."

"I think I kept it."

"Would you mind if I came over and looked for it?"

Tori hesitated, thinking about her son and her vow to keep Justin from seeing him. She decided to hold firm on that score but would let him rummage through the boxes. "I guess it's okay but only if we can agree on a specific day and time."

"Does that mean you'll help me get the pendant back?"

Paul entered her peripheral vision. Distress shrouded his face. She felt his upheaval and uncertainty in her bones. They were the same feelings Candace evoked in her. She needed to know what drove her, how she'd corrupted her husband, why she was willing to kill in order to obtain the pendant. The questions throbbed in Tori's mind. Her need to investigate where the pendant had come from and how it drew its power took precedence over her relationship with Paul. She hoped he would eventually see, as she was beginning to, that the pendant might heal the pain upsetting the lives of all three of them.

The no she'd wanted to yell dissolved in her throat as the pendant's allure called to her. Instead she was surprised to hear herself say, "All right, I'll help."

Before she finished, Paul waved her and Justin to the front end. The mechanic shined his flashlight on the twisted mess of rubber and steel. "It's worse than I thought," he said. "The flat tire and bent rim are the least of your worries. You also damaged the axle and broke the tie rods. This car isn't going anywhere."

"What are my options?" Paul said.

"I can tow it to my shop, but I can't fix it until at least Monday."

"I guess I have no other choice."

The mechanic backed his truck up to the Mustang. As he began to attach the towing equipment, Justin said, "Let's take a cab to my apartment. We can stay there until Paul gets his car back."

"No," Tori said. "I promised my mom I'd be home by tomorrow at the latest."

"And I have to work tomorrow," Paul said.

Justin's eyes darted over to Tori. "Then let's take my car. I'll drive us to Staten Island."

Tori felt a surge of excitement at the thought of him coming to New York. She wondered if her heart was working to forgive him in spite of her mind's loud protests. "Then what will you do?"

Justin thought a moment. "I have to track Candace down."

"How?"

"In the past, she rented high-priced office space in Midtown. She also kept a home in the Hamptons as well as a penthouse on Fifth Avenue."

"You can't just show up and demand the pendant."

"No, but I hired and trained an intern at Donahue Financial named Amanda Martinez. She might feed me some information if given the right incentive. I'll try to contact her in New York. For now, let's get a cab at Kennedy Plaza."

"You go ahead." Paul waved him away. "Tori and I will meet you there."

Justin headed downtown to find a cab.

Paul finalized the arrangements with the mechanic then started walking with Tori. "I didn't tell you this earlier, but I got a call from my lawyer. Linda has raised some issues about the divorce."

"What kind of issues?"

"She's having second thoughts. She wants to meet with me and a mediator."

The startling words caused Tori to stop. A peculiar mix of fear and shock flooded in. She was warming toward Justin, but her response to this news confirmed that she wasn't ready to give up Paul.

"No matter what happens, I will always love you." His hand enveloped hers. "I only wish I knew where all this is leading."

The darkness of the night threatened to penetrate every cell in her body. It taunted her with a dilemma from which she couldn't hide. Although she loved Paul and didn't want to lose him, she couldn't marry him until she'd sorted out her feelings. She didn't know what that meant or how long it would take, but she had to do it, just as she needed to let him work through his feelings for Linda.

The darkness grew tentacles that reached for her. She drew a ragged breath and cursed her inability to quiet her emotions. She couldn't stop thinking about Justin and the pendant. His courage with the young people and his eloquent words had stirred the dying embers in her heart. The possibility that he could reignite her love filled her with hope and terror.

As to the pendant, she felt a compelling need to investigate its history and discover the source of its extraordinary power. Finding out what drove Candace and how the pendant worked might be the only ways to disable it before she used it for evil.

She watched Justin hail a cab in the distance. As its headlights swung onto the street and moved toward her, her feet ran toward them as if unprompted.

22

DESPERATE FOR INFORMATION

Justin was losing patience. Amanda Martinez, a member of Candace's inner circle, was his best hope for stopping her. But he didn't dare discuss such sensitive matters on the phone or, worse, show up at Donahue Financial Management in Manhattan. So he'd dropped Tori and Paul in Staten Island and gone to the Williamsburg section of Brooklyn on Monday night. He'd waited in his ratty Taurus for nearly an hour outside Amanda's brick high-rise condominium. The last time he'd seen her, he'd been a married man and a rising star on Wall Street. Now he was nearly broke, his wife was considering marrying his former best friend, and the richest woman on the Street was trying to destroy him.

His rage at the loss of the pendant tightened his hands into fists. A siren wailed as a squad car whizzed by the restaurants, boutiques, and mom-and-pop shops on Meserole Street. He wondered why, at nearly six P.M., Amanda hadn't yet come home. Perhaps she was working late, having a drink with friends, or grabbing a quick workout at a Midtown gym.

As he considered the possibilities, a car approached from the opposite direction. The silver BMW stopped in front of the awning-covered entrance. He ducked when he recognized Quentin Rathbun at the wheel. Amanda got out, and Justin's rage turned to panic. He wondered why Rathbun had brought her home. Perhaps they'd worked late and he'd done it as a courtesy. Or maybe the reason was more sinister.

The traffic continued to pass, and Justin couldn't tell whether the BMW had left. If he stuck his head up, Rathbun might see him. But if he didn't intercept Amanda before she went inside, he could lose his opportunity to speak with her. More cars passed. Finally he peeked out. The BMW passed by giving him a clear view of Rathbun's profile.

Justin ducked again. He fumbled for his keys, unsure whether Rathbun had seen him, and prepared to gun the engine. Thankfully no tires screeched. After the BMW barreled out of sight, Justin got out and dodged the traffic to cross the street.

He opened the outer door of the foyer as Amanda punched in the combination for the inner door. "Please wait," he said.

Her symmetrical features twisted into a quizzical expression as she turned. She wore a tawny all-weather coat a shade lighter than her skin, with the strap of a cordovan shoulder bag looped behind her neck. Her formerly flawless complexion was creased with the beginnings of crow's feet at the edges of her eyes, a fitting complement to the dark circles beneath them.

"Justin Connelly." She brought a hand to her chest and eyed him from head to foot. "I heard you were back but . . . why are you here?"

"I hope I didn't startle you."

"Not at all. Men who've been dead for two years drop by all the time."

The sarcasm surprised him. She hadn't been sharp-tongued in the past. And since he'd hired and trained her, he'd expected a better welcome. "I don't usually drop in on people, but I have something important to tell you. I didn't want to do it by phone. Do you have a minute?"

She glanced at her watch. "Actually, not much more than that. I've got a meeting tonight. Quentin's picking me up in half an hour. I have to change."

Hearing that Rathbun would return made him glance around nervously. "All right, I'll make it fast, but not here."

She unlocked the door and waved for him to follow her into the lobby. "We can go up to my condo."

"What are you doing at the firm now?" Justin entered a vacant elevator car with her.

She studied the light above the door. "My official title is Director of Communications. I manage Candace's schedule and help with event planning."

When they got off at the fourth floor, he stopped her with a hand on her arm. "You and I were friends, and I've always cared about you. I need to warn you about Candace."

"What are you talking about?"

"Remember the pendant she always wore when she met with the boards of corporations?"

Amanda pulled away and started down the hall. "How could I forget it? I've never known anyone who was so attached to a good luck charm."

When they reached the condo, she raised her key, but he touched her hand. "Before we go inside, there are some things I need to tell you."

"In the hall?"

"I'm concerned that your condo might be bugged."

"You've been watching too much TV."

He removed his hand. "I'm serious. When I trained you, there was a lot I didn't reveal about Candace. She has always played outside the rules to enrich herself. Now she's making plans that could endanger your career, even your life."

"That's ridiculous. She's just ambitious."

"Yes, she is, but why? She's already the richest hedge fund manager on the Street, but she always wants more. I fled to Providence because she sucked me into her illegal activities. I believe she's going to attempt even riskier schemes. I'm telling you this to—"

"Protect me?" Amanda laughed and opened the door. "You've always had an instinct for drama. No wonder you lasted nearly two years on the lam."

He entered the light-filled condominium and swept it for listening devices while Amanda changed. He found none. When she returned, he sat her on a couch in front of floor-to-ceiling windows and a door that led onto a terrace.

"I've come to believe that the pendant is more than a good luck charm," he said. "It's some kind of talisman that allows Candace to persuade people to do her bidding. I suspect she's going to use it for more insider trading, maybe even for racketeering, fraud, theft, and worse."

Amanda glanced out the window then looked back. "Candace pays me a good salary. This job is the one stable element in my life right now. I'm not about to jeopardize it."

Justin remembered Nick Lewis, the Manhattan playboy Amanda had been living with in 2001. Even then Justin had seen how emotionally overextended she'd been, forgiving

Nick's womanizing and allowing him to mistreat her just to keep him in the relationship. Now that Justin had received inspiration from the pendant, he recognized the inner emptiness that had made her vulnerable to heartbreak.

"Are you still with Nick?" he asked.

She sighed. "No. He moved out earlier this month, partly because of my long hours. Candace even calls on Saturday nights."

Justin dug his fingers into the couch. "Since I last saw you, I've been through hell in my marriage . . . literally. I may never win Tori back, but I've learned some lessons about love that might help you."

Amanda's eyes widened. "I've never heard you talk like this. You of all people."

"I had to go through the fire before I could receive a new revelation of love. It's a spiritual process. We only find intimacy with another by becoming intimate with ourselves, and we can only do that by staying connected to the source of eternal love. I'm working on that connection every day now." He paused to gather his thoughts.

"I believe the revelation was inspired by the pendant. Its powers can be used for good or evil. When I fled on September 11th, I took the pendant because I thought Candace was dead. I know she believes in its powers because she sent Rathbun to get it back. He succeeded after nearly killing both me and Tori."

"What does all this have to do with me?"

Justin drew a breath. "I need your help. I have to stop Candace from doing immense damage to people's investments and to the U.S. economy. I can't go to the Feds because they won't believe me. Even if they did, Candace has enough dirt on me to take me down with her." He squeezed Amanda's arms. "If you don't help me, you'll be in trouble when they catch Candace and implicate you as an accomplice. This is your chance to get out . . . and to help bring a criminal to justice."

She thought for a moment. "Candace and Quentin are jerks sometimes, but I need this job. More than that, I want to stay alive. If what you're telling me is true and I betray them, there's no telling what they'll do to me."

"I know it would be a risk, but you may be the only one who can help stop terrible evil from being unleashed. Are you willing to—"

A long buzz cut him off. Amanda glanced at her watch then went to the intercom. "Yes?"

"Amanda, it's Quentin. Can I come up?"

Rathbun's raspy voice cut through Justin like a switchblade. Amanda gave him an agitated glance and raised her arms in a gesture of incredulity. "You're a bit early," she said into the intercom. "I'm not quite ready."

"I have something to tell you," Rathbun said. "It's important."

"All right, give me a minute."

Her eyes scanned the condo. "We need to get you out of sight. You can hide out on the terrace." She closed the venetian blinds and opened the glass door. "When we leave the condo, let yourself out. Just lock the front door."

Justin stepped onto the terrace. A round table and two plastic chairs stood in the center of a narrow rectangle that overlooked Meserole Street. He pressed his back against the side wall as Amanda closed the door and buzzed Rathbun in.

Justin took a few deep breaths and waited until he heard her invite his nemesis inside.

"Sorry I'm early," Rathbun said, "but I have something important to discuss."

"All right," Amanda said.

When Rathbun spoke again, his voice was clearly audible. Justin assumed they were sitting on the couch.

"Candace wants to make sure all her events go well," he said. "She's kept her plans secret but needs help. She wants to give you more responsibility and more money."

"What do I have to do?"

"Just agree to her terms. She offers a high salary but in return demands absolute confidentiality and loyalty. You'll be bumped from a hundred to a hundred and fifty thousand a year."

Silence. Amanda was considering the offer, churning over it. Justin feared it was too lucrative for her to turn down but prayed she would. If she got in deeper with Candace and Rathbun, he would lose any hope of having her as an informant. *No, Amanda, please, don't do it.*

"All right," she said. "I agree."

"Great. I'll tell Candace at the meeting tonight. Let's get going. She'll be waiting."

Justin was stricken. Amanda had known he'd been listening. Not only had she rejected becoming his informant but she'd also embraced a larger role in Candace's plans. She and Rathbun had manipulated Amanda and cut him off from any information about the pendant. Amanda didn't realize that she could lose her soul . . . and maybe her life in the process.

23

THE BABY IN THE BALANCE

"You're going to divorce him, aren't you?"

Tori thought her mother's words sounded like a demand, not a question. She continued to feed baby Justin in the kitchen of her townhouse and didn't answer right away. Saying yes would avoid an argument, but after having heard her wayward husband speak so powerfully, *yes* felt like a betrayal of him. And *no* felt like a betrayal of herself. If she didn't divorce Justin, she would have to recommit to her marriage. How could she do that without losing her soul?

She sliced more chicken for her son and said, "I haven't decided yet."

"What's to decide?" Her mother's eyes flashed with disbelief. "Don't tell me you're thinking about taking him back. He abandoned and humiliated you."

Tori glanced at the clock on the stove. It was almost noon on Tuesday. Justin would arrive in less than fifteen minutes to search for his journal. She wiped her son's face and hands. She had to hurry so her mother would leave before Justin arrived. "I need time to let the whole situation settle," she said.

"If I were in your position, I would've already filed the divorce papers." Her mother scooped the leftovers into a plastic container. "You don't still have feelings for him, do you?"

"Can we talk about this later? I'd like you to be gone by the time he gets here."

"Why? I have to see him sometime. We may as well get it over with." As she cleaned the highchair, she said, "You didn't answer my question."

"When I went to Providence, I was determined to divorce him and marry Paul. After being with Justin, I realized it won't be that easy."

Tori picked up her son and noticed that he needed a diaper change. Frustration surged through her. She had vowed not to let Justin see him. Now he might arrive and ruin her plan to deny him that satisfaction, as he'd denied her any semblance of normalcy. If her mother were still there, the situation could get ugly.

"After what Justin did to you, why would you even consider not divorcing him?" Her mother handed her the diaper bag.

Tori headed through the living room. "Because he's sorry and is a changed man."

Her mother caught up at the stairs. "He can be sorry all he wants . . . and you can say yes to Paul."

As they moved into the nursery, Tori said, "Now that he's back, how can I marry his best friend? Besides, Linda may have had a change of heart."

Her mother fell silent with her mouth agape. "You're joking, right?"

"Do I seem like I'm in a joking mood? Paul told me yesterday that Linda wants to meet with him and a mediator."

"All the more reason for you to accept his marriage proposal right away. What can you possibly see in Justin anymore?"

The baby fussed as Tori changed him. By the time she'd finished, he was crying. "You make all of this sound simple, but it's more complicated than you know."

Her mother picked up the baby, patting his back and rocking him. The clock on the dresser read three minutes past noon. Tori had to get her out of the house. She nudged her toward the bedroom door and handed her the diaper bag. They went down the stairs and out the front entrance. She was relieved to see only her mom's Jetta in the driveway. But as she helped her and the baby toward the car, a dented Taurus parked at the curb.

Tori gulped a breath as Justin got out wearing jeans and a polo shirt. Her frustration morphed into fury at the situation she hadn't created and couldn't control. Justin saw her mother with his son and shot a glance at Tori. She looked away and stepped between him and her mom.

"Am I early?" he asked.

"No, about two years late." Her mother glared and nestled her grandson against her chest.

Tori opened the car door for her.

"Wait a minute." Justin moved toward her mom. "He's my son. I—"

Her mother concealed the boy's face. "What he needs is a happy, healthy childhood. Now that you're back, I fear he won't have one."

Tori cringed. She'd planned to avoid this kind of scene and couldn't have failed worse. She blinked against the sting in her eyes and decided the best course of action now would be to calm her mother. "Everyone should be allowed one major mistake, Mama. Please, just let Justin see his son."

Her mother buckled the child into his seat. "I can't do it. Some men aren't cut out to be husbands, let alone fathers. He's one of them."

The baby started to cry. As her mother tried to comfort him, Tori laid a hand on her shoulder. "Mama, please."

"What he did is unforgivable." She confronted Justin. "To me, you no longer exist."

Justin stared at the ground then met her eyes. "I already apologized to Tori, and I'm working to make amends. Will you hold the past against me forever?"

"Tori can do what she wants. I just can't be around you anymore." The baby cried louder as she settled into the driver's seat and slammed the door.

Tori stared at Justin as tears pooled in her eyes. He stayed close to the window and waved at his son as the Jetta backed out of the driveway and sped off.

"This time I didn't do anything wrong." He glanced at his watch. "I was even a little late."

She met his gaze and brushed away the tears. "Mom's pretty angry. I hope her feelings change, but whatever happens, I won't keep you from your son forever."

He squeezed her hand. "That's the first good news I've heard in a long time. Now where are those boxes of keepsakes?"

24

THE HARDEST WORK OF ALL

Paul's meeting with his estranged wife and a divorce mediator had churned him up so much he barely noticed the traffic on Arden Avenue. He glanced at his watch as he entered Tori's neighborhood in his repaired Mustang. It was nearly two P.M. on a blustery, overcast Tuesday. He'd promised to drop by to tell her the outcome of the meeting before he left for work.

He blew through a yellow traffic light and wondered if it was a sign. After having been separated from Linda for over a year, he was cautious about her new openness to reconciliation. Once he'd started dating Tori, he sensed that Linda was dragging out the divorce. She'd claimed she was busy launching another of her hair salons, but he wondered if old-fashioned jealousy and spite were her real motivations.

At the meeting, she'd seemed genuinely interested in how he'd been. She denied that her desire to meet had anything to do with Justin's return, and she agreed to joint custody of Sadie. Still, he wondered about her motivation. Had she proposed the meeting because she realized she loved him? Or was she just lonely or afraid of being a single mom? Foolproof

"Tori navigates the Internet better than I do."

Paul yanked on the swivel chair. "I've done some research of my own. When a man abandons his wife for a year, the marriage is over." He pointed toward the door. "And so is your visit."

Tori pushed down his arm. "Paul, please."

Justin stood and the chair flew back. "She hasn't divorced me yet. It would be illegal for her to marry another man."

"All she has to do is file."

Justin started to go. "All right, I'll leave, but you can't stop Tori from helping me if she wants to."

Tori blocked Justin's path. "We can't just abandon the research; we're making progress."

Paul shoved him toward the door. "He's manipulated us long enough."

Justin retreated then stopped and faced him. "We have very little time before Candace starts using the pendant in devious ways. This research is our only hope. Amanda Martinez has refused to be our informant."

"That's *your* problem." Paul pushed him again. "On your way."

"You of all people should be sympathetic to my cause. You were there on 9/11. If Candace has free reign, she'll wreak even greater destruction."

Paul faced him nose to nose. "Enough of your lectures!"

Justin didn't budge. "I made a terrible mistake and hurt lots of people, but you know me better than anyone. The guy who ran away wasn't all of who I am. I can only prove that by recapturing the pendant and using it to change people's hearts." He grabbed his arms and shook him. "Can't you get beyond your anger? The pendant can help us fight terrorism with stronger weapons than violence and war!"

Tori burrowed between them and forced them apart. "Please, Paul . . . just give him a chance."

Justin lunged toward the computer and reached for the mouse. "Look at what we've found."

Paul hesitated but then caught a glimpse of some photos of mud-encrusted objects on the screen. The electrifying feeling that had sliced through him when Justin had spoken at the sites in Providence returned. He recalled the miraculous sense that Justin was transmitting a message from another world. He'd resisted it, but now he felt overwhelmed with curiosity about where the pendant had come from and how it produced its powerful effect. "Even if you know what year Candace got the pendant, how does that help?"

"We've researched the major scientific and archaeological discoveries of 1996. The pendant may have come from one of them."

Paul drew closer, compelled by a mysterious desire to know more. Justin scrolled down to an article about the encrusted objects. "In 1996 an expedition to the sunken hull of the *Titanic* salvaged seventy-four artifacts. Some people believe the real reason the ship sank was because of a conspiracy."

Paul shook his head. "Are you saying the conspiracy involved the pendant?"

"We can't draw any conclusions yet," Tori said. "We only know that 1996 was an active year for discoveries. Artifacts were salvaged from *Queen Anne's Revenge*, the ship of the legendary pirate Bluebeard. And there were two significant discoveries involving Egypt."

He rubbed his temples. "This is too much like science fiction for me."

Tori took him by the arm. "You and I need to go for a walk."

"All right, but when we get back, either he leaves or I do."

They went outside and started east on Arden Avenue. When they'd quieted, she said, "I want to hear about your meeting with Linda."

He didn't look at her. "She asked if I'd be willing to explore getting back together. Other than that, we discussed mostly practical matters . . . expenses, living arrangements, Sadie. I needed to talk with you before deciding how to proceed."

"You've told me what happened but not how you feel."

He noticed roadwork ahead and slowed down. "Before Justin showed up, I couldn't have imagined going back to Linda. Now I'm wondering whether I should consider it."

She stared at the sidewalk. "What do you need from me?"

"An answer to my marriage proposal."

"Why? If you go back to Linda, it's a moot point."

"I need to know where I stand with you before I make any decisions about her."

She hugged him. "I love you, and I'm grateful for all you've done for me. But how could I have known Justin would return? I'm not ready to make any commitments right now. You can understand that, can't you?"

Paul stopped as they approached a backhoe digging up a section of the street. The mounds of dirt and asphalt reminded him of the mountains of tangled debris at Ground Zero. Memories flooded in: darkness and smoke inside the North Tower, falling bodies, fires ignited by jet fuel, desperate crowds in the stairwells. A familiar cold sweat broke out as he remembered the hundreds of FDNY personnel who'd died. His feet felt as if they were nailed to the pavement. He fought back the memories and reached for Tori's hand.

"Yes, I understand. I hope you can also appreciate my side. Waiting for you without a commitment is just too hard." He turned and walked back toward his car.

She ran to catch up. "Does this mean you and I are finished?"

Paul didn't answer. He sped up, half expecting the cars traveling on Arden Avenue to stop because the world had been fundamentally altered. Seeing everything go on as usual left him no alternative but to hurry back to the Mustang. As he drove away, his emotions were as unsettled as the gathering clouds.

25

THE PRECIPICE OF RISK

Justin was determined to get Amanda Martinez to give him information about Candace. From the backseat of a taxi parked on Third Avenue at the corner of East 53rd Street, he could see the front of the red cylindrical skyscraper known as the Lipstick Building. It was risky to try to speak with Amanda after work but no more than at her condominium where he'd almost confronted Rathbun. He'd described her to the taxi driver, a man who wore a turban and spoke with an Indian accent.

"Is this woman expecting you?" the driver asked.

"No." Justin didn't want to say anything more but sensed he might have to.

"How will you keep track of her in this crowd?"

"I need your help. There'll be a good tip for you."

The steady flow of foot traffic reminded him of happier days when he'd casually walked these same streets. Now he nearly had to run, glancing over a shoulder to make sure he wasn't being followed. He pondered the risk he was taking, and gooseflesh rose on his arms. He had no alternative. Amanda was the only insider who might be willing to help.

Now that he'd found some clues about the pendant's origin, he had to convince her that she was in danger and that helping him was the only way out.

A light rain was falling. Justin kept a discerning eye on the pedestrians and silently rehearsed what he would say. He hoped to pique her interest by telling her about the major discoveries of 1996 and by associating the pendant with them. Her breakup with Nick Lewis might present an even greater opportunity. If Justin could help her heal, she might trust him.

He glimpsed an attractive Hispanic woman walking toward the corner of East 53rd with an umbrella in one hand and a gym bag in the other. He recognized Amanda's deliberate gait and wavy black hair. "There she is. Pull up beside her."

Amanda turned onto East 53rd. The driver followed her, the cab hugging the curb. Justin rolled down his window. "Amanda, we need to talk."

She glanced at him, surprise etched on her face. She sped up. "You should be in the movies. Your ability to materialize out of nowhere could land you some great roles."

The cab kept pace. "If you get in deeper, you're going to need even slicker tricks. You're already in danger."

"We've covered this subject. Just leave me alone."

Other drivers honked at the slow taxi, but Justin wouldn't be deterred. "I care about you too much to abandon you."

Amanda moved farther from the street. "Now who's being slick?"

He was tempted to get out, but she might cut off the conversation. "Not slick, just concerned. I've been researching the pendant. There could be a mystery behind it that has a very dark element."

She slowed, moved toward the street, and leaned close to the window. "What are you talking about?"

He kept his voice down. "Candace got the pendant in 1996. That year artifacts were salvaged from the *Titanic,* ancient Egypt, and a prehistoric site in Washington State. If the pendant came from any of those discoveries, it's worth a lot of money. It also has the kind of power people are willing to kill and die for. The fullest expression of its power changes lives."

Amanda tapped the door and the driver stopped. "Do you think it could heal a broken heart?"

Justin saw hurt in her eyes that resonated with his own. "It has started to heal mine."

Compassion welled up inside him. The challenges he'd spoken had filled his emptiness with love. He wanted the same for her. He measured his next words.

"Your problem isn't that you lost Nick but that he was wrong for you in the first place. You don't seem to understand what led to your infatuation. Until you learn about what's going on inside you, you'll experience the same heartbreak in all your relationships."

Amanda leaned closer. "I would do anything to avoid that."

"Where are you going?"

"To the sports club on 51st and Lexington."

"Mind if I come with you? I think I can help."

She hesitated with a blank stare in her eyes. Finally she spoke in a soft voice. "All right."

Justin told the driver he would get out there. He paid the fare and the tip. Amanda invited him under her umbrella. "How can you help me?"

"The way I'm learning to help myself."

"Nick and I were close to being engaged. I'd given everything to him. Now it feels as if I have nothing except a high-paying job."

Justin noticed a tremor in her voice and pulled her into an alley near Lexington Avenue. He found some privacy for them behind a tall brick building.

"You have to understand where your neediness comes from. When Nick moved in, it was great for him. Men like sex without commitment. You wanted what scared him most—the security of lasting love. By letting him move in, you put your goal out of reach."

She pulled a workout towel from her gym bag and dabbed her eyes. "I was afraid of losing him."

"You were afraid because you didn't know how to love and care for yourself." Justin shuddered, remembering how he'd craved Candace's approval. After speaking under the pendant's power, he was beginning to see relationships in a new light. He gave her arm a supportive squeeze.

"You thought you needed Nick to be whole, but healthy relationships don't work that way. Only when we're full of love are we able to give and receive love in a way free from manipulation."

She kneaded the towel. "And you think the pendant taught you this?"

"I know it did. I only began to learn these lessons when I spoke to people while wearing it." He grabbed the free end of the towel. "I need information that'll help me get the pendant back. Candace wants more wealth and the power that comes with it. She'll use the pendant to get both, and she doesn't care who gets hurt in the process. Please help me."

Amanda's gaze moved from the brick building to the pavement. She stuffed the towel into the bag and met his eyes. "You're right about Candace. She's greedy. She's also narcissistic. I don't like how she belittles me, so I'll tell you this. She's planning a party on her yacht at Dennis Conner's North Cove in lower Manhattan for Saturday night. Representatives from all the largest banks and financial management firms will be there—Citigroup, Bank of America, J. P. Morgan Chase, Lehman Brothers, Goldman Sachs . . . all of them. She's going to present a plan with major implications for the U.S. economy."

"Is she going to wear the pendant?'

"I assume so. She wears it to all her meetings and whenever she's around groups of people, especially high-powered Wall Street types."

"Where does she keep it the rest of the time?"

Amanda turned away. "I can't tell you that."

"Why not? You just gave me other sensitive information. What's—"

She put a finger to her lips. "Don't push me too hard or I won't give you anything more."

He slapped the brick. "I have to stop her!"

"Then be satisfied with what you've got."

He softened his tone. "I need one more detail."

"What did I just say?"

"What room on the yacht will the meeting be in?"

Amanda glanced around the alley then looked back. "Okay, this last detail. The large stateroom on the main deck."

"What time?"

"You said one more question."

"I lied."

She gave him a disgusted shove. "Seven P.M." Her eyes bored into his. "You're not going to do anything stupid, are you?"

"No. Definitely nothing stupid."

"Good. Leave me out of whatever it is."

"Agreed."

He escorted her to the corner of Lexington Avenue. It was raining harder now, but he didn't care. "You were brave to give me the information." She began to walk away. He raised his voice. "Remember what I said about a deeper connection to your heart. It'll help you get over Nick. I hope you'll let me help you again."

She kept walking.

He returned to the alley and leaned against the building pondering the encounter and his words. *I'm a hypocrite,* he thought. *I tell others how they can heal their heartbreak when I haven't fully healed my own.* The downpour reminded him of the sailboat accident and of his sojourn in hell. A sensation of frigid loneliness sliced through him. Jesus had forgiven him and offered him new life, but he still hadn't forgiven himself.

He stared up and let the rain pelt his face as it had in the storm off Block Island. Each drop reminded him of the grace he'd experienced in hell and of his need to embrace its miracle more fully. Warm pins and needles spread across his shoulders and arms. He was finally ready to grant himself the same forgiveness he'd received from Jesus.

The rain washed down his face and mixed with his tears. He let go of his need to punish himself over his affair with Candace and the rest of his treachery. With each drop, he forgave himself a little more. The wetter he grew, the more his burden lifted. He was ready to confess the affair to Tori, but that would have to wait until the right moment. He had a more pressing concern on his mind.

He withdrew his cell phone. When Tori answered, he described the upcoming meeting on Candace's yacht.

"If she succeeds," she said, "people will lose their homes, their jobs, their pensions. She needs to be stopped."

"I have a plan, but I can't carry it out on my own."

There was a long pause, then: "What do you want me to do?"

Justin turned to leave the alley. "Let's not discuss it on the phone. I just hope you know how to drive a speedboat."

26

THE FOURTH CHALLENGE: REIMAGINED ABUNDANCE

Saturday night was clear. At nearly four A.M., enough light shone on Dennis Conner's North Cove for Justin to make out Candace's one-hundred-and-twenty-two-foot luxury yacht *Independence*. He ditched his fins, kept his head low in the Hudson, and breaststroked to the swim platform at the stern. He hung on to its short lip and glanced back but couldn't see the speedboat Tori had used to drop him off. Good. She'd kept the lights dark and set the anchor as soon as he'd begun the quarter-mile swim.

His wetsuit left his feet and hands exposed so they ached from the cold. If he failed to thwart Candace, America's top banking and investment executives would be mesmerized by the pendant. She would embroil them in a scheme that would devastate the nation's economy. He risked being jailed or killed, but with little time to prepare, he'd found no other means to stop her.

He checked his watertight waist pouch for the laminated statement he'd written against her philosophy of atheism, greed, materialism, and unbridled pleasure. The copies and the waterproof case of CDs that contained evidence of her criminal activities were safe. He rested a moment and listened, shivering.

Faint, tinny voices from a TV wafted over the river. A hopeful sign. If the security guards were watching television in one of the salons, perhaps they'd be distracted during their patrols—or wouldn't patrol at all.

A door slammed on the main deck. His hopes sank. A flashlight beam flickered on the open-air patio above him. The beam swept the area several times then disappeared. He breathed easier until he heard footsteps proceeding aft. He lowered himself into the water up to his nose.

The patrol didn't surprise him. He'd kept the yacht under surveillance the previous night and knew the security detail consisted of at least three men. He had to penetrate their defenses and find a hiding place without being discovered.

Thankfully he knew the yacht well. He'd been on it for business meetings as well as during several private sessions with Candace. The small storage closet at the foot of the stairs in the main stateroom would be the best place to hide. From there he could hear her conversations and know when the gathering broke for dinner.

He kept low and sculled toward starboard. If he hid around the corner of the stern, he couldn't be seen from the swim platform. The clunk-clunk-clunk on the stairs signaled that the guard was descending into the lounge that opened onto the platform. Justin would have to wait to climb on board until the guard left.

The footsteps came closer. Justin held each breath as long as he could and concentrated to keep his teeth from chattering. The footsteps stopped. He smelled cigarette smoke.

The guard had paused to enjoy the Hudson and the lights of the city.

Justin stayed out of sight and remained motionless for several minutes until the guard tossed a glowing butt into the water and walked away. He waited until he could no longer hear footsteps then sculled back, grabbed the ledge, and pulled himself up onto the swim platform. He swung one leg over the rail and stood. The chilly air nipped at his bare feet, face, and hands, but the rest of his body remained warm beneath the wetsuit.

He crouched and withdrew a flashlight from his waist pouch. The beam illuminated a path through the lounge area and up the stairs on the starboard side. He followed the path and climbed to the main deck. Again he heard footsteps. He dashed into the aft salon, switched off the flashlight, and pressed against a wall.

The footsteps approached. He stifled a breath. The footsteps paused. A flashlight beam swept the room. He went as still as a mummy, his heart hammering in his ears. If the beam fell on him, he would have to fight off the guard and flee. An image of being shot dead looped through his mind. His eyes darted from side to side. The beam climbed a wall and zigzagged across the ceiling.

Then it disappeared.

The footsteps continued aft. He breathed easier and waited until the steps faded. He switched on his flashlight and started across the salon. Before he'd taken three steps, he tripped on a footstool and landed with a thump.

He got up. Footsteps approached from both stern and bow. He fled into the stateroom, found the short, square closet across from the semi-circular sofas, and climbed in. Seconds after he'd closed the door, light shone through the crack at the bottom.

"Did you hear something?" a deep voice said.

"I thought so," another voice said. "But no one's here."

"We better hope no one's here. Come on, let's look around."

Everything went black. Justin turned on his flashlight and cleared a space for himself amid shoes and articles of clothing. He had to stretch out. He was going to be there a while.

"Bring your drinks into the stateroom and find a seat."

Justin recognized Candace's voice and shined his flashlight on his watch: 7:13 P.M. His legs ached from having been curled up in the cramped closet for more than fifteen hours. Candace was ready to make her proposal to the finance industry's most powerful executives, so his time for action had almost arrived. Lightheaded from going so long without food, he stared at the watch and anticipated the moment when he would distribute the statements and CDs.

The executives had been gathering and socializing for the past hour. He imagined them milling around or sitting on the long, semi-circular sofas, the men in stylish suits and blazers, the women in neatly pressed slacks and blouses. He'd heard their envious comments about the extravagance of Candace's yacht and their frenzied speculations about the kind of business opportunity she was about to offer.

He waited for them to move into the dining room. When no one was watching, he planned to leave the CDs along with the laminated statements on the vacant sofas. Then he would slip into the Hudson and swim out to where Tori would pick him up.

It was a risky plan, but he knew of no other way to dissuade the executives from signing on to Candace's sinister scheme. He stared at his watch and wondered if it was ticking down the final minutes of his life. When he switched off the flashlight, the darkness engulfed his mind as well as his body.

"Is everyone having a good time?" Candace's voice penetrated the closet door.

"Here, here!"

"You bet."

"Absolutely."

Justin thought the cries sounded forced.

"I invited you here," she said, "because your banks and investment firms are the greatest financial institutions in America. You didn't get to the top by always playing it safe. You're the innovators, the visionaries of our industry. You recognize once-in-a-lifetime opportunities. That's the kind of opportunity I have for you tonight."

Justin felt the compelling energy the pendant gave her words. He sat up and savored every syllable. His arms moved as if unprompted. An overwhelming desire urged him to come out of the closet and join her cause. He only resisted by using the same process that had saved him from the three-headed dogs in hell: he meditated on the ways he'd helped others during his life and filled his mind with thoughts of goodness.

"I'm ready to risk my reputation by developing financial products that can make all of us rich beyond our wildest imaginings," Candace continued. "We have a unique opportunity because of the deregulation. The Fed has given us historically low interest rates and fueled an unprecedented housing boom. I've begun taking advantage of this, and I'm looking for partners."

A man's voice said, "What exactly are you offering?"

"I've created several hedge funds based on mortgage-backed securities, or mortgage bonds. I'm looking for investors. It's a surefire idea because home prices never fall. Real estate always goes up. Until now, the financial services industry has missed out. I'm offering you the opportunity to capitalize on it as never before."

"What happens if the housing bubble bursts and homeowners begin to default? Won't that put the banks at risk when the mortgage-based bonds drop?"

"Don't worry about that. Government regulators have turned a blind eye to this market sector, so we can basically do as we please. Besides, the banks represented in this room are too big to fail. Even if you're faced with massive foreclosures—which will never happen—the government and taxpayers will have no choice but to bail you out."

Justin rose to his knees, propelled by what felt like a vicious whirlwind in his chest. He sensed the power of the pendant. Her words sounded more persuasive than any he'd ever heard.

"This is the kind of opportunity Citigroup has been looking for," a woman's excited voice said. "I just need to hear more details."

A deeper but no less enthusiastic male voice closer to the door spoke. "The same goes for Goldman Sachs."

The Fourth Challenge: Reimagined Abundance

Justin suppressed a scream as voices erupted all over the room.

"Lehman Brothers wants to hear more."

"So does Wells Fargo."

"And J. P. Morgan Chase."

Candace interrupted the cacophony. "I'll spell out more of the details over dinner. Please follow me into the dining room."

Justin felt the floor rumble. He decided to review the words he'd written one last time. In the beam of his flashlight, he read:

> This CD contains evidence of Candace Donahue's criminal history, dating to March 1996. Do not trust her or sign on to her treacherous financial scheme. If you do, you will bring immense suffering on yourself and unsuspecting homeowners. REPORT HER TO THE SECURITIES AND EXCHANGE COMMISSION IMMEDIATELY.
>
> No matter what Candace tells you, remember that true happiness comes from abundance within. The average person—let alone those who work in the financial services industry—will have a hard time grasping this concept because the natural mind thinks in material terms. That's why we must reimagine the meaning of abundance before we can experience the reality of it.
>
> The essence of abundance is spiritual, not material. Those who reject this truth condemn themselves to a life of barrenness and disappointment. You can have vast material wealth but feel empty, lonely, and despairing. True

abundance is a matter of the spirit and cannot be earned: it comes from union with God and deepens this union.

If you lack spiritual abundance, you'll be susceptible to addictions of many kinds. You'll feel as if something is missing and try to heal the feeling in ways that imprison you in dependency. Addiction grows out of the false belief that a substance, process, or relationship can fill the soul's yearning for fulfillment. Abusing alcohol or drugs, overeating or gambling, becoming obsessed with TV or shopping, work or sex—these are but a few of the addictions that enslave an unfulfilled soul. On Wall Street, the gods of money, sex, and power loom especially large, destroying many lives.

Spiritual abundance generates the overflowing faith, hope, and love that breaks the power of addiction. The kind of love you experience in the spiritual realm is of a quality all its own, endlessly creative, tirelessly empowering. This love dissolves your separateness in the embrace of your Creator. Inexpressible peace and joy flood your being as your wounds are healed.

You experience wonder and ecstasy as you've never known. Your past, present, and future become one. You break through to the timeless state of your soul. You enter a higher dimension and awaken to the hidden meaning of your life, and of life itself. Spontaneous gratitude pours into your heart and radiates through every fiber of your being. You feel accepted, understood, forgiven. Light breaks through your darkness and turns it into glorious dawn.

The only word for this experience is rapture. You've been suffocating all your life and now can breathe. You've been in prison all your life and now are free. People who fill their hearts with love for God, others, and themselves will always be rich, no matter how little they own. This reimagined understanding of abundance is like a treasure buried in a field. When you find the treasure, you sell all you have in order to buy that field. Spiritual abundance is the yeast that makes dough rise; it's the best wine saved for last; it's the pearl of great price.

Reject every offer to get rich quick, especially by exploiting others. Money is worth nothing in eternity; it's a danger to your soul. Becoming obsessed with it will make you miserable, and the misery will spread to everyone you care about. In the end you will destroy many people . . . and yourself. If you are hungry, come to the table of spiritual abundance and be filled. If you are thirsty, come and be satisfied; and you will never hunger or thirst again.

When all was quiet, Justin opened the closet door. His pulse throbbed in his fingertips. He entered the plush stateroom and gazed at the sofas. Many of the guests had left notebooks, slip cases, handheld devices, and other personal items behind. He examined them as he placed the CDs and laminated postcards around the room, including on the end tables and footstools. Every one of them proclaimed spiritual abundance as the only lasting wealth.

None of the personal belongings appeared worth taking until he found a small leather purse on the sofa nearest the door to the dining room. Inside he found a set of Candace's business cards. *Her purse!* He rummaged further and touched something hard. He scooped it out and stared, amazed at his good fortune—her Blackberry. He tucked the Blackberry into the watertight container. He zipped the container into his waist pouch as he headed for the aft door. Before he reached it, a gruff voice behind him shouted, "Thief! Stop, thief!"

Justin kept going. Nearly blind with terror, he fled to the outside walkway. Rathbun ran toward him from the stern with fury in his eyes. Justin spun toward the bow. Three more guards rushed him from that direction. Rathbun grabbed for him, but Justin leaped onto the rail and dove into the Hudson.

Frigid water jolted his skin, darkness assaulted him from every direction, bullets zinged all around. He stayed submerged and propelled himself with mighty strokes until he couldn't hold his breath any longer. Finally he surfaced, gulped some air, and dove toward the lights of New Jersey. Their dull glow appeared as distant as the stable life he'd once known—the life he feared he would never know again.

He swam underwater as far as he could then surfaced, sucked in a breath, and dove again. After what seemed like hours, he came up and heard a speedboat. He waved his arms. "Tori, over here!"

He kept waving until the boat veered in his direction and slowed. Tori shifted the engine to idle, rushed to the stern, and helped him up the ladder. She hurried to the controls and jerked the engine into gear.

The boat sped into the night as he lay on the deck gasping.

27

FOLLOWING THE EVIDENCE

Tori was transferring the research folders from her portable file box to her kitchen table when she stepped back in awe. Justin was rummaging through the first two folders concerning the 1996 discoveries. His intensity reminded her how he'd handled his escape from Candace's yacht under a barrage of bullets.

The memory of hauling him into the boat then fleeing at top speed made the hair on the back of her neck bristle. She hoped the financial executives had read his statement and the incriminating evidence against Candace on the CDs. Even if they hadn't, his daring exploit had been worth the risk. Candace's Blackberry had revealed that she would attend the annual gathering of the famed Bilderberg Group in Versailles, France.

"I have a hunch about why she's going to the Bilderberg conference," he said. "The meeting on her yacht was mostly for U.S.-based financial industry executives. The Bilderbergers are presidents, prime ministers, international bankers . . . even royalty. Their power extends worldwide, and this year the meeting directly precedes the G8 Summit in Paris."

"So she wants these international powerbrokers to sign on to her investment scheme then somehow influence world leaders?"

Justin withdrew another folder from the box. "It sounds grandiose, but given what she's already accomplished with the pendant, it would be foolish to underestimate her."

Tori took the folder from him and froze. "I hope she's only interested in money, but if she's after something bigger . . ."

"That's my fear." Justin's expression darkened. "The conference includes the CEO of Goldman Sachs, the Vice President of Fannie Mae, Henry Kissinger, David Rockefeller, Paul Wolfowitz, Thomas Friedman . . . the list goes on. She could use the pendant to influence national and international politics. We have to stop her."

His touch felt surprisingly sensual. Tori noticed his large brown eyes, his thick sandy hair, the intensity of his voice . . . all the qualities that had originally drawn her to him. "Versailles is a long way from New York. How can I help?"

Justin drew closer and lowered his voice. "The conference is notorious for being secret—no media, no uninvited guests, no written reports of any kind. I can't get in on my own, but your press credentials could—"

"Not a chance." She pulled away. "I've already taken huge risks, but to suggest I jeopardize my job . . . well, you've got a lot of nerve."

"I'm only asking because I'm desperate. There are lots of conspiracy theories related to the Bilderbergers. It's an historical fact that they pushed for the European Union in the 1940s and '50s. The continent would be very different without their influence. Who knows what other schemes they're planning. I have to stop—"

Tori grabbed another folder and slapped it on the table. "First you have me drive a speedboat into a hail of bullets. Now you want me to sneak you into a top-secret conference. What'll you ask for next?"

She finished spreading out the five folders. "Before either of us rushes off to Versailles, I suggest we look at my research. If we can identify the pendant's origins and how Candace obtained it, maybe we can learn how to defuse its power or even pressure her into surrendering it. Our chances of succeeding are as good or better as our chances of recapturing the pendant."

"All right, but we have to hurry. It'll take a lot of planning to get me into the Bilderberg conference." He skimmed a printed article then returned it to its folder. "Do you really think the pendant could've come from any of these discoveries?"

She moved closer and felt a surprising rush of excitement when her arm brushed his. "I don't know, but it had to come from somewhere. These are our best possibilities at the moment. I have doubts about both shipwrecks."

"Why?"

"The *Titanic* conspiracy theory has nothing to do with the ship's cargo. It was about insurance fraud."

Justin found the *Titanic* folder and thumbed through the articles. "Do you believe the theory?"

She looked away to discourage any attraction, but it took all her concentration to formulate an answer. "Not for a minute. No reputable scholar believes it. More significantly, *Titanic* sailed only a century ago and carried a fairly generic cargo. In 1996 only seventy-four artifacts were salvaged compared with thousands earlier in the decade. Any connection with an ancient pendant seems farfetched."

Justin held her gaze as if pondering whether to move closer. She remained still. He exchanged the folder for the one marked *Queen Anne's Revenge* and flipped through its numerous pages. "What about Blackbeard's ship?"

She resisted the tug at her heart by adopting a purely professional tone. "*Queen Anne's Revenge* sailed only two centuries earlier than *Titanic*. The thousands of artifacts recovered were all from the eighteenth century—arms, medical instruments, personal effects, jewelry, and the like. I don't see a connection with the pendant there either."

Justin sorted through the folders and picked out one marked *Kennewick Man*. "Here's an archaeological find that's between five and ten thousand years old made in July 1996. A couple of spectators at a hydroplane race found a human skull on the banks of the Columbia River in Washington State. All the bones formed one of the most complete human skeletons ever discovered."

"The Kennewick Man is fascinating, but I doubt it has anything to do with the pendant."

Justin pointed at a section highlighted in yellow. "Several Native American tribes claim the Kennewick Man as their ancestor. Didn't most tribes have shamans? Maybe they used a magical pendant in their ceremonies."

She looked more closely at the article. "But no artifacts were found with the Kennewick Man. Even if the pendant does have Native American roots, how could it have ended up with Candace on the other side of the country?"

"Good question." He pointed at the remaining two folders. "What about those?"

She fought to control her frustration that she hadn't established any clear leads. "I placed those two together because they both involve Egypt."

He finished skimming the pages. "I haven't heard of either of these."

She took one of the folders. "The first involves modern Egypt. King Farouk I ruled the country from 1936 to '52 and amassed a stash of rare coins. After Farouk was deposed, the Egyptian government auctioned off his collection in 1954."

Justin pointed at a photo of a vast array of coins. "This caption says the auction was 'the most significant sale of the century.' But how is any of this relevant?"

"I'm not certain it is. I only know there's a mystery related to Farouk." She withdrew one of the articles and reviewed its tedious story in order to stop thinking about Justin. She pointed at a photo of a twenty-dollar coin imprinted with the image of one bald eagle superimposed on another. "The mystery involves this gold coin, known as a Saint-Gaudens 1933 Double Eagle."

"What's so special about it?"

"Nearly four hundred and fifty thousand of these were minted with the 1933 date, but none became legal tender."

He took the article from her and began to read.

She went on, "FDR took the U.S. off the gold standard that year to prevent runs on the banks during the Depression. It became a crime to own a gold coin. Roosevelt ordered all citizens to turn them in, including the Double Eagles issued from 1907 to 1932. He ordered the U.S. Mint to melt down the 1933 Double Eagles and convert them into gold bullion."

"Okay, so they became valuable collectors' items, but I don't see—"

"Wait a minute. It gets more interesting."

He crossed his arms. "How so?"

"About twenty of the 1933 Double Eagles were stolen from the Mint. The Secret Service recovered all but one. King Farouk had legally purchased and exported that one coin before the Secret Service got wind of it."

"Unbelievable."

"Not as unbelievable as what happened later. The Farouk Double Eagle was seen at the 1954 auction, but it mysteriously disappeared for more than forty years . . . until February 8, 1996."

Justin took the article again and turned to a section she'd highlighted and circled. "The coin was recovered in a Secret Service sting at the Waldorf-Astoria Hotel in Manhattan."

"Exactly."

He raised his palms and shrugged. "What happened to the coin for forty years is mysterious, and the sting operation was dramatic, but I don't see any relationship between the Farouk Double Eagle and the pendant. The tie to the Kennewick Man seems stronger."

"At this point, we don't have enough evidence to say one way or the other." Tori took the article from him, tucked it away, and set the Farouk folder down. "There was also a discovery in Egypt in 1996 of a more ancient nature. It happened near the Bahariya Oasis, about three hundred and eighty kilometers west of the pyramids. An antiquities guard at the Temple of Alexander the Great was crossing the desert when his donkey's leg buckled. The donkey had stumbled onto a cache of more than a hundred mummies."

He looked impressed. "How old were they?"

"About two thousand years. They're the best ever found from the Greco-Roman era."

"I can easily imagine an ancient pendant coming from that."

"So can I, but only if some of the coins pre-dated the Greco-Roman era." She glanced away and wondered if her struggle against her attraction showed in her eyes. "I can also imagine the pendant having come from the Kennewick Man site. The problem is it would take lots of time and money to travel to those places for further research."

"The same goes for getting me into the Bilderberg conference, but what choice do we have? If we don't take the pendant from Candace or find some way to disarm it, there's no telling what destruction she'll cause."

Tori sensed his growing anxiety. She reached for the last folder in the box, marked *Candace Donahue*, and shuffled the documents and notes inside. "There's another approach that may help. What do you know about Candace's background?"

"I know she's a Darmouth grad. She got her MBA from the Wharton School at Penn and then went to work on Wall Street. Why?"

"Because she's as mysterious as the pendant. Why would the richest woman in the country be insanely driven to amass more wealth? If we can answer that question, we might discover where she's vulnerable and how to bring her down."

answers eluded him. All he knew was that he could handle only one woman at a time.

He felt his pulse quicken as Tori's house came into view. She'd provided the emotional connection he hadn't felt in his marriage for a long time, but he couldn't put his life on hold while she sorted out her feelings for her vagabond husband. He saw Justin's car in the driveway and knew what he had to do.

Tori appeared anxious. Paul stepped into the living room and caught a glimpse of Justin in the study. "What's he doing here?"

Tori closed the door. "He came to look through his journal. When he found an entry about the pendant, we started doing research on the Internet."

"I need to talk to him. This arrangement isn't working for me."

She caught up outside the study. "Justin's in the middle of his research. You and I can go somewhere and talk."

"Can't he finish his research at the library?"

"It's better for him to stay here. He may be close to uncovering something important."

"What makes you think so?"

"According to his journal, he talked to Candace about the pendant in March of 1998. She'd gotten it a couple years earlier, the same time she began making huge sums in the stock market."

The revelation piqued Paul's curiosity, but his greater concern was his relationship with Tori. He went and confronted Justin. "Computers have come down in price. Maybe you should buy yourself one."

He peered into the open folder. "What have you found?"

She pulled out photocopies of two documents. "Karen S. Donahue of Flatbush, New York, was granted a divorce after her husband had abandoned her and her daughter. Candace's birth certificate lists Karen Donahue as her mother."

"So what? Thousands of people get divorced every day."

"What happened six years later may be more significant." She held up a photocopy of the police blotter from *The New York Times*. "The divorce was granted in August 1973, when Candace would have been six. On February 27, 1978, Karen Donahue was arrested in Manhattan."

"For what?"

She pointed to the slender column of newsprint.

The color drained from his cheeks as he read the report. "Prostitution?"

Hearing the word sent ice water through Tori's veins, as had happened when she'd first read the charge. "Yes. What we don't know is what became of Candace after the arrest."

"And it'll be tough to find out."

"I'll have to research the foster care system."

He reached for the folder. "We should stay focused on the pendant."

She pulled the folder away. "I have to do both." She sensed tension leaching from him. It bothered her that he was resisting a sound investigative strategy.

"But shouldn't we—"

She returned the folder to the box before he could finish. "We have to fight this war on all fronts. There's probably more information out there about Candace and about the 1996 discoveries. I won't know what's most useful until I find it."

"The research will have to wait until we get back from Versailles."

"Until *we* get back?"

"As I said, I need your help. If we don't act fast, further research will be useless." He laid a hand on her arm. "Can you convince the *Herald* to let you secretly cover the Bilderberg conference? It would be an unprecedented story and terrific for sales. If you could get into the Trianon Palace Hotel, you could sneak me in. I could sabotage Candace's message to the Bilderbergers, and maybe we can recover the pendant."

"You realize, don't you, that the risks we'll take at the Bilderberg conference will be far greater than the ones you took to get onto her yacht?"

"Do you have a better idea?"

Tori grew pensive. "I don't, but I know that John Cormier, the Democratic senator from New Jersey, is a Bilderberger this year. He owes Grant Richards for writing a stellar endorsement of him in the *Herald* during his reelection campaign."

He stepped toward her. "Sounds like a good place to start."

She sensed he wanted to say something more, maybe even kiss her, but she wasn't ready for either. "I think you better go."

Disappointment showed in his eyes. "You don't need to be afraid."

"Yes, I do. Afraid of more hurt, more heartbreak."

"I have fears too . . . about my legal problems, about the dangers of pursuing the pendant. But more than anything I fear a future without you."

Hearing him express his feelings had a peculiar effect. Rather than reassure her, his words brought back bitter memories of the trust she'd offered and the price she'd paid in anguish. The attraction withered away. "Given your track record, I'm not sold on your words or promises."

He pulled away. "Is real love about keeping score? That look in your eyes tells me you still have feelings for me, but you won't let yourself acknowledge them."

She led him to the front door and said nothing.

He glanced back. "I hope you'll ask Grant to let you cover the conference."

"We'll see."

She closed the door and went into the kitchen. The folders sat on the table with their contents protruding. She'd spent hours researching the pendant's possible origins and Candace's background, but she needed to do more. Should she continue? Should she help Justin get into the Bilderberg conference? She felt as if a knife had sliced through her. Part of her loved him; another part feared him. The knife hadn't made a surgical incision, clean and even, but had left the ragged edge caused by a meat cleaver.

She swung a hand in frustration and accidentally hit a chair. It crashed to the floor, hurting her ears and bringing back the sound of Rathbun attacking her.

No matter how divided her feelings were about her prodigal husband, he was right about one thing: Rathbun and Candace had to be stopped. Only when she decided to help Justin did the pain in her ears subside.

28

CHECKPOINT OF DECISION

*P*aul raced through JFK Airport, desperate to catch Tori before she went to her gate. A burly guard motioned for him to slow down. Paul obeyed until he turned a corner; then he ran all the way to the Delta terminal. At the entrance, he paused to check the overhead monitor. The flight to Paris would leave at 5:35 p.m. Tori's mom had warned him that she would be on it headed to cover some important conference, supposedly a once-in-a-lifetime opportunity.

Earlier that afternoon, her mom had returned to the house to pick up a forgotten teddy bear and had heard a cryptic message from Justin on the answering machine. He planned to go to Paris, stay at the Hotel Roma Sacre Coeur, and have Tori sneak him into the conference in Versailles. Paul had left for the airport as soon as she'd alerted him.

He stopped at the rear of the spiraling line to the ticket counter. The rushing sound generated by hundreds of voices in the expansive lobby reminded him of the backwashing waves on the Staten Island shore. The muted roar of competing voices was mild compared with the crashing of raw emotions inside him.

His FDNY uniform accorded him respect as he searched for Tori. His gaze lingered on an attractive woman with olive skin and long black hair before moving to another with a similar appearance. Neither was Tori. He scanned one side of the crowd but didn't find her. He repeated the procedure along the back then along the other side. Finally he stood in front.

When he still didn't see her, he headed for the long lines waiting at the TSA security point. He scanned the faces and nearly despaired. Finally he glimpsed a raven-haired woman with a striking profile near the front of the middle line.

Tori.

He wove through the crowd, barraged by indignant stares, until he was close enough to touch her arm. She drew back, stunned. "Paul. What are you doing here?"

He reached for her hand. "I can't let you get on that plane."

She pulled away. "I have to."

He picked up her carry-on and held it against his chest. "What's going on?"

Two middle-aged men in dark suits glared at him. "Is this guy bothering you, Tori?" the closest one said.

"No, he's a friend of mine."

Paul took her hand and began to lead her away. The other man waved for her to come back. "Don't leave. You'll miss the flight."

"I'll catch up with you."

"We'll wait."

Paul guided her to a quieter spot near the gift shop. "I hope we're still friends, but I'm not so sure. Friends don't make secret plans. Your mom heard a message that Justin left on your answering machine."

"Why do you care? I didn't think you wanted to see me again."

Her words felt like a kick in his gut. He'd only resorted to an extreme measure to send the message that he had feelings. Despite her turmoil with Justin, she had to respect them. Withdrawing from her was the only power he had. He set down the carry-on and held her arms. "What are you and Justin planning to do?"

She pulled free and pressed a finger to her lips. "No one's supposed to know. What else did my mom tell you?"

He moved closer. "She researched the Bilderberg conference and saw Candace Donahue's name was on the list of attendees." He gripped her hand. "I'm not going to let you and Justin do something stupid. Something dangerous!"

"Letting Candace speak at this conference would be stupid *and* dangerous. The NATO countries are preoccupied with the volatile economy and the wars in Afghanistan and Iraq. Candace could persuade the Bilderbergers to influence events in a way that would have catastrophic results."

To hear her speak in such extreme terms made his head ache with frustration. He'd felt the power of the pendant and heard of Candace's success on Wall Street, but the idea that it could influence world events sounded like something out of a fantasy novel. "So you've completely bought into the myth about this scratched-up trinket?"

"I've found possible connections between the pendant and some historic discoveries made in 1996."

"What are you talking about?"

"This scratched-up trinket may have come from an ancient source. I'll follow up on the leads when I get back, but stopping Candace has to be the first priority."

Paul felt his jaw drop. He stared at her and saw someone different from the woman he loved. Her lower lip trembled; desperation filled her eyes. He feared she'd accepted Justin's theories and been swept up in his plan even if it meant risking her life. He tightened his grip on her hand. "Since Justin came back, he's been nothing but trouble. How can you trust him again?"

She wrenched her hand loose. "I already told you I can't just walk away from him. Nor can I do anything that jeopardizes my son's future."

"You're needlessly putting yourself in danger. How is that not jeopardizing your son's future?"

He felt as if she were drifting away from him and he couldn't bring her back. A man in the middle of the ticket counter line caught his eye. He was lugging two large suitcases and had a pack strapped to his back. He kept checking his watch, but the line had stalled. Paul empathized with the trapped man. He was in a situation that he hadn't created and couldn't control. He wanted to move on with his life, but he couldn't let Tori go or stop Justin from endangering all three of them. The expansive terminal felt cramped, as if the walls were closing in.

The intercom announced that the flight to Paris was boarding.

"I have to go," she said. "I'm sorry I didn't tell you about the trip. I was afraid something like this would happen." She snatched up the carry-on and headed toward the TSA security point.

Paul raced to catch up. "Rathbun will probably be there. He almost killed you, remember?"

One of the men traveling with Tori waited for her inside the security area. She hurried toward the impeccably dressed man. "I've already made my decision." She placed her valuables in a bin, tossed the bag onto the conveyor belt, and glanced back. "I need to see it through."

Without a boarding pass, Paul couldn't follow her, but he had to do something. Her determination had given him a new insight: not only did he have to save her from Candace and Rathbun, he also had to save her from herself. He had to fly to Paris and find Justin at the Hotel Roma Sacre Coeur.

29

The Galerie Van Gogh

The plan *had* to work. The mantra looped through Justin's mind as he hoofed it from the Rue de Seine onto the Rue Mazarine in Paris trying to look inconspicuous. He checked his watch again—4:27 p.m. The Galerie Van Gogh closed at five. If Tori didn't arrive from Versailles by the time he walked around the block one more time, their plan would fail.

She would be in a black Mercedes supposedly on her way to the Galerie Van Gogh to purchase a framed print of the eccentric painter's masterpiece *Starry Night*. Justin kept glancing down the narrow street in search of an elegant S-class sedan. The plan called for him to wait in the courtyard-like park on the trendy, one-way Rue de Seine, famous for its many art galleries. He couldn't stay long because he feared he was being followed.

He stole a glance up and down the Rue Mazarine but didn't see the white Fiat taxi in which a man in a blue suit had been riding. He'd noticed the Fiat outside the Hotel Roma Sacre Coeur where he'd stayed, and had instructed the driver of his cab to speed up when the Fiat had tailed them. He hadn't been able to tell if the man was Rathbun, but he braced for the worst. Rathbun could have tapped Tori's cell phone.

His driver had taken a circuitous route and dropped him by the park down the block from the Galerie Van Gogh. Justin hadn't seen any suspicious people, but Rathbun was crafty. Danger could lurk around the next corner.

After walking around the block, he veered back onto the Rue de Seine. The backs of many art nouveau apartment buildings lined the street. The wrought iron bars of their terraces made him think of prison. His feet turned leaden. Before engaging in insider trading, he'd never lived outside the law. Now, if he wanted to stop Candace, he couldn't shirk from straying even farther. The specter of going to jail paralyzed him momentarily, but he forced himself to trudge ahead. If he didn't, Tori would be in danger.

He turned into the urban-style park with its brick paths and a few trees. He sat on a stone bench facing the Rue de Seine. He'd come here yesterday then described the area to Tori. Because of the narrow street and lack of parking spaces, the chauffeur would probably circle the block more than once before he could stop. The gate to the street was open and the traffic minimal. He glanced up when a man entered. He looked alarmingly familiar: athletic build, easygoing gait, blue suit, dark sunglasses.

"Surprised to see me?" he asked.

The words exploded in Justin's mind as he recognized Paul Spardello's deep, resonant voice. He went rigid with shock. "Not surprised . . . speechless. How—"

Paul moved close and told him about Tori's mom hearing the message. "I knew Candace and Rathbun would be at the conference, and that you might involve Tori in something dangerous. I came to protect the woman I love."

Justin felt blood flow up his neck. "And how do you propose to do that?"

"You tell me." Paul dug his fingers into his arm. "I don't know what your plans are, but I won't let you endanger Tori."

A thousand thoughts clashed in his mind. He felt an urge to level Paul with a punch to the jaw but restrained himself. Hitting him would only create a disturbance and jeopardize the plan. He glanced at his watch—4:45. His heart galloped. How could this be happening?

"Tori will arrive soon," he said. "If you really care about her, you'll stay out of the way." He jerked his arm free and gave Paul a shove.

"So she can sneak you into the conference? That sounds even more dangerous to me."

Justin silently cursed himself for allowing his emotions to spill out of control, but Paul was a jerk to have followed him. He bit back a stream of curses. "There's nothing you can do. Just get out of here!"

Paul planted his feet on the ground. "And abandon Tori to some cockamamie scheme? No way."

Justin pushed him again, harder this time, then glanced around the park. The few couples and singles who shared it looked concerned. A plain-looking college-age man turned away from the stylish young woman he was with and stared at Paul. "Is everything all right, sir?"

Paul waved him off. He lowered his voice and moved closer to Justin. "Now suppose you tell me exactly what you have planned."

Justin decided he had no choice but to comply. "Stop Candace from infiltrating the most powerful conference—"

"I know that. How?"

His conscience reminded him that the underlying cause of all this stress was his own terrible treacheries. Paul hadn't done anything wrong; he'd simply fallen in love with a beautiful woman he thought was his best friend's widow. Now the men were bitter rivals. Justin wished he could erase time and regain the fun, seemingly limitless potential of their high school years. But that was lost forever, the casualty of a battle for Tori's heart. Neither of them had chosen the battle, and both seemed powerless to stop it. Change would only come once he recovered the pendant and used it in the service of love and peace.

"Tori will be here any second. She promised the chauffeur a large tip to bring her to the Galerie Van Gogh up the street." He pointed to the right. "I'm supposed to—"

A black Mercedes sedan passed the park. Justin hid behind the two-story apartment building trailed by Paul.

The Mercedes rounded the block. The chauffeur found a space several doors up from the Galerie Van Gogh, an attractive storefront with an art deco design. He parked parallel to the curb, then he and Tori disappeared into the gallery.

Justin headed for the Mercedes. He tried to appear inconspicuous but found it difficult with Paul matching his every step.

30

OPENING THE TRUNK

Tori hurried across the secluded parking lot of the Trianon Palace Hotel praying that Justin hadn't suffocated in the trunk of the Mercedes. She'd looked for an opportunity to unlock it before taking the framed print of *Starry Night* to her room, but she hadn't been able to sneak the deed past the young, world-wise chauffeur.

Instead she settled for secretly unlocking the car's rear door as she'd done outside the Galerie Van Gogh. The chauffeur had helped her with the painting, and she'd given him a hundred-dollar tip, but at her room, he'd rambled on about the French government's opposition to the Iraq War. She hadn't been able to send him away without arousing his suspicions.

Justin had been in the trunk at least forty minutes. She was so worried her legs could barely support her weight. The parking lot lay in the shadow of the ornate white façade of the three-story hotel. A few cars were entering and leaving. It was just after six P.M., but no one was milling around. She hoped Justin didn't suffer from claustrophobia.

The thought of finding a corpse in the trunk spread gooseflesh over her skin. At the same time, a curious giddiness churned in her stomach, the same feeling she'd had when Justin had brushed her arm during their research session. After all he'd done to hurt her, the feeling made no sense, but there it was. She questioned whether she could trust it. When he'd moved closer to her in her kitchen, she'd remembered his treacheries and withdrawn. She wondered if she could ever forgive his running away, but she owed it to herself and her son to try.

She approached the Mercedes holding the photo ID she'd forged, the kind worn on a cord around the neck. Coming to Versailles, she decided, had a dual purpose: opposing Candace and testing the strength of her feelings for Justin. Neither purpose could work unless she avoided Rathbun. She anticipated the thrill of outwitting him with Justin's help.

No one was watching. She opened the rear door of the Mercedes and reached up to release the trunk. She hurried around and yanked it open. He moved. Thank God! He shook his head and pulled himself to his knees. She drew back in terror as an ache of disbelief knotted her stomach.

The man staring at her wasn't Justin . . . it was Paul!

She hadn't been so shocked since hearing that Justin was alive.

"Don't look so surprised." He climbed out and closed the trunk. "I told you I would do anything to protect the woman I love."

"Love?" She threw the badge at him. "You're stalking me!"

"I would never do that." He caught the badge and draped it around his neck. "Rathbun would've recognized Justin. It makes more sense for me to be here."

She turned to walk away. Paul had alienated her at the airport. Showing up at the conference only made it worse. "I can't deal with this."

"Don't blame me for Justin's flawed thinking. I just want to keep you safe."

She maintained a steady pace, concerned about drawing attention. Paul didn't understand that his chivalry felt like control. His arrival had introduced a shocking change of plans and plunged her spirit into chaos. She'd already put her journalism career on the line by posing as an aid for Senator Cormier and sneaking into the conference. Now what would she do? She headed for the back door of the hotel. "I wish you'd fight for me less and consider my feelings more."

"You left me no choice. I wasn't going to let you get killed."

She studied his square jaw and well-proportioned face. He appeared so sincere and well-meaning. She was furious but couldn't just abandon him. She pointed at Justin's photo on the ID badge. "Your name is now James Dougherty. You better hope no one checks the photo until I can switch Justin's for yours."

Paul turned the photo against his suit coat. "I'm here for you. Just tell me what you want me to do."

She led him toward the door. "Keep the badge turned backward and walk with authority. Act like you belong here and know where you're going. I'm in 308. There'll be delegates in the halls and the lobby. We'll blend in with them then split up and meet at my room. Give me time to get there first."

She used her coded keycard to unlock the back door of the hotel. They passed only a few people in the high-ceilinged hallway with its black-and-white-tiled floor polished to a glossy shine. When they reached the lobby, they studied the men and women in fashionable dark suits crowded beneath crystal chandeliers.

She moved ahead and they wove toward the elevators. A stocky, redheaded guard said, "Sir, may I see your ID, please?"

Tori glanced back and felt a rush of panic; the guard was addressing Paul. She hurried to the elevator with Paul behind her and the guard in pursuit.

The elevator was almost full, but two more could squeeze in. Then she saw a handsome, curly-haired man and a glamorous woman with long, coal-black hair standing in front. *Rathbun and Candace.* Tori's heart nearly spasmed. The door began to close. She beat it, and Paul leaped in behind her. The door slid shut before the fuming guard could stop it.

She caught a glimpse of Rathbun measuring her from head to foot. "Well if it isn't my friend from Staten Island," he said. "You're a long way from home."

She stared at the elevator light as her stomach swirled. She dared not glance at Paul and give the impression that they were together. She hoped he was studying Candace and Rathbun so he would know who to avoid at the conference.

"I wouldn't miss Candace's keynote," Tori said. "I'm sure it will be worth the long trip."

Candace wasn't wearing the pendant. She offered a forced smile. "It will be memorable, I promise."

Rathbun intensified his glare. "If we receive the speech with respect, it'll leave a lasting impression. If we don't, there will be consequences."

The elevator stopped on the second floor. Rathbun got off with Candace, Paul, and two others. He glanced back. "I hope I've made myself clear."

Tori said nothing as the door closed and the elevator ascended to the third floor. She got off and hurried down the thickly carpeted hallway to her room. A few people drifted down the hall. Some discussed the day's business, others wrapped up dinner conversations. Finally there was a lull followed by three quick knocks. She looked through the peephole and let Paul in. "Did anyone see you?"

"I don't think so." He ducked inside and she locked the door. "But I need a proper ID or I'll be in trouble."

"That's my next order of business."

He handed her the badge. "I'm glad Rathbun didn't see Justin's photo. I can't imagine what he would've done if Justin had been on that elevator."

"Okay, okay . . . you've made your point. Now that you've disrupted our plan, I've got to call him and devise a new one." She led Paul into the classically decorated, luxurious room. "You were smart not to make eye contact with me on the elevator. Since we got off on different floors, hopefully Rathbun doesn't suspect we're together."

"After how he spoke to you, I want to sabotage Candace's speech."

"Good. We need your help."

"In the meantime, I hope we can talk."

She moved to the window, glanced at the lush shrubbery behind the hotel, then turned toward him. "If you came here to discuss our relationship, I'm not ready for that." She saw the glimmer in his eyes disappear as it was displaced by hurt. She couldn't lie. Her heart was divided.

Living with the conflict was torture. She couldn't explain her feelings to Paul because she didn't understand them herself. After what Justin had done, she would have expected to hate him forever. Instead she found herself inexplicably drawn to the father of her son. She'd been a widow for twenty months, thinking her husband had died the most horrendous of deaths. The overwhelming relief and gratitude she felt had somehow softened the hurt of him running away. And then there was the pendant . . .

She took a blanket off the king-size bed and tossed it onto the velvety green sofa. "You can sleep here." He smiled as she reached for the camera atop the dresser. "Now for that photo for the ID badge."

31

THE FIFTH CHALLENGE: LIBERATED SERVICE

Only a perfect execution of the plan would sabotage Candace Donahue's keynote address. Paul's moment to act was minutes away. His energy felt as electric as the atmosphere in the elegant ballroom of the Trianon Palace Hotel. The one hundred and twenty international businessmen, politicians, financiers, and royalty were taking their seats. He stayed toward the back under a glittering crystal chandelier and focused on Tori near the front.

British banking magnate Edward Fairchild stepped to the podium and announced the start of the event. The Bilderbergers still milling around bustled to their seats, as did Paul at the end of a row. Tori turned, and he gave her a stealthy wave. She tipped her pen in his direction. He silently wished her success with that pen, which was really a digital voice transmitter. The plan called for her to be as secretive and skillful in using the transmitter as she had been in obtaining his photo ID.

She gave him a quick smile. Something broke loose in a vulnerable place inside him. Her eyes were richly dark and warm, features that had mesmerized him for the past year. He'd received intimate messages from those enchanting eyes but wondered if he ever would again.

A hush fell over the ballroom. He fingered the all-important mobile phone in his pocket. Edward Fairchild began his introduction of Candace, a woman he said "epitomized the spirit of innovation and entrepreneurship needed to transform the global economy into an engine of abundance for all nations." As if on cue, she entered from the back and strutted up the center aisle to the podium, nodding to acknowledge a standing ovation. She was as stunning as the most glamorous movie star, sensuous and inaccessible, which created an aura of fascination.

The applause reverberated in the covert wireless receiver in Paul's ear, making him wince. So this was the woman who'd caused Tori so much anguish. She was slightly taller than medium height and meticulously coiffed. She wore a sleeveless teal dress with coordinated jewelry and spiked heels with the pendant around her neck.

Paul's time had arrived. So far he'd avoided a confrontation with the stocky, redheaded guard who'd chased him in the lobby. He could sabotage Candace's speech only if he continued to elude that guard as well as the others. If he didn't, he would be arrested as a trespasser since his name wasn't on the official list of attendees.

Candace thanked the Bilderbergers for including her in such distinguished company and giving her the privilege of addressing them. Power flowed from her words. The feeling reminded Paul of the spontaneous combustion of a chemical fire. This was the first time he'd heard her speak while she wore the pendant. He understood why Tori and Justin were so concerned.

Her piercing green eyes cut to his marrow. All other noise, all other activity ceased, as did his awareness of the outside world. Candace appeared radiant, goddess-like, as if glorious light shone on her.

"The greatest privilege we have," she said, "is that of helping others. No calling could be higher."

Her simple words cast a spell on Paul. They crackled with sensual energy and coaxed his heart toward her. His fingertips tingled and sent a jolt of energy up his arms and into his chest. It took all his willpower to look away as she continued.

"The media criticizes us for being secretive as well as wealthy and powerful, but our real purpose is to help the people in this world live up to their potential."

Paul was only able to extricate himself from her allure by rehearsing the plan. He left his seat and headed for the door behind him. Everyone's attention was riveted on Candace. The room was as silent as a cemetery.

He entered the foyer and turned right. At least a dozen people milled around or talked in small groups. He had to get to the audio-visual closet. The hallway that led to it lay through the door at the end of the foyer. Candace's voice resounded in his earpiece.

"I want to speak to you today about the best way . . . really, the only way . . . to help others. You must first help yourself. I want to give you the chance to do that in a manner and on a scale never before imagined."

Earlier in the day, Paul had walked through the plan. If he weren't deterred, it would take him less than a minute to reach the A-V closet. He dug out his mobile phone, punched in Justin's number, and glanced back to make sure no one was following him. He slipped through the door and waited until Justin answered. "Do you have the car?"

"Yes."

Paul veered right and went through another door. He sped up when he reached the hall that ran parallel to the ballroom. "What kind?

"A black Audi."

"Where are you?"

Justin sounded tense. "Outside the hotel, just beyond the security zone."

Paul stopped at the A-V closet and opened the door. "We'll be there as soon as we're done. Are you ready for me to patch you in?"

"Ready."

The tall, box-like control console for the ballroom's public address system was surrounded by amplifiers, wires, and speakers on the side shelves. Paul had to unplug Candace's microphone before she convinced the Bilderbergers to buy in to her grandiose investment scheme. He grabbed the patch cord from his pocket.

Candace said, "I've started a new hedge fund called the Trans-European Cooperative. The concept is simple. You invest your funds with me on Wall Street, backed by my stellar record of returns, and I share the profits with you. My goal is to strengthen Europe and cement the destinies of the European countries with that of the United States."

Paul plugged the cord in to his mobile phone and spun the PA console around.

"If you invest in my plan," Candace said, "those of us in this room will be major players in shaping the post-9/11 economy, and we'll all—"

Paul unplugged the cable to her microphone and inserted the patch cord hooked to his mobile. He laid the phone on top of the console, locked the door from the inside, closed it behind him, and ran from the room. In his earpiece, he heard the audience in the ballroom let out groans of frustration.

"My microphone just died." Candace's voice was one of the loudest.

"What's going on?" several people said.

"So much for luxury services."

Paul raced up the hall and through the first door before he slowed. In his earpiece, he heard Justin begin to address the Bilderbergers.

"Don't be alarmed," his voice said. "Ms. Donahue's speech has been preempted so you can hear a life-changing message. I need to warn you about Ms. Donahue's scheme. She doesn't really want to help others. Investing with her won't increase your wealth or power. She's manipulating you to increase her own."

Paul paused to catch his breath and heard hotel workers behind him banging on the locked door of the A-V closet. He left the hallway and entered the foyer.

Justin said, "You have the power of wealth and political influence, but another kind of power is far more dynamic . . . the power of truly serving others. That sounds counterintuitive because we think the most powerful people are those who can make others do their bidding. But these people are often the unhappiest. They think of themselves first. Only those who find another way to live receive the gift of lasting happiness."

Paul walked through the foyer and reentered the ballroom. The Bilderbergers flowed into the aisles confused about what was happening. A half-dozen hotel workers tried with little success to get them to sit down. Tori had left her seat and was moving toward the side aisle to meet him in back.

Justin said, "The desire to have power over others comes from the ego, that part of ourselves driven by selfishness and fear of insignificance. The ego's prison is built around me, me, me. Its warden is our lust for status and recognition. Its guards are the idols we make of our needs and desires. In this prison, we worship ourselves, not the true and living God who is the only source of freedom and joy."

Paul waved, silently urging Tori to hurry. Rathbun went to the podium accompanied by two heavily muscled men and an athletic woman, all wearing dark suits. They conferred with Candace, then Rathbun gestured toward Tori's empty seat. An expression of alarm came over Candace's face. Her gaze searched the area and landed on Tori. She pointed and said something to Rathbun and the others. Paul nearly screamed. He needed to warn Tori but had no way to do so. Rathbun led the others off the platform and plowed through the crowd.

Justin's tone intensified. "The freedom we crave comes when we let go of our desire for wealth, power, success, fame, and the like. Surrender to love. We succeed when we stop obsessing about our own needs and put the needs of others first. This is the way of the soul. We discover our oneness with the entire human family. We realize we can only achieve our full potential by helping others achieve theirs."

Paul waved at Tori again. She acknowledged him with a nod but couldn't see Rathbun and his security detail. He mouthed, *Hurry!*

Justin said, "When you heed the call of your soul, you'll grow beyond the bondage of the ego. You'll share your power and work toward mutual goals. No longer will you need to be the center of attention. No longer will you be jealous of the gifts or accomplishments of others. No longer will you compete with anyone but yourself. You'll always win because you'll pursue love above all things."

Tori had almost reached Paul. Rathbun and the guards were jammed up twenty feet behind. Paul sprang forward, grabbed her hand, and pulled her through the crowd toward the foyer. "We have to hurry. Rathbun's right behind us with three of his guards."

Justin's words rang in his earpiece. "Few people find this simple but elusive liberation, but you can find it. It's as close as your own heart. You can surrender to love this very moment and put others ahead of yourself. You'll begin a journey that starts in this world and continues for all eternity. On this journey, you become the person you long to be. Through generosity and service, you help God heal the world."

Paul shoved a man out of the way in the foyer then another. Fortunately lots of people were fleeing the chaos in the ballroom, so he and Tori blended in. They hurried through the crowded halls into the lobby and out the front door. Through generosity and service, he thought, we help God heal the world. Then they came into the security zone where police swarmed. One of them asked where they were going.

Tori flashed her ID badge. "Into town to get some dinner."

"Just the two of you?"

Paul's pulse raced. "Yes, we just want some French cuisine and—" He heard running footsteps. "Sorry, officer, we have to—"

He glanced back. Rathbun and the guards had come out the front door and were sprinting toward them. Paul dodged the officers and pulled Tori along. They bent low as they ran for the waiting Audi. He and Tori leaped into the backseat. The roar of the engine and the shriek of tires couldn't drown out the pop, pop, pop of gunfire as Justin spirited them into the twilight.

32

AT THE SALISBURY HOTEL

The rapping on the door of room 571 at Manhattan's Salisbury Hotel sounded frantic. Startled, Tori set her laptop on the queen-size bed where she lay in jeans and a sweatshirt researching the pendant. She'd been waiting for Justin, but he'd taken longer than expected to get to the hotel on West 57th across from Carnegie Hall.

The knocking grew louder as she cautiously approached the door. This would be her first meeting with him since returning from Versailles. After the Bilderberg conference, she feared that Candace and Rathbun would seek revenge. She'd sought refuge at the Salisbury while her mother took Justin Jr. to stay with Aunt Elizabeth in Jersey City. In the meantime, Justin had staked out Tori's house, and Paul was keeping watch at her mother's. The surveillance would protect her from Rathbun, but Justin and Paul also hoped to trail him. That might lead to information about Candace's next move.

The rapping echoed ominously in her ears. She peered through the peephole and let Justin in. "Thank God you're safe."

He stepped inside and hugged her. "I feel the same about you. I'm glad you're here and not at your house."

"Why? What happened?"

She yearned to hold him longer. The problem was, reconciling would make her vulnerable to being hurt again. It would also complicate their relationship and possibly hamper their efforts to recapture the pendant. But her feelings had grown so powerful she found them impossible to ignore.

He laid both hands on her shoulders. "Rathbun circled your block in his BMW around seven o'clock. He slowed and eyed your house but kept driving when he saw the lights were off and the driveway was empty."

She forced herself to pull away. "Did you follow him?"

"Only until I got stuck in traffic on Amboy Road." He moved farther into the older-style, modestly furnished room. "I decided it would be more productive to come here and help you sort through your research."

"You may be right. With Candace's tight security, our only hope may be to find the source of the pendant's power and disable it. It would help to know what's motivating her." Tori faced him in the center of the room. "We have to hurry. She mesmerized the Bilderbergers. Some of them will invest venture capital with her, and she'll use her gains to tighten the connections between the European and American monetary systems. Once she controls the banks on both sides of the Atlantic, she'll be able to influence the destiny of every Western country."

His eyes narrowed. "Have you found any new information?"

"Some." She picked up one of the folders from the bed, withdrew a colorful pamphlet, and handed it to him. "Have you heard of the Chapin School?"

"No." He thumbed through the pamphlet.

"It's Manhattan's most elite all-girls school. Anne Morrow Lindbergh, Jacqueline Bouvier Kennedy, and Sigourney Weaver are among the famous alums."

He returned the pamphlet to her. "So?"

"Candace Donahue graduated from Chapin."

He frowned and sat down in a chair beside the bed. "How could a girl whose mother was jailed for prostitution pull that off?"

"I couldn't get access to her foster care records, so I don't know for sure. All I found is that a man by the name of Gustav Phelps paid her tuition."

"Who's he?"

"You can bet I'm going to find out." She set the *Candace Donahue* folder on the bed and pointed at the others beside it. "As to where the pendant came from, I believe my initial hunches were right. The artifacts from the *Titanic* and *Queen Anne's Revenge* aren't old enough, so I don't see any connections between them and Candace."

He sorted through the folders. "What about the Kennewick Man?"

"That one's still in play, but I don't think we should pursue it first."

"Why not? The possible link to Native American shamans sounds like exactly what we're looking for."

The glint in his eyes reminded her of his younger days when he'd been a tireless dreamer. It was as if a light had pierced her heart and illuminated a part of her she couldn't access on her own. How she longed for those younger, more carefree days when they'd both believed anything was possible. She felt herself drawn to him—to what they'd once had together, to what they might still recreate.

Something gave way inside her, a tension that had grown unmanageable, a resistance that had finally broken down. She found herself forgiving him and letting go of her rage despite every inclination not to. A peculiar warmth flooded her followed by a newfound peace. She didn't know if she could ever take him back as her husband, but the burden of guilt and blame had lifted, and she felt free.

"I think we should focus on the Egyptian discoveries first," she said. "If neither pans out, we can come back to the Kennewick Man."

"Are you sure you're not jumping to conclusions?"

She sat on the edge of the bed with her laptop and navigated to a website that displayed photographs of an excavation in the desert. "This article tells about that cache of mummies. It was found in 1996 near the Bahariya Oasis. The article claims that the Bahariya Inspectorate of Antiquities kept the discovery secret for a time, supposedly for fear of thievery, but I'm suspicious of that."

"Why?"

She pointed to a long paragraph. "Read this."

As he read, she noticed the faint crow's feet that had appeared at the edges of his eyes. They suited him, lending an air of maturity to his otherwise youthful appearance. His message to the Bilderbergers came back—the authority of his voice, the wisdom of his words. He seemed so different from the man he'd been twenty months earlier. She couldn't decide which surprised her more . . . how much he'd changed or how attractive he'd become to her.

He finished the paragraph and raised an eyebrow. "This article says artifacts were scattered all around the mummies—earrings, bracelets, pottery, wine jars, even statues of women in mourning. The archaeologists also found Ptolemaic coins, even one with an image of Cleopatra. The artifacts are intriguing. What are you suspicious about?"

She brought more photos up on the screen. "If the pendant was one of the artifacts, it could have been stolen and sold in the United States. The only problem is that the mummies are from the Roman era. The pendant is probably much older."

"It could have come from ancient Egypt and been kept at the Bahariya Oasis for centuries. Or maybe it came from one of the Roman mystery cults. Who knows?"

She moved higher on the bed and folded her legs beneath her. "We need more information, and I have an idea how to get it. First let me show you this." She navigated to a website with photos of gold coins. "I found some intriguing material on the Farouk Double Eagle."

He picked up the folder marked *Farouk* and thumbed through the papers. "That coin was minted in 1933. How could it have anything to do with the pendant?"

She pointed at the screen. "The Double Eagle was originally part of King Farouk's collection of over eight thousand items. He also collected priceless art and antiques. It's possible that the collection included Egyptian artifacts, maybe even ancient ones."

"How can we prove the pendant was one of them?"

"We can't . . . unless we find some connection to the Farouk Double Eagle."

He gave a cynical laugh. "That seems like a long shot."

"Maybe, maybe not." Tori took the folder. "Remember, the Double Eagle was seen at the auction of Farouk's collection in 1954 then disappeared for forty years. What if the coin wasn't the only item that went missing?"

"That's total speculation. If we're pursuing Egyptian discoveries, the artifacts found with the mummies seem like the better bet."

"Except for one detail." She pointed to a highlighted section of an article she'd found that morning. "After the Secret Service confiscated the Farouk Double Eagle at the Waldorf-Astoria, they stored it in their vault in Seven World Trade Center. It was removed a few months before the building was destroyed on September 11th. The coin became the Mona Lisa of the collecting world and sold at auction last year for $7.6 million."

Justin read the section. "So you think there's some connection between the pendant and Seven World Trade Center?"

"I don't know, but that building was in the same complex as the North Tower where you and Candace worked."

He stepped back and cupped his chin. "I agree that the proximity is striking, but it doesn't prove anything. Since Seven World Trade Center is gone, we'll never have any physical evidence."

"I still think the lead is worth pursuing." She put the folder down, aware that her attraction hadn't diminished but increased. She looked away as her heart raced. "We can do it in conjunction with researching the mummy artifacts."

"What are you suggesting?"

"We should consult with Dr. Jonathan Koestler, head of the Egyptian Art department at the Metropolitan Museum.

He may be able to tell us if those engravings on the pendant are more than just decorative."

"Are you saying they might mean something?"

"It's not impossible. Do you remember any of them specifically? Could you sketch a few?"

"I'm no artist but I'll try."

Tori grabbed a tablet and a pen from the nightstand. "Good. A sketch will give us something specific to show Koestler."

Her hand brushed his and he met her eyes. He tossed the tablet and pen on the bed and took her hand. "Have you forgiven me yet?"

"It doesn't happen all at once . . . I'm working on it." She tried to turn away but couldn't. She'd seen strength and integrity in Paul's eyes, but in Justin's she glimpsed a missing piece of her soul. She'd seen it before, long ago when they were learning of their mutual passions for music and art, for Asian food and frozen yogurt and walks in Central Park when autumn leaves blanketed the path. Most of all, she'd seen it in the youthful idealism that had caused her to fall in love with him.

Now, after the light in their marriage had been extinguished by his deception, she'd seen a glimmer again in his willingness to sacrifice everything for his spiritual message. Those eyes belonged to the man she'd loved more than any other. She felt drawn to him as if for the first time.

He pulled her toward him. "I'm different now. I swear. If you give me another chance, I promise to be the kind of husband and father you deserve."

His lips met hers. Before she could even think of resisting, she leaned in and matched his passion with her own.

His musky scent evoked memories of their earliest dates. Her mind told her this was crazy, that taking him back would never work, that she would end up devastated again. But her heart yearned to restore the intimacy they'd once shared and to raise the unified family she could only have with him.

She forgot they were in a hotel running from a ruthless man, forgot they were trying to stop a maniacal woman from destroying thousands of lives or even national economies. Touching his lips transported her to happier times—to walks on the Staten Island shore and dates in Manhattan, to their wedding day and the ecstasy of making love under a canopy of stars. Her legs felt unable to hold her. She stiffened her knees and closed her eyes and saw light instead of darkness. Hope that they could rebuild what they'd lost welled up.

"Does this mean you'll let me see my son?" he asked.

"I'll have to think—" The chirping of her phone cut her off. She picked it up and saw Paul's number. "Hi, where are you?"

"At the Grand Hyatt Hotel on 42nd and Park. I trailed Rathbun from your mom's house. He went in through a service entrance and stayed about a half hour. He just drove off."

"Any idea what he was doing there?"

"None. I couldn't see where he went or who he talked to."

She sighed in frustration. "That doesn't tell us much."

"Have you found anything on the pendant?"

"I'm still working on it. Justin's here." The line fell silent, as if they'd been cut off. "Hello?"

"Justin's there?" His voice sounded strained.

She bit her lip, feeling guilty about the kiss. "Yeah. We're ready to follow up on some leads."

"Do you need help? I'm not far away."

His request caught her by surprise. He sounded so sincere and well-meaning. How could she say no? "We definitely need your support. You can help most by trailing Rathbun and finding out what he's up to. If Candace is planning some new initiative, we have to know about it."

"Okay, but what will you do?"

"Justin and I are going to the Metropolitan Museum tomorrow to check out one of the leads."

"Where is he staying tonight?" His tone was sharp.

She glanced at Justin and didn't answer right away. "It won't be here, if that's what you mean."

Tori heard a click. She felt the lingering tension but refused to apologize for having kissed Justin. She hadn't divorced him. Why shouldn't she kiss her husband? It had felt right . . . until she'd heard Paul's voice.

She went to the window and stared out at the glimmering city. She didn't want to hurt either of them, but it would be impossible not to. The thousands of lights seemed to blind her. They gleamed brighter than she'd ever seen and with rare hopefulness—the opposite of what she felt.

Love was supposed to be fulfilling. Why did it feel like torture? Her eyes burned and the lights grew blurry. She glanced back at Justin. He sat on the floor beside the bed watching her reflectively. The sight brought back something he'd said at the Bilderberg conference, something about peace being found not through control but through surrender.

33

An Encounter at the Museum

"The Louvre has the Mona Lisa, but we have the Temple of Dendur," Dr. Jonathan Koestler said.

Justin stood with Tori in the back of the tour group at the Metropolitan Museum of Art. The bald, white-bearded director of the Egyptian Art department pointed at the centerpiece of its collection. The Roman emperor Caesar Augustus had built the temple on the banks of the Nile around 15 B.C. The United States had received it as a gift from the Egyptian government.

As the group dispersed, Justin pushed to the front with Tori. They admired the temple's rectangular shape, two stately columns, and open-fronted sanctuary. The sweetness of the kiss still lingered on his lips along with hope and excitement in his heart. He leaned over and kissed her on the cheek.

"I don't recall giving you permission to do that." She shot him an indignant glance.

"Since when does a husband need permission to kiss his wife?"

"Since his wife is still trying to figure out how she feels about him."

But she'd kissed him passionately yesterday. Didn't that mean she loved him again? She redirected his attention toward Dr. Koestler, who was answering tourists' questions.

Justin noticed the peaceful water in the reflecting pool that nearly surrounded the eighty-two-foot-long sandstone temple. He wished his spirit could absorb some of the pool's serenity. He was churning over the revelations about Candace's background, about how to find out what she planned next and whether Rathbun would track them down. Even more, he dreaded telling Tori about his affair. He couldn't hide it forever, but first he wanted to reestablish their intimacy and regain her trust.

Her vacillating attitude brought to mind how he'd treated her before September 11th. At the time, he'd thought of love as a romantic feeling. The gradual loss of that feeling in their marriage had left him empty, and he'd tried to heal himself with Candace. His terrifying near-death experience followed by the inspiration from the pendant had transformed his thinking. Now he saw love as a lifetime commitment that shaped two people's souls through joy and pain.

He longed to prove himself worthy of her trust. The longing felt like a stab wound in his chest. He tried to ignore it by returning his attention to Dr. Koestler, but the ache wouldn't cease.

A spry elderly woman asked Koestler if Jacqueline Kennedy had really been part of the U.S. delegation that had received the Temple of Dendur. The distinguished lecturer appeared impatient with the question. "Where did you hear that?"

"I read it in a magazine. The ceremony was in 1965."

"There's your answer then." Koestler appeared relieved as he glanced at his watch. When he turned to go, Justin followed him.

"Do you have time for a couple more questions, sir?"

"I'm sorry, but I'm late for a meeting." Koestler headed away from the exhibit area.

Tori caught up to the pair. "It'll just take a minute."

Justin withdrew his sketch of the pendant from his pocket. "I'm looking for some information that only an Egyptologist can provide."

Koestler didn't slow down. "About what?"

"About some artifacts discovered with a cache of mummies. The cache was found in the Egyptian desert in 1996."

"There was such a discovery, near the Bahariya Oasis." Koestler left the Sackler Wing and briskly moved through the open space outside it. "I remember it well because at the time the museum was reinstalling more than nine hundred objects from the Amarna Period into newly designed gallery spaces. There were more than one hundred mummies in the Bahariya cache. Incredible."

"Were any artifacts from that discovery acquired by the museum?" Justin couldn't stop his voice from trembling.

"No, definitely not. None of them were allowed to leave Egypt."

Tori ran ahead of them. "The real reason we're interested is because we're looking for information about a pendant."

Justin handed Dr. Koestler his sketch. The Egyptologist stopped. His expression darkened and his demeanor turned guarded. "Was this pendant three or four inches long and made of burnished acacia?"

Justin nodded.

"And those stick figures you've drawn, were those images engraved on the pendant's surface?"

"That's right." Justin bit his lip then asked the question he most wanted answered. "Could those engravings be hieroglyphics?"

Koestler ignored the question. His tone grew harsh. "Where did you get this pendant?"

Justin felt the wind rush out of him. Why would a renowned Egyptologist turn hostile unless he was hiding something? "It belonged to a friend of mine."

Koestler snatched the sketch from Justin and shook it in his face. "Who is this friend of yours?"

He jerked back. "Why do you want to know? Is there a problem?"

Koestler flung the sketch aside and grabbed his collar. "Just answer my question! How did your friend get this pendant?"

He tried to disengage without hurting the older man. "I don't know. That's what I'm trying to figure out."

"I bet you are. Anyone who has anything to do with that pendant should be in jail. A good man is dead because of it."

Sweat beaded on Justin's forehead. "What are you talking about? Why would I—"

Koestler waved a hand then latched on to his arm. "Security! Detain this man immediately. Call the police!"

Justin tried to yank his arm away. They wrestled until Tori pulled the Egyptologist off. Justin ran toward the corridor outside the Rogers Auditorium dodging frantic museum patrons. He and Tori headed for the open space outside the Met Store into the Great Hall at the front of the museum.

They fled out the 82nd Street entrance and kept running down Fifth Avenue until they reached the secluded woods of Central Park. When they finally slowed, Justin put an arm around Tori and drew her close. This time she took his face in her hands and found his lips. The kiss tasted even sweeter than the previous one because she initiated it. He let it last for a long, blissful moment thinking that when it ended he would muster his courage and confess the affair. But before he could speak, she pulled away.

"Let's get a bus on Fifth Avenue." She started to run. "We'll be safer in a crowd."

He hurried to catch up. When she offered him her hand, he took it. The confession would have to wait for a better time.

34

A Suspicious Delivery

*M*attie's Café, a second-floor coffee shop on West 43rd, was a good place to hide from the Met's security guards. Justin's seat by the window gave him a clear view of the towering *New York Herald* building across the street. Tori had gone to her office to further research Dr. Koestler and the Egyptian discoveries. Justin suspected he knew more about the pendant than he'd let on. Why else would he have had such an extreme reaction to the sketch?

An equally urgent question was whether Quentin Rathbun had staked out Tori's office. By killing her, he could lay to rest any fears about what her research might reveal. By killing both of them, he would eliminate the only significant threat to his and Candace's possession of the pendant and their conspiracy's success.

Justin fingered his can of pepper spray and sipped his coffee. The traffic flowed by in a blur of color—yellow taxis, red tour buses, white FedEx vans with purple and orange letters. He caught a glimpse of a family of four on a double-decker bus and watched them until they disappeared. Prior to September 11th, he couldn't have imagined wanting a family of his own. Now there was nothing he wanted more . . . along with an intimate marriage.

Candace stood in the way. He and Tori couldn't truly be intimate until he'd confessed the affair and eliminated the threat to their lives by bringing her to justice. He had to recover the pendant even if it meant implicating himself in her pre-9/11 insider-trading scheme.

He noticed a tall, broad-shouldered deliveryman in a gray uniform wheeling a dolly toward the entrance to the *Herald* building. He looked like Rathbun. Justin stood for a better view and dialed Tori. She picked up as he left the café and raced down the stairs.

"I think Rathbun just entered the building," he said.

"Are you sure?"

"Not completely, but we can't take chances. He's disguised as a deliveryman." He dodged oncoming traffic. "You've got to get out of there."

"I'm almost done with my research. I need—"

"*Now*, Tori. I'll meet you. If we leave through the loading dock, he'll never find us."

Justin entered the building and approached the security desk. A heavyset woman was on duty. He urged himself to remain calm. "I'm Tori Connelly's husband. That deliveryman who just came through here . . . did you get his name?"

"I'm sorry, sir. I'm not allowed to give out that information."

Justin showed her his driver's license. "I don't think that guy's a deliveryman at all."

She handed him a clipboard. He signed in and she buzzed him through. "Send security to Tori's office right away."

He rushed into the lobby but didn't see the deliveryman. All three elevators were in use, so he ran past them and found the door to the stairs. He sprinted up three flights. The door at the top opened onto a wide mezzanine. It wrapped around to the offices that overlooked the pressroom on the first floor.

He rushed toward Tori's office. She met him halfway. His heart turned over when he saw her terror. He had to protect her. "Quick, we'll take the stairs."

The elevator door opened before they ran past. The deliveryman stepped off and eyed them with a withering stare.

Rathbun.

Justin stepped in front of him and pushed Tori toward the stairs. "Now you're using disguises like a common criminal? You used to teach me the latest stock algorithms. What happened to you?"

Rathbun brandished a knife. "What I'm protecting is more valuable than any stock. And I won't rest until it's secure."

He lunged. Justin parried and shot pepper spray in his face, dropping him to his knees. Fleeing into the stairwell, he followed Tori down.

Rathbun's footsteps pounded above them.

At the basement level, they opened a door into a garage-like room. It was filled with refrigerator-size control modules and enormous double rolls of paper. The paper swirled into printing machines that hummed and rattled a cacophony of noise.

The narrow aisle that ran through the room led into a warehouse-like space with rows of conveyors at its center. He pulled Tori behind one of the printing machines in the first room. Bundles of newspapers spiraled down the rollers in S-curves to the loading bays in the warehouse, clickety-clack, clickety-clack.

He peered around the machine and saw Rathbun in the aisle rubbing his red, watery eyes. He walked between the conveyor belts and glanced around. Justin gripped Tori's hand. His palm was slick with sweat. He prayed that Rathbun would leave through the loading dock so they could escape out the main entrance. Instead he spun around and came back up the aisle with his knife drawn.

Justin drew back and readied the pepper spray. Footsteps approached. When Rathbun appeared, Justin sprayed him with one hand and pushed Tori out with the other.

Rathbun wiped at his eyes. "You're a dead man!"

He stabbed wildly. Justin dodged, and the blade careened off the machine.

"That's where you're wrong. I was dead when I was working for you and Candace." Rather than hatred, he felt pity for a man so enthralled with a woman that he would kill for her. He seized Rathbun's wrist. "Now I have a new life that makes your Wall Street riches look cheap and tawdry."

He twisted the knife loose. It disappeared into the whirling rolls of paper. Rathbun flailed wildly, but the pepper spray had blinded him. Justin rammed a shoulder into his gut and drove him down the aisle. Tori helped shove Rathbun into the warehouse onto a conveyor belt. Justin sent him spiraling toward the loading bays between bundles of newspapers.

Justin grabbed Tori's hand and raced for the stairwell. "We've got to get out of here."

"Let's go through the lobby." She started up the stairs. "We have to get to Queens right away."

"Why?"

In the lobby, she surged ahead with a brisk but unobtrusive pace. "I found a couple of leads in the *Herald's* archives."

He pulled even with her on the street. "New leads?"

"I'll tell you about it in a minute." She began to run and pulled her cell phone from her jeans. By the time they reached the Port Authority at 42nd Street and 8th Avenue, she'd called Paul and asked him to go to the *Herald* to track Rathbun from there.

Justin located a train to Queens and led her through tunnels and turnstiles. Once on the platform, she waved him behind a secluded pillar to the far left away from the waiting crowd. She kept her voice low.

"The leads explain why Koestler got so agitated. His predecessor was a renowned Egyptologist named Dr. Dieter Gruenwald. He was murdered on April 13th, 1996, but the killer was never caught."

The news hit Justin like the blast from an open furnace. "So what's the connection to Queens?"

"Eleven days before Gruenwald was murdered, a Secret Service agent by the name of Daniel McCarthy was killed by a subway train at the World Trade Center stop. I contacted McCarthy's brother. He lives in Queens. We have to interview him and see what he knows."

Justin fell silent and stared at the tracks. He'd always thought that falling onto them and getting crushed by a train would be a horrifying way to die. If the horror that had befallen Agent McCarthy was in any way related to the pendant, they were entangled in something far more perilous than he'd imagined . . . a peril in which he'd involved the woman he loved.

She drew closer to him. "I also found out more about the man who put Candace through the Chapin School."

"This guy Gustav Phelps?"

"Yes. He was a wealthy venture capitalist with a posh apartment on the Upper East Side. He and his wife took in foster children. In May 1988 he was convicted of the sexual abuse of a teenage girl."

Justin did some quick figuring. "Candace would've been in college at the time."

"Right. According to police records, she initiated the allegations then became a key witness at the trial. My guess is that she was trying to save another girl from the suffering she'd endured. I also found that she's a major donor to Refuge Commons in Westchester County. It's a safe house and recovery program for abused girls."

The train's headlight appeared in the distance. He glanced at Tori and bit his lower lip to keep it from trembling. As the lead car approached, his gaze fell on the dull, silvery shine of the third rail, the one that conducted high-voltage electricity to the trains. An equally powerful jolt of terror pierced his gut.

35

THE SECRET AGENT'S BROTHER

The low-lying clouds over the Jamaica section of Queens looked threatening. Tori hoped it wouldn't rain before she and Justin had walked the last couple blocks to William McCarthy's house on 104th Street. Her haunting memory of Dr. Jonathan Koestler's tirade seemed out of place in this quiet, orderly neighborhood. She wondered whether he'd reacted hysterically to the sketch because the pendant was somehow behind the murder of Dr. Dieter Gruenwald . . . or because Koestler had killed him in order to take his job and feared being accused.

She glanced at the clouds again. They appeared darker, as if preparing to unleash a downpour. She suspected Koestler had seen the pendant around the time of Gruenwald's murder. What she didn't know was whether the murder was related to the death of Secret Service agent Daniel McCarthy. His brother had sounded curt when she'd called him from her office. At first he'd said he didn't want her meddling. She understood his hesitation. She wanted to know about his brother's Secret Service assignment and his activities prior to his death, about the accident scene and the coroner's report . . . everything. When she'd told him about Gruenwald's unsolved murder, William McCarthy had reluctantly agreed to meet.

A dreadful sense of apprehension twisted through her. She feared being drawn into a murder investigation that might involve the agency sworn to protect the President of the United States. Justin took her hand. His touch confronted her with another source of apprehension—where her relationship with him was headed. Her fingertips went numb against his skin.

When they arrived at McCarthy's single-family clapboard bungalow, she tried to put her ominous thoughts to rest. The thick-chested man let them in without a handshake and with an irritated expression on his chubby face. He showed them into the cluttered living room and offered them seats on a tired-looking couch. He sat across from them in an easy chair and asked, "Why do you want to pry into my brother's death after all these years?"

Tori noticed stains on the carpet and streaks of soot on the wallpaper. "I have no intention of bringing you pain, but your brother died eleven days before the unsolved murder of Dr. Dieter Gruenwald, a renowned Egyptologist. We're looking for leads in that case."

A storm erupted in his basset hound eyes. "You aren't suggesting the two deaths were related, are you? My brother died in a tragic accident."

"This question may be hard for you to hear," Justin said, "but are you sure it was an accident?"

He frowned. "That's what the New York City detectives and the Secret Service concluded after their investigation. I have no reason to doubt them."

His uncritical acceptance of the verdict puzzled Tori, especially since he showed no emotion. "Were there any witnesses?" she asked.

"Only one—the motorman on the subway car that killed him, a man named Franklin Scott. All he saw was a body falling in front of his train."

"No one on the platform saw anything?" Justin asked.

"It was after one-thirty in the morning. The station was deserted. Besides, it happened right where the train enters the station, away from where the passengers wait."

The early hour of the accident made Tori suspicious. Tragedy could strike at any time. Was it just a coincidence that this one had occurred when no one else had been around to witness it? Or had this "accident" been carefully planned? "Where do you think your brother was going at that hour?"

He shrugged. "I've always assumed he had worked late and was on his way home."

Tori stared into his stormy eyes and noticed how frequently he blinked, a possible sign he was lying. "It was a Saturday. Why would he have been working?"

"I don't know. The Secret Service had a lot going on in Seven World Trade Center. It wasn't unusual for agents to be there twenty-four seven."

"Was there an autopsy?"

"Yes. No alcohol or drugs were found in his blood, and he hadn't had a heart attack or stroke or anything like that."

Tori bit her lip. She wanted to pose her next question carefully. Before she could speak, her cell phone vibrated. Paul's number was on the display. Her breath caught in her throat. Her first impulse was to let the call go into voice mail, but he might have news about Rathbun or Candace. She apologized and took the call.

"I can't talk long; we're with William McCarthy. Were you able to track our man?"

"Yes," Paul said, "and you'll never guess where he went. The Grand Hyatt."

The revelation gave her pause. "Did you find out what he's up to?"

"I couldn't get close enough. That's why I called. We could probably learn more if you came to the hotel with me. You're better at investigations."

Hearing the insistence in his voice reminded her of what a good man he was, of how much she respected him. "Okay, we'll go tomorrow. I'll call you."

She hung up. "Had you been in touch with Daniel before he died? I'm wondering about his state of mind."

McCarthy grew indignant. "If you're asking whether he committed suicide, the answer is no. Daniel was in excellent health and had everything to live for."

"Can you tell us anything about his assignment with the Secret Service?" Justin said.

"All I know is he worked in the offices in Seven World Trade Center. He never told me what he did."

Tori noticed that McCarthy looked away when he answered, again blinking. She wondered if he knew what his brother had done and for some reason wouldn't tell. She followed his wandering eyes until he met her gaze. "Could anyone have wanted Daniel dead, say, for revenge or something like that?"

McCarthy leaned forward with an intense expression. "My brother was a federal agent. If his colleagues thought he was murdered, they would've feared for their own lives and pursued the case with extra vigor. I'm satisfied that they didn't suspect foul play."

"But if he were murdered, how do you know the crime wasn't orchestrated from within?"

His expression soured. "I guess I have more confidence in the Secret Service than you do."

She decided to change the subject. "Do you have any photos of Daniel?"

He hesitated as if pondering what to say. Then he nodded and went up the staircase at the far end of the living room. When he returned, he handed her a five-by-seven color photo of a pleasant-looking, sandy-haired man with the physique of middleweight wrestler. She examined it carefully then gave it to Justin.

He studied it for a long moment before his eyes grew wide. "I think I've seen this man."

"What do you mean?" Tori gave him a curious look. "When?"

Justin kept staring at the photo. "I vaguely remember him coming into Candace's office. She called him Danny."

His voice sounded strained, as if he'd choked up then fought down the emotion. The color had drained from his face. He didn't just recognize the man in the photo; he was responding emotionally to him.

"My brother had many friends," McCarthy said. "Everybody called him Danny."

"Are you sure you only saw this guy once?" Tori asked. "How did Candace know him?" It bothered her that Justin was now the one diverting his eyes.

He just shrugged. "I don't know. I only remember seeing him once." He returned the photo to McCarthy.

"Can you show us any other materials related to your brother?" Tori asked.

"No, I really can't. It's getting late. I have other things to do."

She suspected that he was hiding something. She might need to investigate further. "We should be going. May I use your bathroom?"

McCarthy turned stone-faced, as if trapped between resenting the request and knowing it would be impolite to refuse. He finally nodded and pointed to a door near the entrance to the dining room.

She went into the spacious bathroom and unlocked the latch on the double-hung window above the radiator. She waited a moment, flushed the toilet, washed her hands, and returned to the living room.

William McCarthy let her and Justin out the front door and said a curt good-bye. It was drizzling now, and neither of them had brought an umbrella. As the rain wet her cheeks, she remembered all the tears she'd wept for the husband she thought she'd lost. Now she had him back, and their hearts had bonded again. But his obvious discomfort with Daniel McCarthy's photo made her wonder if he was hiding something.

"You got very quiet when you saw that picture," she said. "How come?"

Justin slipped an arm around hers and kept walking. "I guess the photo brought back memories of working for Candace and how many regrets I have about that time in my life."

His answer made sense. She wanted very much to believe him, so she dropped the matter. She was more troubled about William McCarthy's abrupt and evasive answers.

"McCarthy knows more than he told us," she said. "He seemed curious about Gruenwald's murder but didn't ask many questions. Nor did he give us much information about his brother's death. In fact, after he showed us the photo, he ended the interview. I wonder what else he might be hiding."

"I do too, but we'll probably never know."

"Yes, we will." She gave him a cryptic smile. "I unlocked the window in the bathroom. When I get back from the Grand Hyatt, we'll check out McCarthy's house further. But this time we'll do it when he's not home."

36

TRYING TO FIGURE IT ALL OUT

A man's heart differs from a woman's in only one way. The thought haunted Paul as he waited for Tori outside the Grand Hyatt Hotel. Men and women were equally susceptible to the temporary insanity called falling in love, but when ecstasy turned into misery, men had a greater tendency to bottle up their pain. When the bottle exploded, it often turned into depression or chemical dependency, violence, or even suicide. On a sun-bathed Manhattan morning, Paul nursed his hurt over losing Tori and couldn't get those repercussions out of his mind.

The doorman gave him an irritated glance. "May I help you, sir?"

"No, I'm just waiting for a friend."

He moved farther from the entrance. Was Tori still a friend? He glanced at the steady stream of professionally dressed men and women entering the hotel. With his blazer and slacks, he blended in with them, even without the tie. But he was a firefighter. He wasn't one of them and never would be.

Unlike Justin.

If Tori needed a businessman for a husband, Paul didn't qualify. He couldn't compete on that front with his former best friend. Prior to Justin's return, Paul wouldn't have considered reconciling with Linda, but he found himself softening toward the idea, playing with scenarios that might make it work. He felt as if the rays of the sun had scorched his heart.

The pendant was the wildcard. It seemed to have made Justin a different man—someone Paul could respect again. After hearing Candace and Justin speak at the Bilderberg conference, the pendant's power was undisputable. He might never be friends with Justin again, but he'd seen the terror caused by unfettered hatred on September 11th. If the pendant unleashed an outpouring of love and understanding, it would bring new hope to a wounded, terrified world. He had to help recover it.

Tori's arrival jarred him out of his thoughts. "I'm relieved you're all right," he said.

"So am I." She gave him a hug. "I've had some scary moments since I last saw you."

He led her farther from the entrance and told her everything he knew about Rathbun's visits to the Grand Hyatt, which wasn't much. "We should pose as corporate representatives planning a conference. We can request a tour of the hotel. Then we'll ask about upcoming conferences to find out if any involve Candace."

"And what if we don't get any answers?"

"Then I'll make up an excuse to leave the tour early. You'll keep the event planner occupied while I obtain the information secretly."

After they'd agreed on the details, he led her through the hotel's revolving door to the escalator up to the lobby. The background noise created by the fountain made him comfortable enough to ask her about the leads she'd found.

She moved closer. "So far I don't see a link between the murder of Dr. Gruenwald and the accidental death of the Secret Service agent. But I think McCarthy's brother knows more than he's willing to say." She whispered, "The only way we can find out if he has any of Daniel's materials is to break into his house."

When they got off the escalator, Paul took her to a secluded corner of the lobby's sitting area. "Are you crazy? You could end up in jail."

"There's no other way . . . and we need your help."

He gave her a withering glare. "I break into homes to help people, not snoop on them."

"What if he has information about the destruction of Seven World Trade Center? His brother worked in the building, and there are conspiracy theories related to the building's collapse."

He smirked. "I've heard them. Supposedly Larry Silverstein, the leaseholder, ordered the building pulled after it had burned all day. Then the fire department intentionally imploded the building." His eyes narrowed. "You don't believe that, do you?"

She scanned the lobby. "I don't know. I saw online videos of WTC7 crumbling onto its base, not onto the streets as the Twin Towers had. The building's debris flew so fast it damaged surrounding properties. That's a sign of an explosion.

The CIA, the Secret Service, and the Securities and Exchange Commission all rented space there. Their files along with the criminal cases they contained were destroyed and now can't be prosecuted for lack of evidence. The implosion may have been orchestrated by one or more of those criminal defendants."

Paul was shocked to hear her pursuing that line of thought. The mystery of Seven World Trade Center's destruction had been satisfactorily explained by the official inquiry: excessive heat had weakened the building's structure and caused it to collapse. If she'd found new information, or if William McCarthy had some hidden in his home, its revelation would be highly controversial.

"Daniel McCarthy died five years before September 11th," he said.

"He could've had information that one or more of the criminals wanted suppressed. If a conspiracy didn't bring down the building, what did? Its collapse couldn't have been caused by excessive heat. Fire doesn't burn through steel. William McCarthy might be hiding evidence that will uncover the truth. As a firefighter, you have an obligation to help us."

Paul started toward the front desk. "No promises."

Once he'd crossed the lobby, he asked the first available clerk about event planning. The young man called the catering office and arranged for them to meet a woman named Debra Monteiro.

Paul said nothing as he and Tori rode the half-full elevator to the mezzanine. They walked toward offices that overlooked the lobby. A petite, energetic African-American woman greeted them. She introduced herself as Debra Monteiro and took them into her contemporary office.

"So you're interested in planning an event?" She offered them seats.

"We might be," Paul said. "A conference on leadership for business people. We'll need space for both plenary sessions and breakout meetings."

"We can certainly accommodate your needs. It's just a matter of availability."

"I imagine that lots of groups use your facilities," Tori said.

"Of course."

"Have you ever heard of a businesswoman named Candace Donahue or her partner, Quentin Rathbun?" Paul asked.

Debra stiffened. "I'm sorry, but that information is confidential."

"Then can you show us the meeting rooms?" Tori said.

"Of course." She moved toward the door. "They're on the fourth floor. Follow me."

Paul glanced at Tori and hoped she could execute the plan they'd discussed. He followed her and Debra Monteiro into the hallway. Debra closed the door behind them. When they'd gone past two offices, Tori stopped. "I forgot my pad and pen in your office. Do you mind if we go back?"

"Not at all," Debra said.

They returned to her office where Tori picked up the pad and pen. On the way out, Paul diverted Debra's attention by asking how long she'd worked at the hotel. Before she answered, she called back to Tori, "Just pull the door closed. I already locked it."

She told them about her three-year history with the hotel then took them to the fourth floor. A few of the spacious ballrooms were in use, but she kept up a steady stream of conversation, telling them about room dividers and the potential for hosting groups from fifty to two thousand people.

When Paul excused himself to use the restroom, he headed for her office. Tori was supposed to have left the door unlocked. Two catering staff workers in white uniforms on the elevator were deep in conversation and didn't question him. He got off to find a tall woman in a blue suit walking the hallway. He diverted his eyes. She walked past.

When he came to Debra Montiero's door, he looked all around. He reached for the knob. If it didn't turn, he'd have no other way to get information about Candace's event. A moment of panic gripped him. His stress intensified as he turned the knob. He relaxed when the door opened.

He left the lights out and quickly went through Debra's desk drawers but didn't see any planning calendars or notes. He struck a key on her computer. Fortunately she'd left it on hibernate. He used the mouse to find her files and clicked on *2003 Schedule.*

He worried that the light from the screen would allow anyone in the hallway to see him. He heard people walking by. A man's voice said, "Wait a minute. Let me ask Debra. She'll know."

A key slipped into the lock. Paul dove for the crawlspace under the desk. The knob rattled, the door opened. The man said, "She's not in. I'll leave her a note."

The man flipped on the light. Paul held his breath. The man's penny loafers appeared beneath the desk. He opened a drawer. Paul's heart slammed against his rib cage. If this guy took much longer, Debra would wonder why he hadn't returned.

After what seemed like forever, the man left, and Paul went back to the computer. He scrolled through the 2003 file until he found the May schedule. He clicked on a reference called *The Donahue Vision Challenge*. A brief description appeared: *A day of empowerment for Hollywood producers, TV executives, and print and broadcast media innovators.* The date was May 21, 2003 . . . less than a week away.

Paul forced himself not to glance around to see if anyone had followed him upstairs. Tori was nearly finished with her tour. He winked at her, and she wrapped up her conversation. Debra walked them to the elevator and promised to provide any further assistance they might need. When the door opened, Paul was relieved to see that the car was empty. They got on and the door closed.

"Did you find anything?" Tori asked.

Paul stood close to her. "Candace is hosting powerbrokers from the media and the entertainment industry next week."

"If she corrupts them, they could destroy our country from within." As they passed through the lobby to the escalator, she said, "We'll have to meet with Justin at the Salisbury and come up with a strategy. The break-in at McCarthy's house will have to wait."

Out on the street, Paul hailed a cab. He instructed the driver to take them to the Salisbury. The car merged into the traffic and became surrounded by revving engines and blaring horns. Tori stared at her hands and steepled her fingers.

"There's no easy way to say this." She turned toward him with her lips trembling. "I've decided to take Justin back."

She paused. When she continued, her voice was unsteady. "I know I'm hurting you, and that's the last thing I want to do. But I have to do what's best for me and my family. You seem to be considering the same thing."

Paul stared out the window. The traffic on the street and the crowds on the sidewalks were obscured by the wetness of his eyes. She was right. The mediation had changed his thinking about his divorce, but he still felt the sting of her decision. Their relationship had offered balm for their wounded hearts and hope for their uncertain futures. Now it was coming to an abrupt and improbable end. He considered ordering the driver to stop so he could flee to a safe place where he could absorb the shock. But none existed . . . for either of them. The honest pain in her eyes stopped him.

"I don't know what to say. You were my—"

She pressed the tips of her fingers to his lips. "It's all too much to explain. Who would have thought that my runaway husband would come back? Or that he'd have a powerful near-death experience and discover a miraculous pendant? All I know is that the world needs Justin's message. I'm trusting the truth of it to guide us."

"Have you told him yet?"

"No, but I plan to soon."

A peculiar sensation swept through him. He had no desire to try to change her mind. Instead a surprising peace settled over him as if sent from some mysterious source. He glanced ahead and noticed how scratched and murky the Plexiglas between the back and front seats was. When he gazed through the yellowed material, he saw the driver and the oncoming cars as a blur, as if he were viewing them underwater.

His thoughts about the pendant were similarly obscured. He questioned how a worn piece of jewelry could empower the words of the person who possessed it. He pushed against the Plexiglas with his palms, desperate to ward off the surge of curiosity attacking his doubt. To acknowledge the pendant's power would be to let go of logic and take a frightening leap of faith. His hands fell limp at his sides. Something broke free in a part of him not fully under his control. He could resist no longer. His spirit began to soar. The more he surrendered, the clearer he could see.

He had to act. He needed to help stop Candace and recapture the pendant. Not out of loyalty to Tori and Justin but out of a growing personal commitment to the cause. By the time the taxi arrived at the Salisbury Hotel, he'd begun working out a plan to disrupt Candace's event and allow Justin to speak.

37

The Sixth Challenge: Inspired Creativity

The management of the Grand Hyatt Hotel dreaded having the fire alarm go off during a standing-room-only event. What Debra Monteiro didn't know was that Paul Spardello had posed as a fire inspector and started the alarm's trouble indicator. By sabotaging the detection system, he'd forced her to call a repairman. She'd never met Justin Connelly, so when he arrived in a cap and coveralls with a toolbox in hand, she had no reason to question whether he was an imposter. She led him to the alarm command center at the rear of the Commodore Ballroom and left him to his work.

On the way in, Justin had admired the historic, two-thousand-seat venue with its art glass chandeliers and metal grillwork reminiscent of neighboring Grand Central Station. He disarmed the beeping trouble indicator while powerbrokers from the worlds of film, television, advertising, and broadcast media watched an introductory video for Candace's keynote.

He slipped off the cap and coveralls then put on a necktie he'd hidden inside the toolbox. He grabbed the copy of the remarks he'd prepared. His only hope of delivering them was to snatch the pendant from Candace and win over the crowd within the first paragraph. Otherwise security guards would haul him off the stage.

He ran a comb through his hair and straightened his suit coat. As far as he could tell, he was appropriately dressed for the formal occasion. He stuffed the coveralls and cap into the toolbox and carried it to the door of the command center. Once he walked through the short corridor behind the speaker's platform, he would have only seconds to tear the pendant from Candace's neck and preempt her speech with his own.

He opened the door and heard Candace's voice on the hotel's PA system. She was commending the shapers of American culture for their courage and creativity in offering the public imaginative images and unforgettable dramas.

"I've called you together," she said, "to build a coalition that will transform America in the twenty-first century. Antiquated thinking has put up obstacles for too long, especially from the influence of faith-based communities and organizations."

He ventured through the corridor into the backstage area. He saw Candace from the side and set down the toolbox. She stood at the podium in a sleeveless evening gown of rich purple. The bodice was low-cut, and the pendant clung to her neck. Diamond earrings glimmered whenever she turned her head. She was stunning.

"Your visionary films, TV shows, and commercials already have the religious zealots on the defensive," she said, "but my initiative will liberate our country from its oppressive Puritan roots. You'll increase your power and profits as never before."

The audience interrupted with a rousing ovation. Justin charged. The applause ceased. He exploded across the stage and reached for the pendant. Rathbun and two burly security guards rushed from the audience. Candace jerked her head away too late. He tore the pendant from her neck. Euphoric, he turned to the microphone, but Rathbun and the guards wrestled him to the floor.

Candace stopped them. "Don't worry, I know this man."

"So do I." Debra Monteiro carved a path through the chaos. "He sneaked in by posing as an alarm repairman. I can have him arrested."

"No, don't do that." She pulled Rathbun and the guards off him and convinced them to wait backstage. "He's a former employee of mine. He's been trying to do something like this for a long time. I've decided that the best way to handle the situation is to let him speak."

She nudged him toward the podium. He wondered why she was saying bizarre things and giving him this rare opportunity. It must be because he possessed the pendant. She'd lost her ability to oppose him. The thought of speaking under its power kindled fire in his bones. Perhaps his battle with Candace was finally over. He could convert the crowd to the ways of God and goodness and peace. He chided himself for ever having doubted this ultimate outcome.

Candace waved a hand to quiet the ballroom. "You've got five minutes."

Justin pulled the speech from his pocket. "Ms. Donahue commended you for your glitzy images and spectacular dramas, but I have a different perspective. Too many of your productions idolize wealth and encourage greed. Too many glorify violence and glamorize promiscuity. Rather than call out the best in your viewers, you bog them down in passivity and cynicism. You have the most powerful communications technology ever invented, but rather than fulfill your viewers' longing for inspiration, you cater to their baser instincts. You're getting rich undermining the faith and values of the American people!"

Boos erupted from several sections of the audience. Justin ignored them.

"Most of us can't measure up to your images of youth and beauty, wealth and success. We buy the products advertised because we believe we can't live without them. We accept that world of distorted values because you make it look irresistibly luminous. I'm talking about the win-at-any-cost world of professional sports and the over-sexualized world of situation comedies. I'm talking about the cutthroat world of reality TV and the bloody world of action movies and interactive games."

He was shocked to hear snickers. Catcalls wafted across the ballroom.

"Enough of this anti-American diatribe!"

"Who are you, the values police?"

Had the pendant lost its power? He gripped it harder.

"I'm speaking as a man who was lost in betrayal and cowardice. I know how painful it is to confront our shameful and vicious tendencies. We disguise our darkness as light or deny the darkness exists. Even worse, we project our darkness onto others and see them as evil and ourselves as righteous."

"Enough of this nonsense!" yelled someone near the stage.

"Hear me out," Justin said. "We express ourselves through dazzling high-tech mediums from TV programs and blockbuster films to the Internet and computer games. But we can't truly be free living in darkness. Only by evolving spiritually can we access the kind of creativity that transforms us and our world. I'm talking about opening our imaginations to the divine in prayer and meditation. When we do this, we bring inspired art into the world—the kind of art that brings out the best in those who create it as well as those who encounter it."

Laughter and cries of derision broke out. The hostility baffled Justin. Why wasn't the pendant mesmerizing the crowd? He moved closer to the microphone. "I invite you on a journey of inspired creativity. To accept is an act of courage. As you connect with the image of God inside you, you'll receive the spiritual light that brings goodness, truth, and beauty into the world."

A man in front with shoulder-length blond hair stood. "What are you, some kind of fanatic?"

Justin spoke faster. "Never doubt your creative ability. There's genius in you that longs to be expressed. As God has made you unique in all the universe, so are your gifts and talents without equal. Bathing them in spiritual light will heal and satisfy your soul. You'll need the support of others who also seek the light. The bond you share will end your loneliness. As you produce art that inspires the world, you'll find your highest joy, and advances will be made toward justice, community, and peace. The journey begins when you get honest about your darkness and commit yourself to follow the light, no matter the cost."

"Now I know you're a fanatic," the man said. The crowd laughed but Justin kept speaking.

"I invite you to take the first step tonight. Use your talents to build a spiritual culture on earth. If we own our darkness, we can transcend it. The good things can finally be ours—loving, respectful relationships, clean air and water, racial harmony, interfaith understanding, an end to poverty, each person achieving his or her God-given potential. Don't be afraid! In this new world, we'll live in harmony with one another and with the loving providence that is the source of all—"

Candace nudged him away from the podium. "Your time's up."

He resisted, but the crowd shouted him down. He finally stepped aside.

Candace stooped, removed a pendant from her ankle, and fastened it around her neck. She leaned toward the microphone. "This man obviously doesn't share our vision of unbridled self-fulfillment in America."

The crowd applauded. Justin stared at the pendant in his hand. Its engravings looked like random scratches. Those on the pendant that Candace wore appeared orderly.

He'd been duped.

She and Rathbun had predicted he would launch an assault and had made an imitation.

She shook a finger in his direction. "This man's ideas are so antiquated and silly that no thinking person believes them. In the post-9/11 world, we need less, not more, religion. We'll never be truly free until we complete our evolution into a religionless society. It's time to pursue the birthright of privilege and pleasure guaranteed by the Declaration of Independence and the Constitution of the United States!"

Justin felt the stage shake from the thunderous applause. Seeing the pendant's effect on the influential entertainment and media professionals left him in awe. Her plan had worked;

he'd become an object of ridicule and scorn. Worse, he'd lost his best opportunity to recover the pendant. If he tried to leave through the back, Rathbun and his guards would beat or kill him.

His only hope was to flee through the ballroom. He descended the stairs and dodged men in tuxedos and women in evening gowns. The light from the chandeliers reflected off the women's jewelry and assaulted his eyes. The glitzy images reminded him of the tawdry artificial light in hell. He remembered fleeing the three-headed dogs, growing exhausted and drawing on inner strength he hadn't known he possessed. He reached inside to find that strength again.

The crowd had fallen under the spell of the pendant and was too preoccupied to stop him. He emerged into the foyer and blended in with other hotel guests. To recapture the pendant seemed more impossible than ever. His best hope now was to find a way to disable it. That meant breaking into William McCarthy's house in search of more leads. Not until he rode the elevator to the lobby and fled out the front door did his heart stop pounding.

38

BREAKING AND ENTERING

"Hurry, I can't hold you much longer," Justin whispered. Tori worked harder at opening McCarthy's bathroom window. The window budged, so she knew he hadn't relocked it after their visit. Her feet wobbled on Justin's shoulders as the darkness obscured her vision. She'd already removed the screen and was trying to shove the window up. "Can you lift me higher?"

His grip tightened around her ankles. She felt her body rise. When she leaned an elbow on the outer sill, the added leverage helped her lift the window. She grabbed the ledge with both hands. "Okay, shove me as high as you can."

She swung one leg over the sill and let herself down onto the radiator inside the bathroom. The apprehension in her gut felt as hard as the metal beneath her feet. She and Justin had made sure McCarthy wasn't home. They were still taking a tremendous risk, but they had no other choice. If this man possessed items or materials from his brother's home, they might contain clues about whether his death had been a tragic accident or something more sinister. The clues might indicate whether any of the tenants in Seven World Trade Center—or even the government—had wanted Daniel McCarthy dead. Most of all, they might shed light on where the pendant had come from and how Candace had obtained it.

After Justin's humiliation at the Grand Hyatt, Tori was more worried than ever about the spread of Candace's conspiracy. The Queen of Wall Street had brought the heads of the largest Manhattan banks under her control along with the most powerful Bilderbergers and the elites of the film and broadcasting industries. If she and Justin didn't stop her soon, Candace would turn America into a spiritless, materialistic wasteland and reap billions in the process.

Tori jumped down and used her flashlight to find McCarthy's back door. She let Justin in knowing that if they found nothing useful, she would have to revamp her investigation and start over. She pushed those ricocheting thoughts out of her mind and led him through the kitchen. They crouched low and hurried through the dining and living rooms and up to the second floor. They found only one room there, a bedroom furnished with a queen-size bed and nightstand, an armoire, a dresser with a mirror, a computer desk, and a widescreen TV. She caught an unpleasant whiff of body odor and recoiled when a cat ran out of the bathroom.

Justin opened several dresser drawers in rapid succession while she rifled through the armoire. "It didn't take McCarthy long to bring us the photo. If he has other materials somewhere, they're probably close by."

She saw no file cabinets or storage boxes, just clothes strewn on the floor and a clutter of papers on the computer desk. She examined the papers and searched under the bed and in the bathroom but found nothing. She noticed a small door near the entrance that she'd missed when they'd come in. She opened the door and turned on a light. The long, narrow storage space contained rows of cardboard boxes with lids. She waved to Justin. "This way."

She ran the beam of her flashlight over the unmarked boxes and began to open them. The boxes contained books, Christmas decorations, household items, and the like. Not until she and Justin reached the far end of the space did she see the words *Danny's stuff* written in magic marker on the last three boxes. She opened the first one as Justin dug into the second.

"Just old clothes in here," he said.

She shined her flashlight and sorted through the contents of her box. "Only some books and training manuals in this one."

She closed the first box and opened the third. It contained a row of file folders, each one marked. She riffled through them and found old correspondence and various commendations Danny had received for outstanding service. One of the files was marked *Photos*. She pulled it out and thumbed past an autographed photo of Danny with President Ronald Reagan and another of him with President Bill Clinton. Then she held up a five-by-seven color print, hardly able to believe what she saw. "Justin, look at this."

The photo showed the pendant beside the 1933 Double Eagle with several other jewels and old coins. She laid the photo on the floor, pulled her cell phone from her pocket, and took two snapshots of it. "This may hold a clue to where the pendant came from."

Justin looked more closely. "It's certainly intriguing."

She was almost too excited to speak. "It appears that the pendant was tied to the Farouk Double Eagle. Perhaps they both came from King Farouk's vast collection. If so, they were probably stored together in the Secret Service vault. If Danny had access, he could've been murdered by someone who was after these treasures."

"But why photograph them?"

Tori put her phone away and returned the file to the box. "Probably to prove to some interested party that he could obtain the treasures. I suspect that party was Candace Donahue."

Justin stared at her, appearing confused. "Why?"

"Because Danny McCarthy was probably dating her when he died."

He showed no expression. "How do you know that?"

"You said you saw Danny in Candace's office, right?"

"So?"

Tori tightened her grip on his arm. "Was it around April 2nd, 1996?"

Justin thought a moment. "It very well could have been. Why?"

She jabbed the air with a finger. "Because that's the day Danny was killed by Franklin Scott's train. If Candace had illegally obtained the pendant from Danny, he was the only one who could implicate her. I doubt he fell in front of that train. I suspect that Candace pushed—"

"It must be fun to play detective."

The voice spoke from near the door, sending a jolt through Tori. She turned, and her heart leaped into her throat. William McCarthy was pointing a handgun at them.

"You came and asked about my brother," he said, "but you were really casing my house. Now you'll answer to the cops. Come out of there."

She moved toward him. "Don't you care that your brother was probably murdered?"

"Shut up!" McCarthy kept the gun steady and stayed near the door.

She walked past him onto the landing. "If you call the cops, we'll tell them about Danny's stuff. Tampering with evidence in a murder case is a federal crime. They'll want to know about those photos you're hiding."

He shoved her then did the same to Justin. "What's in those boxes is none of your business."

She stopped in front of the stairs and turned. "Why are you so uptight about Danny's stuff? Did someone pay you to keep quiet?"

"I said shut up!"

"No, you need to hear me. I may have just seen evidence that your brother was murdered."

"If you make wild allegations, you better be able to back 'em up."

She gave him a fierce look. "There's a photo in Danny's belongings that may implicate him in a federal crime. He may have stolen a valuable artifact from the Secret Service vault. Whoever put him up to it may then have murdered him."

Justin stepped between them. "Now the choice is yours. Do you want to bring Danny's murderer to justice? Or do you want to protect your brother's reputation?"

McCarthy's hands began to shake. "How do you know these things?"

Tori pushed Justin aside. "We've been doing research. We have to find out about the Egyptologist I told you about, Dr. Dieter Gruenwald. I have a hunch that your brother's death was related to his."

Justin reached toward the gun. "You can either have us arrested or you can help us solve this case."

McCarthy shook his head as his arm trembled. Seconds passed. Finally he said, "I've always wondered about that picture." He lowered the gun. "All right, I'll help you."

Tori led both men down the stairs then took Justin aside. "I looked up Dr. Gruenwald's obituary. He lived in Brooklyn with his wife. We need to go see her."

Tori promised to keep McCarthy posted on any developments and took Justin's hand. They went out the front door and headed a couple blocks up 104th Street toward his car. Just beyond the house, she wrapped an arm around him. "You know what I really hate?"

"What?"

"Having a gun pointed at me."

He adjusted his gait so that it matched hers. "As I recall, the break-in was your idea, not mine."

"It doesn't matter. Almost getting shot has some advantages. It makes you realize what's important."

"I can think of safer ways to find that out."

"So can I, but this is the way that worked for me." She locked her eyes on his. "I don't want to die with regrets. What I would regret most is not taking you back as my husband."

∼

Tori's words hit Justin like a blast of Staten Island humidity. He'd been trying to confess his affair, but danger kept getting in the way. He would have no better opportunity than now, but he hesitated to speak. He berated himself for being a coward then reminded himself that any man in his position would be afraid. After having come so far in his attempt to regain her trust, he blanched at the thought of losing it again. But he couldn't have an intimate marriage unless it was built on complete honesty.

"Since you brought up regrets," he said, "I should tell you mine."

"You already did."

"I left something out."

"What could be worse than running away on September 11th?"

He swallowed and forced himself to speak. "The reason I did it."

"You already told me the reason." She didn't look at him and kept walking.

"There's more." He had the urge to throw himself in front of one of the cars traveling on the street. "I was having an affair with Candace."

Tori stopped and pulled away. "You couldn't possibly have said what I think I just heard." She stared at him. Her eyes were cauldrons of aching confusion.

He struggled to speak. "It was the stupidest thing I've ever done. I don't have any excuses. All I can say is how sorry I am." He reached for her arm.

She shoved his hand away. "If I had McCarthy's gun, I might use it on you."

He forced himself to go on. "The affair only lasted a few weeks. I realized I didn't love her. Despite the problems in our marriage, I knew I was being unfair to you. I had just told her I wanted out when the plane hit the North Tower."

She ran a hand through her hair and shook her head. "And the affair was part of why you ran to Providence?"

"Yes. Candace and I made it out of the building, but she got hit by a piece of debris. She'd stopped breathing. I carried her to a fireman, thinking she was dead. Then I took the pendant and ran."

"Why did you want it?"

"I don't even know. I was in shock. Later, I decided to carry the pendant on my key ring to remind me of how terribly I'd failed and how much I needed to change." He reached for her again. "Can you ever forgive me?"

She pulled away from him and hurried toward the car, brushing away tears. "I don't know. I really don't know."

39

WHAT DOES IT MEAN TO LOVE?

Paul trudged across the parking lot of the Parkhurst Elementary School feeling anxious about what Linda would say. Sadie's kindergarten class had just let out. At least twenty children swarmed the slides, swings, monkey bars, and bouncing bridge. He didn't see his daughter but spotted Linda in a group of parents watching from the surrounding grass. She looked the part of the successful businesswoman she'd become. Her chestnut hair had been pulled back, and her appealing features were accentuated by small gold earrings and a tasteful application of makeup.

The asphalt felt as if it were hardening around his feet. He was staggered by sadness over having lost the intimacy they'd once shared. That same sadness had haunted him since Linda had begun to expand her Staten Cuts Beauty Salon into a multi-site business. Her long hours, coupled with the stresses of his firefighting, had left them little time for each other. Whatever time they'd managed to find had grown increasingly tense.

The simmering alienation had boiled over after September 11th. The trauma of that day and his despair over having lost so many buddies had plunged him into a depression that Linda couldn't penetrate, let alone heal. She'd finally said she needed more from a marriage than a mutual exercise in loneliness and hostility. When he'd moved out in February 2002, Tori's friendship had saved him. They'd both lost marriages in the wake of that horrific day, and their mutual love for Justin gave them a powerful bond.

It had taken Paul a year to accept that his feelings for Tori had grown romantic. Finally he'd asked her out. Their relationship helped both of them stop despairing and start laughing and enjoying life again. With Justin's return and Linda's proposal of mediation, Paul was fighting a new battle with confusion.

He stared at the asphalt and noticed the fissures running through it. He thought of the freezing and thawing that occurred during the winter and how the process would eventually turn the parking lot into a sea of potholes. He forced himself to keep going. Something similar might happen to his heart if he didn't resolve the grief of losing both Linda and Tori.

He scanned the playground and spotted a girl with auburn curls and a nose and cheeks dotted with freckles. *Sadie.* He waved until she saw him and waved back. Then she went on playing. The quick interaction reminded him of the frantic nature of their relationship—always forged on the run, always squeezed between his schedule and Linda's, always interrupted when Sadie left his apartment after the weekend and returned to her mom's house.

He glanced at the fissures again, convinced that their jagged, chaotic designs ran through the scaffolding of his inner life, and that the scaffolding threatened to crumple because of his lost time with his daughter. The worst part for a take-charge man like himself was being helpless to stop the gradual disintegration. Because he left for work as Sadie got home from school, it was impossible to have more time with her. He bit his lip, frustrated by his inability to change the situation. He cringed at the metallic taste of blood.

The optimism and innocence in her eyes wouldn't let him stop hoping. An insistent voice urged him not to belabor the breakup with Tori. For his daughter's sake, he needed to move on and be open to reconciling with Linda. But did she really love him? Nothing could change until she said yes and proved it with her actions. Even then reconciliation would require a three-alarm effort.

He approached the chain link fence at the edge of the playground and watched the children. After a couple minutes, Linda caught a glimpse of him and stared in surprise. She came over, looking sleek in taupe slacks and a crisp white shirt under an evergreen blazer, one of her typical business casual outfits.

"What brings you here?" The corner of her mouth twitched.

"I was in the neighborhood and thought I'd stop by." He searched her eyes, relieved that the twitch suggested he wasn't the only one who was nervous. Part of him felt as alienated from her as ever; another part hoped they could find a way beyond the pain. "I need some advice from a savvy business woman."

"After all I've put you through, I never thought you'd call me that."

He detected a glint of warmth in her gaze. "I'm not talking about how you manage your salons."

"That's the only kind of business I'm in."

"I thought so too until we met with the mediator. Now I wonder if you're in the business of trying to put lawyers out of work."

She laughed. "I wouldn't have suggested mediation if I wasn't."

He rubbed one foot against the fence. "Tell me honestly. Does my relationship with Tori have anything to do with this?"

She laughed harder but it sounded forced. "Are you serious?"

Her response set warning lights flashing in his mind. "If you want me involved, we have to be honest with each other."

She took hold of the support pipe at the top of the fence. "All right, maybe I was a little jealous."

"You don't have to be anymore."

Her eyes widened.

He gripped the top of the fence but stayed clear of her hands. "She's taking Justin back."

"And you think *I'm* the one putting lawyers out of business?"

He pulled himself closer. "We both know it's more complicated than that. If you suspect I'm here on the rebound . . . well, there's some truth to that too." He crossed his arms on the support pipe. "Do you want to withdraw your offer?"

"No." Her lips tightened into a thin line. "But I'm under no illusions that reconciling will be easy."

"Nor am I." He wondered if it was even possible. "What I need is an intimate partner, not just a roommate who helps pay the bills."

"We want the same thing. I only initiated the divorce because I thought an intimate marriage was no longer possible with you."

"And you think it's possible now?"

"I don't know but I'm open to trying." She put her hand on his. "Recently you've seemed more like your old self. After September 11th, you got so moody, so irritable. I finally stopped trying to reach you."

He turned away and swallowed hard. "I've changed a lot since then. I'm different from the man you wanted to divorce."

"Then maybe the business venture you mentioned isn't such a bad idea."

As she spoke the words, an unexpected wave of the old sadness washed over him. "I don't know, Linda, I—"

Sadie screamed. A jolt of terror knifed through him as he ran for the playground. To his amazement, Linda overtook him, broke through the other parents, and scooped up their daughter like a mother eagle rescuing her young. Sadie wailed and brushed woodchips from her face. A blond woman with a ponytail also tried to comfort her.

"It's all right." Linda patted her on the back. "What happened, sweetheart?"

"Sammy pushed me!" She pointed at a rather homely boy wearing a mischievous expression.

The woman with the ponytail grabbed Sammy's hand, made him apologize, and began to pull him away. He fought to stay put.

Paul wrapped an arm around his wife and daughter. Sadie eventually quieted and begged to play again. Linda dusted her off. More woodchips fell to the ground. Paul felt his resistance begin to fall with them. The emotion of the moment took him back to September 11th . . . to the smell of jet fuel, the taste of sooty air, the pandemonium of debris raining down on running, screaming people.

His fireman's instinct had kicked in and sent him into the North Tower to rescue as many as he could. He'd been there for them though he hadn't known them and would never see them again. Sadie would be part of his life forever. He desperately wanted to be there for her, but he couldn't tolerate a one-way relationship with her mother. It had to be mutual or he couldn't go back.

Linda let Sadie go play and waved him toward a bench near the fence. She sat down and patted the seat next to her. He hesitated. There was so much hurt between them, so many unresolved issues.

She took his hand. "Let's not talk about the problems. Just being together is a victory."

He sat down, struck that she was right. He thought of the pendant and the powerful effect it had had on audiences in Providence, Versailles, Manhattan. He was committed to helping Justin and Tori recapture it, but if Linda was serious about reconciling, how could he justify not telling her about it? He composed his words carefully.

"I'm exhausted by the problems too, but there's one I haven't told you about."

"Not another business venture, I hope."

"Actually, you might call it something like that. Justin's business dealings have gotten him into a lot of trouble."

"Let me guess: The trouble has something to do with Wall Street and why he ran away on September 11th."

"Like I said, you have good business instincts."

She drew her hand away. "My instincts are directed toward earning an honest living. The Wall Street crowd plays by a different set of rules. They make obscene amounts of money then, when they get into trouble, they expect the rest of us to bail them out."

"Justin is indeed in trouble." Paul leaned toward her and lowered his voice. "Insider trading. He wasn't the instigator, though; his boss and her assistant were. If I told you the details, you'd never believe me."

"He should go to the police."

"He can't. He'd go to jail too."

"So what does he plan to do?"

Paul peered into her smoldering eyes, dark blue like the night sky beyond the stars. "He's trying to take his case to the public. I've been helping him."

She put a hand on his thigh. "You aren't in any trouble, are you?"

"Not with the law. But helping Justin could get dangerous."

"Then I hope you'll back off."

"I can't. Helping him has taught me some lessons I needed to learn . . . especially about marriage."

She gave him a puzzled look. "I'm listening."

Paul couldn't tell her about the pendant. She wouldn't believe him. He decided to focus on just one of the many lessons. "When Justin was in his coma, he had a powerful near-death experience. He came back believing that marriage works best when both partners are evolving spiritually. That's my perspective now too. I hope it'll become yours as well."

Her expression turned skeptical. "Why would you listen to a man who abandoned his wife and son for nearly two years?"

Paul kneaded his fingers against the wooden bench. "Is that all you're going to say? What about the concept?"

Linda stood and took his hand. "Can we just drop this? I'm not ready to talk about Justin." She gave him a hug.

The boy who'd pushed Sadie was crying now, refusing to let his mother take him to the car. Paul had never seen the boy before, but he empathized with his anguish. He remained stiff, paralyzed by a flashback of the day he'd moved out. He believed that marriages should be saved if possible, but the process required a level of vulnerability that scared him. He'd been hurt in the past. Was he ready to put himself in a position where it could happen again? He resisted the hug as the question gnawed at him. Then he caught a glimpse of Sadie running on the playground. Her face was animated with delight.

He took Linda in his arms.

"I'm not asking you to move back in," she said. "I just wondered if we could grab a cup of coffee sometime. I've got some news to share with you."

"Will you bring Sadie?"

"Let's make it ice cream then." She pulled away but kept holding his hands. "This news really is about my business. I've decided to sell my salons."

He braced himself to keep from falling off the bench. "Those are the last words I thought you'd say."

"I've been thinking about it for a while, but I finally listed them a few weeks ago. I've already had some inquiries."

"Could any of this be related to why you proposed mediation?"

She stood and scanned the playground for Sadie. "I'll give you a call, okay?"

He hesitated, speechless with surprise and disbelief. He glanced at the hazy sky, the playground equipment, the other parents. His hope that he and Linda could love each other again clashed with his fear that he still loved Tori. He tried to stand but couldn't.

Then he met Linda's gaze and she smiled.

"Okay," he said.

And he got up and headed for the Mustang.

40

AN EXCRUCIATING INVESTIGATION

Tori climbed the stairs of Mrs. Ursula Gruenwald's well-kept brownstone. Each step echoed her heartbreak over Justin's confession. Part of her craved revenge. Hearing about his affair with Candace was like drinking toxic water. He should have to drown in it. She glanced at him. His gaze was directed straight ahead, and her mind flashed an image of him thrashing naked in the freezing waters of the East River.

Another part of her respected his honesty. If she really loved him, perhaps she should forgive even the profoundest of betrayals. Her eyes roamed to the carved wooden arch above the door. Its intricate curls and loops reflected the jumble of her conflicted emotions. Justin had caused her immense anguish, yet the messages he'd spoken with the pendant had revived her passion for him. Because of that, and because Candace posed an imminent threat to economies on both sides of the Atlantic, she couldn't just abandon him and drop the investigation. A knot tightened in the pit of her stomach. She had no choice but to keep working with him and hope she could eventually unravel it.

Her immediate task was to question Mrs. Gruenwald. Seven years after the elderly widow's husband had been murdered, she was still traumatized and living in the Park Slope section of Brooklyn where they'd raised their three children. Tori had asked to meet in order to share some new information about the case. But Mrs. Gruenwald had refused when she'd learned she was a reporter.

She rang the doorbell with a shiver of trepidation. The outcome of her investigation depended on whether Mrs. Gruenwald would cooperate. If not, it would be impossible to pry specifics about the theft of the pendant from the close-lipped Secret Service. Nor could she go to the police and risk getting Justin arrested. Finding the photo of the pendant with the Double Eagle had been a stunning revelation, but Mrs. Gruenwald's response to their visit would either move the investigation forward or end it in disappointment.

An ache of anxiety spiraled through her as she rang the bell again. She caught Justin's eye and saw genuine pain and remorse. The arrogance of his Wall Street days was gone, replaced by a humility that evoked her desire to forgive. She wondered if that desire would ever grow stronger than her hurt.

The door opened a crack with the security chain still attached. Mrs. Gruenwald spoke in a heavy German accent. "What do you want?"

Tori could see only one of the older woman's hazel eyes, a sliver of her forehead, a swatch of her white hair. "Forgive me, but I'm the woman who called about—"

Mrs. Gruenwald's eye grew fiery. "I told you I did not want to speak with you. Leave or I will call the police."

Justin waved imploringly. "We have information the police—"

"Do you not understand the word *no?*" Mrs. Gruenwald started to slam the door.

Justin blocked it with a foot. "Please. You're the only one who can sort out this information."

Mrs. Gruenwald kicked at his foot. "Now you are harassing me."

A note of indecision emboldened Tori. "We've discovered another possible murder. It could be linked to your husband's."

Mrs. Gruenwald appeared skeptical but her gaze softened. "How?"

"By the circumstances. The other death was ruled an accident, but we have evidence against that conclusion."

Mrs. Gruenwald intensified her one-eyed stare. "What are you talking about?"

Using her cell phone, Tori pulled up the snapshot she'd taken of the photo of the pendant beside the Double Eagle. "This. If you let us, we'll tell you more."

Mrs. Gruenwald scrutinized every inch of her face. Seconds passed. Finally the chain slid free and the door opened. She led them through a tastefully decorated Victorian home with high ceilings and paintings of ancient Egypt on several walls. She invited them to sit down in the dining room. "Tell me about this photograph and why you think it has anything to do with my husband's murder."

Tori let her examine the snapshot more closely. "There are engravings on the wooden pendant. Someone deliberately photographed it with those jewels and that gold coin, known as a 1933 Double Eagle."

"How do you know about that coin?"

"I researched it. The coin came from the collection of a former king of Egypt. The Secret Service seized the coin in a sting operation. The other possible murder involved a Secret Service agent killed by a subway train eleven days before your husband died."

Mrs. Gruenwald frowned. "Why would this pendant have anything to do with my husband's murder?"

Tori pointed at the engravings. "It's just a hunch, but I wonder if these markings are Egyptian hieroglyphics. Perhaps your husband translated them and was murdered as a result."

"My husband did many translations. Who would want to kill him for one of them?"

Tori ran a finger over the phone's screen. "The pendant is probably a valuable ancient artifact. The engravings may reveal where it came from."

"And you think the same person who murdered my husband pushed the Secret Service agent in front of the train?"

"Precisely." She closed the phone.

Justin leaned forward. His voice was firm. "We think the agent, Daniel McCarthy, stole the pendant from the Secret Service vault in Seven World Trade Center. Someone else wanted the pendant, and that person murdered McCarthy in a way that made it look like an accident. The train hit him just after 1:30 A.M. on April 2, 1996, at the entrance to the World Trade Center station."

Tori put the phone in her pocket. "If Dr. Gruenwald's translation revealed the origin and value of the pendant, the killer may have feared that your husband would go public with the news." She took the risk of touching Mrs. Gruenwald's motionless hand. "Do you have access to any of your husband's papers? If we could find his translation, it could break this case open."

Her face went pale. "This is all quite shocking." She hesitated then said, "But I will do anything to help. My husband kept an office on the third floor. It is still as he left it because I get frequent requests from scholars to review aspects of his research. After his death, the Metropolitan Museum gave me his papers. If you want, you can go through the translations, but I warn you, there are lots of them."

Tori followed her up a wide staircase that led from the entrance of the house to the second floor. She felt hopeful about finding new evidence but warned herself against expecting tidy answers. Justin caught up when they reached the landing. Mrs. Gruenwald turned a corner and opened a door to a steeper set of wooden stairs.

Tori and Justin each took one of her arms and helped her climb to a remodeled attic. The large room contained six long bookshelves in the center. A desk near the window was flanked by a potbelly stove. Mrs. Gruenwald ambled to a row of five tall file cabinets that lined the wall by the door.

"These cabinets contain all of my husband's work." She opened the top drawer of the cabinet on the far end nearest the window. "This drawer has his notes from his translations."

An ache throbbed in Tori's chest as she thumbed through the material. There were files on Cleopatra and another Egyptian queen named Hatshepsut. Other files covered numerous pharaohs: Ramses II, King Tut, Thutmore III, and more. Thankfully Dr. Gruenwald had designated files for the translations he'd done each year.

Tori flipped to a folder marked *1996* and found pages full of hieroglyphics from various projects: *Ancient Egyptian Math Problems, Markings from Tombs near the Giza Pyramids, Insights into Egyptian Astronomy,* and several other topics. These hieroglyphics hadn't been translated.

Then she came to a file that stopped her heart. It was marked *Pendant*. Inside was a sheet of paper that listed a column of English letters next to a column of hieroglyphics. The letters read, *FROM MOSES STAFF*. The file also contained several scholarly articles.

Tori held the front of the file cabinet to calm herself. "Look at this."

Justin scanned the translation and let out a muffled cry. "Could this mean what I think it means?"

She read the highlighted sections of the articles. "This translation suggests the pendant came from the staff of Moses. These articles explain the meaning of the staff in the Bible, how Moses used it to liberate the Hebrews but how it also unleashed great suffering on the Egyptians."

The translation trembled in Justin's hands. "Amazing." The word came out slowly in a voice filled with awe.

Mrs. Gruenwald had been straightening the desk. She came over. "Did I hear you mention Moses?"

"Yes," Tori said. "Why?"

Her voice grew animated. "My husband made a reference to Moses that I've never understood. It was an offhand comment on the morning of the day he was murdered . . . something like, 'Well, no one can ever again say that Moses wasn't mentioned in Egyptian hieroglyphics.' He mumbled the words under his breath as he left for the museum. I don't think he even knew I heard him."

"Do you remember anything else about that morning?" Tori asked.

"One thing stands out. When Dieter kissed me good-bye, he smelled of cologne. I asked him why he had put it on, since he never had before. He got upset and said it was his business. I should not worry about it."

Tori lay a hand on her shoulder. "I know this is hard for you, but can you tell us anything about the crime scene?"

Mrs. Gruenwald glanced away and drew a slow breath. "My husband was found in his car in a parking lot on the Hudson at the end of Dyckman Street. He had been poisoned with a hypodermic needle, but the detectives found very little evidence in the car."

An expression of recognition came over Justin's face. "Candace took a group of us to a restaurant on Dyckman Street, a quaint Italian place."

Tori thanked Mrs. Gruenwald for her help and promised to keep her informed of future developments. Then she hurried Justin toward the door.

"Here's what I think happened," she said. "Candace got the pendant from Daniel McCarthy and learned how valuable it was. She pushed him in front of the train to cover her tracks. To get Dr. Gruenwald to translate the hieroglyphics, she seduced him. When she learned the pendant was made from the staff of Moses, she wanted its power, so she had to protect the secret. That's why she murdered Gruenwald—to silence him, and so the discovery wouldn't cause a media frenzy."

Justin appeared shaken. "This goes beyond anything I could have imagined."

"Now we know why the pendant bleeds . . . because Moses used the staff to turn the Nile to blood. And your face was radiant like his when he came down from Mount Sinai." She grabbed Justin on the second floor landing. "A piece of the staff of Moses would have enormous power."

"As we've seen."

"Yes, but there's more to the story. Did you read the articles in the file?"

"I skimmed through several."

She squeezed him. "One of the highlighted sections gave me chills. It was an interpretation of the incident on Mount Horeb when Moses threw down the staff and it became a serpent."

"From the book of Exodus?"

"Yes. Some Rabbinic scholars believe that serpent was the very one that tempted Eve in the Garden of Eden . . . the embodiment of Satan."

Justin stepped back and bumped the wall. "So a pendant made from the staff could wreak untold destruction and suffering?"

"According to the articles, yes. They note that the staff brought plagues of blood, hail, locusts, frogs, and the like upon the Hebrews' enemies. In the wrong hands, it could cause a massive cataclysm."

"Candace and Rathbun have no idea what they're playing with."

"Maybe we don't either." Tori continued down the stairs. "Another article stated that Jesus Christ will wield the staff of

Moses at his Second Coming. He'll use it for the highest good of all—ushering in peace on earth. That means the pendant might hold the key to the future."

Her mind swirled with wonder and terror. Never had the world situation been more precarious; never had humanity been more in need of spiritual guidance, and she'd heard extraordinary wisdom come from her wayward husband.

She glanced at him. Sadness ringed his eyes but his jaw was firmly set. She admired how he'd placed himself in danger in pursuit of his mission. He'd risked his life for her and had mustered the courage to confess his affair. She couldn't hold on to her anger and hurt forever.

She wanted to forgive. To rebuild their marriage for the sake of each other and their son. She resolved to tell him as soon as she got the chance. Right now they had to recapture the pendant before Candace used it to plunge the world into its darkest age ever.

She stopped Justin as they left the house. "Time is running out." She struggled to catch her breath. "Either we recover the pendant or—"

He didn't let her finish. He ran to his car and waved her along. "Our best hope is to infiltrate Candace's inner circle, and I know just where to start."

41

Terminal Memories

A certain ritual had become part of Paul's afternoon journeys from Staten Island to his Manhattan firehouse. Before he boarded the ferry, he stopped at the waterfront esplanade adjacent to the terminal to remember the fallen heroes of September 11th. The ritual reminded him of why he kept working as a firefighter and gave him inspiration for the night ahead.

But on this overcast afternoon in early June, inspiration eluded him. He sat staring across New York Harbor haunted by the emptiness of the Manhattan skyline where the World Trade Center towers had stood. The breakup with Tori had left a similar void inside him, and he feared that Linda couldn't fill it. As of yet, he hadn't returned her phone calls.

He rose from the bench, pulled the collar of his windbreaker around his neck, and started toward the terminal. He caught a glimpse of the Statue of Liberty and thought of the people of New York City. A shiver rippled from the base of his neck down into his gut. New Yorkers had gone on with courage and resilience after September 11th. So must he.

As he approached a ramp that led up to the terminal, he heard a voice behind him call, "Paul, wait!" He turned and saw Linda hurrying toward him.

"I was hoping to catch you," she said. "I knew you'd be here."

"Since when did you start following me?"

"Since you stopped returning my calls."

He dug his hands into the pockets of his windbreaker. "I have to go. I'll miss my ferry."

She pulled even with him. "After what you told me about Justin, I'm worried about you."

"I have to help him. When it's all over, I'll tell you why. Right now, you couldn't possibly understand."

"Try me."

"I can't." He pulled ahead of her on the ramp. "I have to get to work."

"And maybe you'll save someone's life tonight." She fell a step behind him and raised her voice. "Your work is all about giving people second chances. That's what you're doing for Justin. I deserve a second chance too."

Her words cut through him. He hadn't expected her to fight so hard for their marriage. An image of the first time he'd kissed her good-night flashed in his mind. The sheer ecstasy of the moment came back followed by a memory of their pushing Sadie in a swing when she was three or four. His resentment and fear began to thaw.

"I believe in second chances," he said, "but there's a lot of bad history between us."

"History can be remade." She caught up and held his arm. "I'm in the process of remaking mine. That's why I came here . . . to tell you I got an offer on my business."

"Congratulations." He stopped and gazed into her unsettled eyes. "Just don't say I asked you to sell your salons. I've tried to support your dreams."

"Yes, you have. I want to sell because the salons take me away from you and Sadie."

He glanced at the people running a gauntlet of taxis, cars, and buses as they rushed toward the terminal. Something released inside him. He felt as if the wind blowing against his body had penetrated his vital organs and swept away years of tension. "What will you do now?"

"That depends on whether you can accept my sincere apology." She held both his arms. "And whether you're able to forgive me."

He stared deeper into her eyes and saw sincerity there. A tear trickled down her cheek. Her renewed commitment to their marriage made her appear more beautiful than ever. "Forgiveness doesn't happen all at once." He took her in his arms. "But I'm willing to take the first step."

"So am I." She pulled him closer. "Because I love you."

He wanted to respond, but the tightness in his throat made it impossible. He let go and headed up the ramp. After a few steps, he swallowed hard and turned. "I'll give you a call, I promise. We have to follow through on that ice cream date."

Then he rushed into the terminal.

42

Another Subway Station

*I*f Amanda Martinez didn't step off one of the next trains, it would mean she had decided to remain loyal to Candace. Justin paced the platform of the Delancey Street/Essex Street subway station in Manhattan and looked for his former protégé in each new horde of disembarking passengers.

He checked his watch: 7:51 P.M. Tori had called him nearly half an hour earlier after having tracked Amanda to the New York Sports Club on Lexington Avenue. They'd spoken in the locker room where Tori had been safe from Rathbun. She'd told Amanda that new information about the pendant had surfaced, information that would have radical implications for Amanda's relationship with Candace. Justin would wait on the platform at the Delancey Street stop. If she wanted to hear more, she could speak with him there.

Justin had liked the plan because it protected him from any encounters with Rathbun, but Amanda should've arrived by now, and he was having second thoughts. A billboard across the tracks caught his eye. It featured a silver-haired rock guitarist singing into a microphone as sweat poured down his ruggedly handsome face. The rocker looked familiar. The ad was for a concert by John Silverstone.

Memories flooded in. During the late nineties, Candace had managed Silverstone's investments and been romantically involved with him. The two of them had been on a getaway in Rome when the tech-stock bubble had burst on Wall Street. Silverstone's manager, Kyle Hudson, had called Justin in a panic and ordered him to sell the rock star's plummeting shares of Enron Broadband. The memory made his temples pound louder than the squeal and whoosh of the incoming trains. He'd saved Silverstone millions. He'd also realized how jealous he'd been of the rocker . . . and how ripe he'd been for his own affair with Candace.

A train pulled away. He leaned against one of the steel pilings that dotted the dimly lit station. The shame he felt over the affair fed his rage and terror over the murders of McCarthy and Gruenwald. But his disbelief and awe regarding the origin of the pendant were more overwhelming. If it really had come from the staff of Moses, the pendant was either the most dangerous or most enlightening artifact ever discovered. The results depended on who possessed it. He struggled to make sense of the impossible discovery— *bizarre . . . shocking . . . miraculous . . . unbelievable.*

Another train ground to a stop and delivered a stampede of passengers. Justin felt the energy of their forward surge flow through him. He couldn't explain why someone like him, a man who'd failed so miserably, would be given the chance to recapture the pendant and inspire humanity's spiritual evolution. Whether or not Amanda got off the train, he couldn't shirk this mission.

He searched the harried faces, but the crowd of passengers thinned out. She wasn't among them.

He fished out his cell phone and called Tori. "Are you sure Amanda took the F train?"

"No, I didn't go with her to the station."

"It's about eight o'clock. What time did she leave the club?"

"About seven fifteen."

Justin tried to remain calm but found it impossible. "She should've been here by now."

"What will we do if she doesn't come?"

He hadn't allowed himself to consider that, so he said the first thing that came to mind. "Maybe we'll try to break into Candace's office . . . I don't know."

"There has to be some way to surprise them."

"We have to figure out what she's planning next." He pushed away from the piling. "Can you get back to the *Herald* and do some research? I can meet you—"

The arrival of another train stopped him. He moved into the open and eyed the disembarking passengers. He was in the middle of the platform and didn't see anyone who looked like Amanda. Then he headed toward the front of the train and saw a petite, dark-haired woman. She wore a stylish white sweat suit with navy piping and carried a vinyl gym bag.

"Tori, I'll call you later."

He hung up as the woman turned toward him—*Amanda*. He dodged through the thinning crowd. "I wasn't sure you'd come," he said.

She gave him a close-lipped nod. He led her to the secluded area at the front of end of the platform. "You're brave to hear me out."

She glanced around nervously. "I came because my life has changed for the better since I started applying the insights you shared with me. I think I'm finally over Nick."

"The pendant inspired those insights . . . the pendant Candace wears."

"Oh, yes, that." She sighed. "The jewelry you're paranoid about."

It frustrated him that she was as cynical as ever. He wondered if she'd fallen under the pendant's spell at Candace's behest. "You may think I'm paranoid but now I have evidence. Tori and I found proof that the pendant is actually an ancient artifact that gives its possessor miraculous powers of persuasion."

She started to leave. "This is getting more bizarre every day."

"Amanda, wait." He held the sleeve of her sweat suit. "The evidence I have is undeniable. How you acted at the Grand Hyatt is part of it."

"What!"

He let her pull her arm away. He couldn't stop her from leaving, so he spoke quickly. "You witnessed how Candace and Quentin set me up. I know you fell for their scheme because I saw you laugh at me. Think back to the Grand Hyatt event and to the Bilderberg conference, and to the party on Candace's yacht. You were as mesmerized as the others." He drew closer. "But I know you, Amanda. You're not mean enough to laugh at a humiliated friend or gullible enough to believe in Candace's message of happiness through materialism, pleasure, and power."

She diverted her eyes. "Like I told you before, the woman pays me a good salary, and I need the job."

Her smooth, tawny skin appeared as perfect as a model's. He remembered his naiveté in allowing Candace to seduce him, and an overwhelming urge to protect Amanda welled up inside. He cupped a hand beneath her chin. "Is it worth losing your soul for a paycheck? I can feel yours slipping away."

"You're wrong. I've been applying your insights about loving myself and finding wholeness within instead of from a man. I feel a lot better about my life."

"See, you *do* believe in the power of the pendant." Justin nudged her back to the more secluded area. A train pulled into the station. He waited for the rumbling to stop then whispered in her ear. "Now I know where the power comes from. Tori and I learned that a renowned Egyptologist translated the hieroglyphics. They mean 'from Moses staff.'"

She headed for the train. "Do you expect me to—"

"Believe me?" He stepped in front of her. "No . . . at least not right away. But according to some Bible scholars, Moses' staff can bring either great good or great evil into the world depending on who wields it. You've seen people fall under Candace's spell when she wears the pendant. Don't you see what she's trying to do?"

"No. What?"

"She's spreading a conspiracy by corrupting the most powerful bankers, politicians, and shapers of American culture. She convinced them that physical beauty, greed, selfishness, and prestige and pleasure bring happiness. She's gaining a following in the United States and Europe. Nation after nation will collapse. That's what she wants. It's all part of her plan to become the wealthiest and most powerful person in the world."

Amanda rolled her eyes. "I shouldn't have gotten off that train."

"I was as big a doubter as you are. I remember questioning Candace's sale of her massive Enron holdings in June 2000. The stock was at ninety dollars a share. I was sure it would go higher, but she predicted the opposite. When I asked why, she stroked the pendant and claimed that it had never let her down. I ridiculed her for being superstitious and told her she should stop trusting in good luck charms. But she got the last laugh. By December 2001, Enron was bankrupt, and she'd made millions in the process. When I heard Candace speak and saw her obsession with the pendant, I remembered that incident and many others like it. I became a believer."

"She already has billions and the power that comes with wealth. Why does she need more?"

He suppressed an impulse to show his exasperation. "I don't have time to tell you about the abuse she suffered growing up. She was a deeply wounded woman, and then she almost died on September 11th. The attack was horrifying enough, but I suspect that losing the pendant compounded the trauma. Now I fear she's capable of unimaginable crimes in order to never feel vulnerable again."

"Like I said, you're the one who's paranoid."

"Call me what you want." He was losing her. Without her help he would be murdered or sent to jail. He latched on to her arm, determined to make every word count.

"Candace may already suspect that you tipped me off to the meeting on her yacht. Who else could've done it? Tori and I have evidence that Candace murdered two men to obtain the pendant. If she suspects you of betraying her, you could be next. You're at a crossroads, Amanda. If you don't help us, you'll eventually get in so deep you won't be able to get out. There's still time to do the right thing, but soon it'll be too late."

She shifted her weight from one leg to the other and stared at the departing train. Finally she faced him. "I don't know . . . it's just . . . well, if I give you more information, I'm putting myself at even greater risk."

"Not if Tori and I recover the pendant and send Candace to jail."

"That's a big *if*."

"I can't make the decision for you. It's dangerous to help us, but it's more dangerous if you don't."

She hugged her gym bag. "Do you really believe she murdered two men?"

"I'm betting my life on it."

The words sounded foreboding. It staggered him to think he'd fallen prey to such a sick, cruel woman. But he couldn't allow his past stupidity to hamper him now. This could be his last chance. He took hold of the gym bag.

"The pendant was stored in the Secret Service vault in Seven World Trade Center. Candace pushed Agent Daniel McCarthy in front of a train to get it and then injected Dr. Gruenwald with poison after he translated the hieroglyphics."

She broke free and walked to the end of the platform. She paced back and forth then stared at the tracks for a long time.

Finally she returned. "You've made me suspicious. I can't let murder go unpunished."

"Are you ready to help me?"

She glanced around nervously then nodded.

He embraced her and felt her shaking. "You're a brave woman, Amanda."

She pulled away. "Candace is meeting with international dignitaries at the United Nations next Wednesday."

This was the first time he'd heard of such a meeting, and it shocked him. "What countries are these dignitaries from?"

"I don't know. She didn't tell me the details." Amanda's expression turned grim. "All I know is that the meeting is at ten A.M. My job is to make sure her limo gets her there a few minutes early."

"Candace has already spread her influence in Europe through the Bilderberg Group. If she addresses the delegates to the U.N., she'll gain an international following." He took her hand. "You have to help me recover the pendant. It's the only way to stop her from corrupting the masses worldwide."

She dug her purse out of her gym bag and found a pen and a scrap of paper. She held the paper against the purse and began to write. "This is the address of Candace's mansion in East Hampton along with the combination to the safe in her first-floor study. The study is a few doors away from the main living room. Whenever Candace isn't wearing the pendant, she keeps it in that safe. The mansion has a security system, but if you can break in and unlock the safe, the pendant will be yours."

Justin glanced at the paper then stuffed it into his pocket. "Thank you. You won't regret it."

Another train arrived. Amanda stepped on board. He headed for the turnstiles, blending in with several dozen passengers who'd stepped off the train. The cavernous station sprawled around him like an ancient catacomb. He went with the flow of the foot traffic and wound through the walkways and corridors until he reached the exit stairs. He hustled up them and ran into a downpour on Delancey Street.

The pelting rain reminded him of the storm on Block Island Sound. The terror and chaos he'd felt when he'd been pitched into the sea came back. He pondered the dangers of breaking into Candace's mansion, and the same brutal feelings blew through him again. The break-in could be a stunning success . . . or another trip to hell. He frantically hailed a taxi and prayed it wouldn't be the latter.

43

A Mansion in the Hamptons

No visitor to Candace's East Hampton mansion would have imagined that such decorative architecture and pristine grounds had been obtained with sophisticated lies and calculated murders. Paul knew the truth. Hearing it from Justin and Tori had shocked and sickened him. But when they'd told him that the pendant had been fashioned from the staff of Moses, he'd refused to believe them. Only after they'd showed him the evidence and he'd reflected further on its miraculous power had he begun to accept their conclusion. Now he had to take decisive action.

Quentin Rathbun buzzed him through the iron gates. Paul pulled his Mustang into the parking circle. The afternoon sun had dipped behind the sprawling, Colonial-style mansion's massive façade leaving the entrance in shadows. Rathbun greeted him. Paul hadn't seen Candace's stock analyst-turned-thug boyfriend since he and his guards had chased him and Tori at the Bilderberg conference. Never before had Paul been involved in deceit, but now he was compelled by circumstances to do business with Rathbun and Candace. He stepped out of the car and felt the shadows penetrate his bones.

Rathbun led him across marble floors to a living room with cathedral ceilings and wall-to-wall windows with ocean views. Candace sat on a contemporary overstuffed couch wearing black slacks and a cream-colored cowl-neck sweater. She shook his hand and offered him a graceful Queen Anne armchair. "Your willingness to meet with us came as a surprise, to say the least."

"I'm in a delicate position," he said. "I saw no way to accomplish my goal other than to help you accomplish yours."

She took a puff of her cigarette. "I thought you and Justin were friends."

"At one time. That has changed."

"I see." She flicked ashes into a tray on the coffee table. "And now you're willing to work with us?"

"You can't reach your goals and I can't reach mine as long as Justin is in the picture."

Rathbun, handsome in his black turtleneck and herringbone sports coat, sipped his drink. "And you think you can help us . . . how shall I say . . . solve the annoying problem we have with him?"

Paul held his voice steady. "Yes, I'm prepared to do that."

"So what's your plan?"

"Let's not make this harder than it needs to be. I know a place I can bring him. I suggest the meeting be between just Mr. Rathbun, Justin, and me. But I'll only do it if you promise Tori won't be hurt or even involved."

Rathbun stared at Candace. "What do you think?"

She nodded. "It sounds workable but I need to hear more details. Let's start with how much you're asking."

∽

Tori peeked behind the mansion and waited for the hefty security guard at the other end to round the corner. The finely manicured lawn sloped down to the rocks above the Atlantic. She hoped Paul was carrying out his part of their plan.

The mansion's alarm system had recently been upgraded and was too sophisticated to disarm. She and Justin had hid in the backseat of the Mustang and crept out after Paul had entered the mansion. He was supposed to keep Candace and Rathbun occupied by making a phony offer to betray Justin. Paul would cast himself as the aggrieved party in a love triangle: Justin had stolen Tori from him; he could get her back only by having Justin murdered. Tori and Justin were to enter the mansion through the rear, steal the pendant, and sneak back into the Mustang in time for Paul to spirit them away.

She glimpsed the guard as he turned the corner. If he was circling the entire mansion, he would take about ten minutes to come back around. She and Justin had to synchronize their robbery with his patrols to avoid him after they'd stolen the pendant. She estimated they had five to seven minutes. She peeked out again, saw no one, and began to run, keeping low, with Justin at her side.

They sprinted behind the multi-car garage and tried its two doors. Locked. They came to the pool and tugged on the sliding glass doors. Locked. They kept going. Amanda had said the guard, Max Urquhart, lived in an apartment in a secluded back section of the mansion. Once they entered the alcove outside his door, the study lay down a long hall that led to the main living room.

At the middle of the property, Tori tried the guard's door. Hopefully he'd left it open when on duty. Excitement surged through her when the knob turned. She entered the alcove with Justin. They stayed close to each another and passed the apartment door, which had been left open a crack. They ran up the wide carpeted hallway. They had to go through the door at the other end to access the inner hallway that led to the center of the mansion. She bit her tongue in frustration. The door was locked.

She glanced at Justin. He hurried back to the guard's quarters. She followed him into a studio apartment where unfolded laundry lay on the couch and dishes stood in the sink. She searched frantically for the key, flinging open kitchen cupboards and rummaging through drawers, but didn't find it. She searched the countertop, frustrated and anxious. Then she felt Justin's hand on her back.

He held up a key. "It was hanging on a nail inside the front closet. Let's go."

She followed him into the hall and closed the door behind them. He tried the key. She held her breath then exhaled when the door pushed open. They rushed up the hall passing a library, an exercise area, a den, and several other rooms. As they approached the study, she heard a faint murmur of voices from the living room up the hall.

She held a finger to her lips. They crept into the study. Justin switched on his flashlight. The room was spacious with a closet to the left, bookshelves to the right, and a desk holding a computer and a lamp facing the window. On the floor in one corner stood a small black safe. A combination keypad and door handle were centered on its front panel.

Justin handed her the slip of paper with the combination. They knelt in front of the safe. He shined the flashlight on the keypad as she punched in the numbers. She pulled down on the handle with her temples pounding. She prepared to snatch the pendant, close the safe, and flee.

She opened the door.

The pendant wasn't there.

A small gold locket on a thin chain lay at the bottom of the safe. She glanced at Justin. His face was so white he appeared ready to faint. She picked up the locket, opened it, and read the inscription. *To Candace, my lover and friend, from Justin.*

The blood drained from Tori's face. The locket was identical to the one he'd given her. It was even inscribed with the same words . . . but to Candace. Her stomach convulsed, her face twisted with fury. Without thinking, she slapped him hard enough to knock him backward. He careened into the desk, and the lamp fell with a crash.

"Max . . . Max? Are you in there?"

The cry came from the living room followed by footsteps. Thankfully the lamp hadn't broken. Justin scooped it up and set it on the desk. Tori held on to the locket, closed the safe, and motioned toward the closet by the door. Hiding inside was their only hope. She climbed in, tempted to keep Justin out so that Rathbun would beat and kill him.

His pleading eyes disgusted her. She hated him with a fierce passion, but leaving him to face the threat would endanger both of them. She scooted over to make room. They squeezed in with a vacuum cleaner and an assortment of jackets and empty hangers. Touching him filled her with revulsion.

Footsteps entered the study. "Max, is that you?"

She recognized Rathbun's voice. If he opened the closet, he would kill them both. Her cheating husband deserved it.

The footsteps left the room. Apparently Rathbun had seen no one and had returned to the conversation with Paul.

She waited a moment then opened the closet door. She didn't look at Justin as they ran for the backyard. Rage and disbelief echoed in her mind. How could he? How *could* he?

She raced down the hall and fled through the door that led past the guard's apartment. She half hoped he would catch them. Why would it matter if she died? She'd ruined her life by loving the wrong man. Every step was torture, sending shockwaves of anguish up her legs and into her heart. Tears nearly blinded her.

When she reached the backyard, she paused to look for the guard but didn't care where he was. She ran for the rocks along the shoreline, which lay low enough to hide her from anyone on the grounds or inside the mansion. She lost track of where she was and whether Justin was with her and how to get back to the Mustang. She just kept running and climbing, hoping that a bullet would kill her or a wave would wash her out to sea and end the nightmare her lost and broken life had become.

44

THE LONG RIDE HOME

"Okay, let's see the pendant."

Paul's words cut through the bitter silence in the Mustang. Tori crouched behind the passenger's seat with her head down and her fists digging into the vinyl. It had taken a fall on the rocks to jolt her back to reality. As furious as she was at Justin, she'd had no choice but to sneak back to the car. They'd managed to elude the guard and climb in without anyone seeing them.

Her tongue was so dry she couldn't speak. Paul was unaware of the tectonic shift that had occurred for both the investigation and her marriage. She pushed off the floorboard and into the backseat. Justin did the same but more slowly. She forced her eyes open and glanced around. Candace's mansion faded into the distance. She dreaded drawing Paul into the ache that throbbed in her chest, but he deserved to know.

"We didn't get the pendant," she said.

He shot her an incredulous look. His wide-set eyes, glistening with hope and fear, accentuated the numbing awfulness of her discovery. He kept glancing back. "I heard a noise. Did it have anything to do with your not getting the pendant?"

"Yes. The pendant wasn't in the safe." The words ripped through her with cruel, unforgiving menace. She and Justin should have the pendant and be on their way home. Instead she had a locket that revealed the depth of his treachery. She opened her palm. "This is what we have instead."

"What is it?"

"Maybe Justin can tell you."

She glared at the man next to her. She no longer knew him. He avoided her eyes. She wondered what had happened to him, how a man with such promise had become a slave of passion and ended up in misery. She'd planned to forgive him and discuss rebuilding their marriage and family. How could she ever do that now?

He reached out to touch her arm.

She pushed his hand away.

He sought out her eyes. "I was going to tell you. Really, I—"

She swallowed the acrid taste of bile. "Don't even try to explain."

"Will you two please tell me what's going on?" Paul slowed the car.

"Candace put the locket in the safe instead of the pendant," Justin said. "She must've discovered that Amanda was betraying her."

"That's all you're going to say?" Tori said.

He bit his lower lip and closed his eyes.

She leaned forward. "Could you please speed up, Paul?"

"I'm already over the speed limit. I don't want to get a ticket."

"I wouldn't mind speaking with a cop right now."

Paul gave her a quizzical look in the rearview mirror. "What? I thought . . ." He trailed off.

She turned to Justin. "Seeing you in handcuffs might be therapeutic."

He slapped the door. "Don't you see that I was set up? Amanda must've talked. Candace planted the locket to destroy my marriage. She wanted revenge and knew how to get it."

She twisted the sleeve of his shirt. "Did you tell Candace you loved her? Look me in the eyes! I need to know."

Staring out the window, he stuck a fist in his mouth. Then he said, "I've been trying so hard to be a better husband. I was going to tell you about the locket."

"I don't know what's true anymore and what isn't."

Her anguish worsened. He didn't understand that his words were worthless. The locket had been sacred to her, a powerful symbol of her husband's love that had sustained her through her grief. By giving Candace the same gift, he'd desecrated their marriage in an irreparable way. She shot him a piercing stare and climbed into the front seat.

Paul said nothing. It was as if a bomb had exploded in the car. They rode along the shore in dreadful silence. She studied the waves crashing on the rocks and sand. With the windows closed, she couldn't hear the surf. The violence happened silently as each breaker pummeled the beach with foam and spray. The violence pounding her heart was silent but no less vicious.

45

Chapel of Refuge

**TORTURE SUSPECTED IN CASE OF
BODY FOUND ON EAST HAMPTON BEACH**

The headline in *The New York Herald* shocked Justin. The article reported that the police had identified the body of twenty-seven-year-old Amanda F. Martinez of Brooklyn, a victim of extensive lacerations and stab wounds. He read the article with overwhelming remorse and grief. Candace's evil knew no bounds. No wonder security at her mansion had been so lax. She'd set him up after learning about the break-in by torturing Amanda. He buried his face in the paper and railed against Rathbun, whom he suspected of carrying out Candace's orders. He couldn't stop shaking. He blamed himself for Amanda's suffering and death. It was as if the terror of hell was assaulting him anew.

He was all alone. He didn't know where to go or how to control the thoughts that reproached him. And since Candace had deceived him with the locket, he wondered if the meeting at the U.N. was also a deception. He needed to figure out what she planned to do next. But he couldn't do that until he cleared his mind.

He fled to St. Paul's Chapel, a refuge past which he'd walked many times when he'd worked in the World Trade Center. He entered the sanctuary at nearly six P.M. in search of solace. He turned off his cell phone and walked the long center aisle alone. Stately Corinthian columns supported the ample gallery, which was illuminated by cut glass chandeliers. A large window of obscured glass stood behind the high altar. The pews were still scuffed from having served as makeshift cots for recovery workers after September 11th.

A cacophony of curses assailed his mind. Every one of them pilloried his life and his choices. The golden cross on the elevated white pulpit loomed overhead. He slipped into a pew in front of it and bowed his head as tears burned his eyes. He'd lost everything—his new life in Providence, his career, his relationships with his wife, his son, and his best friend.

Candace had the pendant.

Amanda was dead.

Because of him.

He'd been hopeful about the spiritual power the pendant had unleashed through him and about becoming the husband and father he longed to be. But Candace had ended it all. Now she was on the verge of plunging the U.S. or even the world into economic chaos and moral and spiritual ruin. What had begun with illegal stock transactions and sexual indiscretions had degenerated into a life that wasn't worth living.

The darkness encroaching behind the window invaded his soul. He cried out to a God who seemed absent at best and vindictive at worst . . . if God existed at all. It was as if Justin were trapped in an underground cave, lost and alone.

Then a door opened on the right, and a man wearing a charcoal blazer and a clerical collar entered. A bit taller than average, he had wire-rimmed glasses and wispy white hair. "The chapel will be closing soon," he said, "but if you want to stay longer, I'll lock the door from the outside. You can close it behind you when you leave."

Justin started to get up, but the gentleness of the priest's voice prompted him to sit again. He thought of Moses and his staff. "Do you have a minute, Reverend?"

The priest turned to leave. "I'm sorry. I have to get to a vestry meeting."

Justin stood. "I won't take much of your time, I promise."

The priest had already opened the door.

"Please. It's important."

He glanced at his watch and closed the door. "Quickly, please."

"Do you know anything about the staff of Moses?"

The priest approached him. "I wouldn't have been granted holy orders if I didn't. Why?"

"I'd like to learn more about it." Justin cautioned himself not to say too much. The priest would never believe the perils he'd survived or the intrigue about the pendant. He only hoped this man could help him understand how the staff worked. It was the only way he could stop Candace. "Moses used the staff to perform miracles, right?"

"Yes."

"But how did he discover its powers?"

The priest laid a hand on the front pew. "Moses had his shepherd's staff with him on Mount Horeb. God spoke from a burning bush and commanded him to throw the staff down."

"That's all?"

"When Moses obeyed, the staff became a serpent. God told him to pick the serpent up, and when he did, it turned into a staff again."

Justin raised an eyebrow. "And then he started performing miracles with it?"

"No." The priest moved into the pews and leaned against one. "The staff became a serpent a second time."

"Really?" Justin sat down again. "When?"

"Moses went to Pharaoh's court with his brother, Aaron. They demanded freedom for the Hebrews. To show Pharaoh they meant business, Aaron threw the staff down. Again it became a serpent, but Pharaoh's magicians duplicated the feat with their staffs."

"So Moses had only one of many miraculous staffs in Egypt?"

The priest smiled. "The serpent from Moses and Aaron's staff devoured the magicians' serpents."

The story sounded like a child's fairy tale. But he'd witnessed the power of the pendant. "What do people think of these stories today?"

"Millions of Jews, Christians, and Muslims believe that an all-powerful God would have no trouble turning a staff into a serpent or a serpent into a staff."

Justin hadn't thought much about the miracles in the Bible since he'd been a teenager. Now his life and the destinies of countless people around the world might depend on how well he understood the staff. "What do you think the miracle of the serpent means?"

"Scholars a lot smarter than me have asked that question. The closest I can come is that God needed to convince Moses of his power and used the staff to do it."

Before Justin had witnessed the power of the pendant, he hadn't believed in miracles. But he'd seen Candace use that power to gain riches and an international following, and his own words had utilized its power. He still needed more insight into how and when miracles were most likely to occur.

"The miracles . . . they only happened when Moses obeyed God. Is that right?"

The priest reached into a rack, withdrew a Bible, and opened it. "You've pretty much summarized what this book teaches. Human beings can only help God perform miracles by surrendering completely to God's will."

When the priest glanced at his watch, Justin pressed further. "If the staff were still in the world today, do you think the same principle of surrender would apply?"

He laughed. "That's a very hypothetical question." He flipped through the Bible as if trying to focus his thoughts. "I can best answer by emphasizing that Moses' entire life depended on the staff. Without it, he couldn't control or defend his sheep. Throwing the staff down was an act of ultimate trust. Only when Moses gave up all he had did the miracle occur. I believe the same is true for us. Miracles happen in our lives when we surrender our will totally and completely to God's will."

The priest was becoming philosophical. Justin needed him to be more specific. "What does surrendering to God's will mean in practical terms?"

He leaned back and held the Bible to his chest. A faraway look glinted in his hazel eyes. "I think it means we no longer live to satisfy ourselves. We make maximum use of our gifts and abilities, but we don't try to control outcomes. We give our best but turn the results over to God."

The answer reminded him of some of the statements he'd made under the pendant's influence. Gooseflesh crawled down his neck just as when he'd spoken while wearing the pendant. "What if someone wanted to use the staff for evil?"

"Only Moses and Aaron possessed the staff, and they used it for good. The staff helped them free the Hebrews from slavery in Egypt."

Justin worried he might raise suspicions by asking too many questions, but he needed information. "Suppose someone had stolen the staff from Moses and Aaron. Could that person have used it for evil?"

The priest ran a hand over the cover of the Bible. "That's an intriguing question because there were times the staff caused great suffering. Moses used the staff to turn the water of the Nile into blood. He also brought plagues of hail and gnats and locusts against the Egyptians. Later he used the staff to part the waters of the Red Sea, but after the Hebrews had crossed, he brought the water down on the Egyptians and drowned them." The priest's eyes lit up as if he'd had a revelation. "Yes, I imagine that in the wrong hands the staff could've been used for evil."

Justin felt as if the walls of the chapel were closing in on him. The priest had confirmed the conclusions Dr. Gruenwald had kept in his file. Candace was committed to using the pendant for evil. If he hoped to stop her, his commitment to using it for good had to be stronger. "What happened to the staff?"

"No one knows." The priest returned the Bible to the rack. "The last time it's mentioned in the Bible, it's used by Moses to help the Hebrews in battle."

"And then it disappears?"

"Not exactly. Later traditions say that the staff was passed down to King David and was used as a scepter by the kings who followed him. Finally it vanished when the Temple was destroyed. According to these traditions, the staff will reappear when the Messiah wields it at his coming and brings peace to the world."

Before, Justin wouldn't have believed any of this speculation. Now he knew that some version of it must be true. The staff of Moses had to have been miraculously preserved. It was the only explanation of the pendant's power that fit the facts. He was more motivated than ever to stop Candace. "One more question, please?"

The priest eyed his watch.

"Do you believe that a person can ever be so bad that God stops loving him?"

He laid a hand on Justin's shoulder. "I'm Reverend Robert Sherman. If you have something to confess, I'll stay and listen."

Tears brimmed in his eyes. He glanced at the cross on the pulpit then at the high altar. A wave of nostalgia for the times he'd spent in church as a boy swept over him. He desperately wished he were young again and could undo the harm he'd caused. If he could go back, he would make better choices. He would have more integrity and become the husband and father his wife and son deserved. Although he couldn't go back, the priest's kindly eyes gave him what he needed to hope again.

"Thank you, Reverend Sherman, but you've already given me more than you can imagine."

"Then at least let me answer your question." He laid both his hands on Justin's shoulders. "I believe that God never stops loving us. No matter how terrible our deeds have been, there's always hope for redemption."

Tears wet Justin's cheeks. He owed Jesus everything for having given him a second chance. Now he needed Jesus' help to prevent Candace from using the pendant for evil. He shook Reverend Sherman's hand and mumbled another thank you.

He was prepared to risk anything to recover the pendant, but he doubted whether he would find Candace at the U.N.

46

COUNTDOWN TO CATASTROPHE

Tori left the *New York Herald* building and headed up 43rd Street. She feared that a demonic conspiracy was playing out somewhere beneath the cloudless night sky, but on that mild Saturday in June, the city's glittering lights camouflaged the peril. She jostled through the streams of pedestrians on the sidewalk. No one suspected that the richest stockbroker on Wall Street was plotting to rule the world's nations by controlling their wealth. If they knew of her intentions and believed in her powers, they would ask the question that swirled in Tori's thoughts: where will Candace use the pendant next and how can she be stopped?

The question haunted her in spite of her rage at Justin. She sped up, reached for her phone, and punched in his number again. She'd grown angrier and more frustrated each time she called his cell and got his voice mail. He hadn't returned her messages. This time when he didn't answer, she hung up and called Paul in desperation. His voice sounded cautious, but her fear of the debacle Candace could cause emboldened her. "I need your help."

"I'm reluctant to get involved any further," he said.

She felt something deflate in her heart. She squeezed the phone. "Candace's plot will put millions of people out of work. They'll lose their homes, their savings . . . and face a jobless economy for years to come."

"How can you be sure?"

"I've researched which powerful economic and political insiders she has won to her cause. Entire financial systems will collapse and ignite widespread revolutions. I need your help to—"

"Slow down," he said. "Do you really think it'll be that bad?"

"Worse."

There was silence before he said, "All right. Where should I meet you?"

"Amanda's condo."

∼

When several residents entered the condominium building at the same time, Tori sneaked in behind them. She hid briefly in a stairwell then let Paul in. They rode the elevator to the fourth floor in silence. She stayed by the elevator to keep watch while he went to Amanda's door with his small pry bar.

He pried at the door. The clanking and squeaking of metal against metal echoed in the hall. The light above the elevator descended to the lobby. It stayed there briefly then jumped to the second floor. The clanking and squeaking continued. The light moved to the third floor. Tori's breath caught in her throat. A few moments later, the elevator door opened. Its whoosh and rattle covered a bang down the hall.

A young couple stepped off with their toddler. Not wanting to raise suspicions, Tori got on. If Paul isn't inside by now, she thought, the couple will discover him. She rode to the fifth floor, got off, and took the stairs down to the fourth.

No one was in the hall.

She hurried to Amanda's door and knocked lightly. No answer. She stared at the rust-colored door as her fear of economic upheaval and political chaos turned her vision the same shade. The door opened a crack. She stepped inside and nearly bumped into Paul. She brushed past him into the contemporary condo. "We're looking for anything that will tell us about Candace's plans."

She glanced around. The kitchen was clean and orderly. No papers lay on the table or countertop. The couch, easy chair, and end tables in the living room were also tidy. She peered into the study across from the kitchen. An L-shaped computer desk sat in the back corner with stacks of letter-size papers covering one side. She waved Paul in and turned on the computer as he sifted through the papers.

The computer powered up and gave her access without a password. Amanda's files contained correspondence, résumés, and articles from the Internet. She came across a photo of a smiling Amanda eating pizza with a darkly handsome man. Tori thought of her tortured body washing up on the East Hampton shore and bit her trembling lip.

Paul glanced up. "Did Amanda have a boyfriend?"

She nodded. "His name was Nick. Justin said he was a playboy who broke her heart."

She rolled her chair back and thumbed through mortgage statements, credit card offers, appeals for money from charities and universities. As a single woman, Amanda had handled these matters alone. Tori feared a similar future. After the incident with the locket, she doubted she could rebuild her marriage. Since it appeared that Paul was going back to Linda . . .

The pages shook in her hands. She would have to raise her son as a single parent. Finding a man to love her would be harder than ever. Before Justin returned, she'd enjoyed a soulful, fulfilling relationship with Paul. She could have married him but instead had risked everything for the man who'd abandoned her. In the end, she'd lost both.

She flipped through the pages to hide the tearstains on them. Then she wiped her eyes on her sleeve and shoved a bill of some kind at Paul. "You should send me one of these for all the pain I've caused you."

He gave a dismissive wave. "Your husband's the one who should pay."

"He may not be my husband much longer."

"You've decided to divorce him?"

The question ripped through her. After Justin's confession, she'd wanted to forgive and even take him back as her husband. But seeing the inscription on the locket had changed everything. "I haven't decided what to do yet. But whatever happens, I owe you an explanation about the locket."

"None is necessary."

She ran a hand over her eyes then told him about the inscription.

"And you're still considering taking him back?" Paul said.

She flipped through one stack of papers then another. "Aren't you doing the same with Linda?"

He tossed some mail-order catalogues on the desk. "Yes, and I don't know what I'll decide."

Tori clutched a pile of papers before giving the remaining stacks a cursory examination. "There aren't any clues here. I'm going to check the rest of the condo."

She hurried into the guest bedroom with every nerve ending frayed. The bed was neat, the dresser and closet empty, the bathroom immaculate. She headed for Amanda's bedroom.

Paul met her at the door.

She brushed past him. A red comforter had been heaped into a mound on the bed; discarded clothes and towels trailed from the closet to the bathroom. She took hold of Paul's arms. "It's ironic that we ended up in the same position. If you figure out what to do, please let me know. I could use some advice."

"So could I." He reached out to give her a hug.

She spotted a handbill wedged between a jewelry box and a perfume bottle on the dresser. The oversize card stock had been emblazoned with *John Silverstone Concert at Shea Stadium, Saturday, June 7, 2003, 8 P.M.* At the top in large letters were the words *BACKSTAGE PASS*. In the left margin, Amanda had scribbled, *Must have Candace's limo there by intermission.*

"Here's the clue we're looking for."

He read it. "I've been hearing about that concert for weeks. The police and fire departments will monitor it."

She led him back to the computer and navigated to John Silverstone's website. "The concert's being broadcast internationally on TV, radio, and the Internet."

"I bet there's a reason Candace is scheduled to arrive at intermission."

Tori shut down the computer. "She's probably going to use the concert to speak to millions of people under the power of the pendant. We have to stop her."

"But there's only one pass."

Tori pulled him toward the door. "I'll have to confront Candace alone. You can drop me off outside Shea and wait for me there."

"What about Justin?"

"I left messages. He hasn't called back."

"You expect me to let you—"

"We have no other choice. It's already 8:30." She led him out the door and broke into a sprint.

47

THE SEVENTH CHALLENGE: TRANSFORMED FAITH

The ear-splitting cheers of sixty thousand fans in the old Shea Stadium approved another rousing song by legendary American rock star John Silverstone. Justin pushed through the crowd wearing a fake beard, sunglasses, and a stocking cap. He headed for the towering stage against the centerfield wall as a multicolored light show revolved around the night sky. The energy of the next song thundered through the music and surged through the frenzied singing and swaying of the fans. The combination nearly lifted him off the ground.

The events that had brought him this far amazed him more than the pyrotechnic spectacle. After Candace had tricked him with the locket, he suspected that her meetings at the U.N. were also bogus. He tailed her limo on his bike from the Lipstick Building to a woman's clothing shop in the East Village then to a nearby shoe store. The first shop, Condo 370, featured the latest high-end fashions for women. The second, Soleful Creations, specialized in trendy footwear. Definitely not clothing for the U.N.

He'd searched numerous online listings of social and artistic events but hadn't found a solid lead until he'd seen a full-page ad in the *Times* for the Silverstone concert. A theory about her strategy had emerged. She'd used the pendant to spread her conspiracy. Her venues were increasingly ambitious as the stakes rose. He kept asking himself what her next move would be if she were trying to win the allegiance of entire nations through a venue other than the U.N.

He'd remembered her relationship with Silverstone and wondered if she'd opted for a grassroots approach. It all began to make sense. Silverstone's concert would be heard by millions via TV, radio, and the Internet. By speaking during the show, Candace could deceive an international audience. The masses would support her move to control the world's economy and make her supreme dictator.

Kyle Hudson, Silverstone's manager, owed Justin a favor for having saved the rock star millions during the tech-stock collapse. Justin had asked if Candace would appear at the concert. When Hudson confirmed the appearance, Justin had collected on the favor by requesting a backstage pass.

He approached the area marked *authorized personnel only* and thought of people worldwide. If Candace succeeded, they would lose their livelihoods, their homes, their savings, their freedoms. The terror that surged up through his feet made him feel as if every hair on his skin had been singed. A security guard stopped him.

"Didn't you see the sign?" The guard had to shout above the wail of horns and the squeal of guitars.

Justin showed him the small rectangular pass. "Silverstone's manager gave me this."

When the guard blocked his way, Justin dug out his cell phone. "All right, I'll call him. His name is Kyle Hudson."

He started to punch in the numbers. Only then did the guard wave him through.

He forged ahead, bracing himself for a possible confrontation with Rathbun. Several scenarios clashed in his mind. In one he saw himself trying in vain to grab the pendant; in another he yelled for the police to arrest Candace and Rathbun for murder; in the third, Rathbun pummeled his face. In each scenario, Justin was the one arrested. When he was brought to trial, his insider trading came to light. He was convicted and sentenced to a long prison term. The scenarios haunted him but he kept going.

He climbed the stairs onto the rear of the stage. Silverstone sang out front. He wore a long-sleeve white shirt beneath a black vest. His shoulder-length hair had been dyed to match his name. Accelerating guitar riffs and horn arpeggios accompanied his hit "Love Me Till Morning." Behind him were a straggly-haired young man at an electronic organ, the equally unkempt bass and lead guitar players, and the boisterous, thrashing drummer.

The backstage area was crowded with instrument cases, mixers, lightshow equipment, technicians hovering over control panels. Justin hid behind an amplifier. He scanned the entire stage for Candace and Rathbun but, to his surprise, didn't see them.

Never had so much ridden on an entrance from Shea Stadium's dressing room to its high-tech sound stage. Rock & Roll legends like the Beatles, the Rolling Stones, the Who, Creedence Clearwater Revival, and many others had been driven through the tunnel onto the field to claim their share of musical immortality. Tori raced toward the dressing room for a different reason—to prevent Candace Donahue from speaking at intermission. Images of deprivation and mass murder under Hitler, Stalin, and Mao played in her mind. If Candace succeeded, she would unleash even greater oppression and suffering.

Every muscle in Tori's legs ached as she raced past a few photographers and security guards holding up her pass. Since leaving Amanda's condo, she'd been trying to decide how best to stop Candace. With security tight, she had no weapon but neither would Rathbun. Should she reason with Candace? Appeal to her better nature? Threaten her? Attack her? There were no good options. Paul had dropped her outside the stadium and was waiting in the Mustang. All she could do was try to snatch the pendant and flee.

Silverstone's hit song "Love Me Till Morning" echoed off the walls of the tunnel:

> *Don't leave me in darkness.*
> *Don't leave me tonight.*
> *Love me till morning.*
> *You're my only light.*

Tori's stomach wound as tightly as the exposed pipes above her. Her ears rang, and her body drew taut as she reached the dressing room. Two muscular guards dressed in black jeans and matching skintight T-shirts flanked the door. "What do you need?" the nearest one said.

"A word with Candace Donahue."

"Who are you? How do you know—"

"It's urgent. It—"

The door opened.

Candace emerged in sleek black slacks and a tight-fitting red jacket. Rathbun was at her side wearing a mock turtleneck and dark blazer that complemented her outfit. He saw Tori and shielded Candace with his body. "How did you get in here?"

Tori held up the pass and willed her tongue not to stutter. "I'm taking Amanda's place."

Rathbun tried to shove her aside and lead Candace around her. "Stealing could get you into a lot of trouble."

Tori blocked the way. "So could murder."

Rathbun shoved harder. "I don't have time for your absurd accusations."

"You're not the one I want to talk to. I need to speak with the woman who had the affair with my husband."

Candace glanced at her watch. "I have no time for this. I've—"

Tori lunged and swiped at her neck. "I won't let you speak with that pendant on!"

Rathbun wrapped his arms around Tori. As she fought him, the alcohol on his breath made her feel sick and disgusted. She kicked his leg. He winced and pulled her away from Candace with the assistance of the two guards.

"It's okay Marino, Hurley," Rathbun said. "I know this woman. She just needs a couple minutes to calm down."

He pulled her into the dressing room and closed the door. Before she could resist, his hand covered her mouth and his other arm wrapped around her neck. He pulled her onto the floor. Something pinched her neck. "Nighty-night, sweetheart."

Those were the last words she heard.

~

Justin stayed hidden among the technicians and equipment at the back of the stage. When "Love Me Till Morning" climaxed in a torrent of flashing lights and bone-crushing sound, the teeming crowd roared its approval. Silverstone and his band strutted back and forth waving and bowing. Before the cheers died down, Candace entered from the back accompanied by two guards who looked like nightclub bouncers.

Seeing the pendant around her neck made Justin's breath catch in his throat. With her striking black and red outfit and her glamorous bearing, she looked like a music industry diva. Despite exuding beauty and style, she appeared even more sinister than she had at the Grand Hyatt. Loathing and disgust thrummed in his chest.

"We're going to take a break." Silverstone turned to leave. He saw Candace and froze, apparently stunned.

Stroking the pendant, she strode to the front microphone. "This concert is being carried all over the world via satellite and the Internet. I have a message about how peace can finally come on earth."

Justin tried to move but couldn't. Silverstone and his band stared and were also apparently immobilized. Her guards positioned themselves beside her and eyed the crowd. A hush descended as if someone had been shot.

"Even the most superficial analysis of today's world will single out religion as a major cause of violence and war. The Twin Towers stood only a few miles from here. Those buildings are gone because of religious fanaticism, but the damage extends far beyond a single act of terrorism. Look at the Middle East today. Study history. Unspeakable crimes have been committed in the name of God. It's all unnecessary and preventable."

Her words echoed in Justin's thoughts. The equipment and people around him seemed to blur; he saw only her. The truth of her words sounded irrefutable. Their harmonious, melodic tone made him think he was hearing a captivating love song. His heart raced as if it had been injected with Red Bull. The only way to avoid being seduced by her message was to pray. He closed his eyes and silently implored the God of Moses and Jesus to help him and to enter the hearts of the masses.

"We have reached a critical moment in history," she said. "We've seen the terrors that religion is capable of—attacks on innocent civilians, war and suffering, guilt and shame and oppression. Join me in creating the religionless future humanity deserves. Once we acknowledge that there is no God, we know there is no heaven or hell. All we have are our own lives and one another. Choose to make the most of them."

Affirming cries sounded all over the stadium: "That's the truth!"

"Finally, a future without the curse of religion."

Justin covered his ears, desperate to protect himself from Candace's spell. He prayed silently, *I surrender my will to you, O God. I let go of all my personal desires and place them in your hands. Only you can stop this evil woman. I offer myself to help you . . . even if I die.*

"There's no limit to what we can accomplish. We'll end all the dissension religion causes. With our technological advances, we'll eradicate disease and create a higher standard of living in every country. The future I want for you is filled with wealth, freedom, fulfillment, and peace. You can have that if you become completely self-sufficient. My goal is to help everyone grow as rich as I am. Only fools sacrifice the abundance of now for some unproven reward in the afterlife."

Her words had lulled the massive crowd into a trance-like state. The people appeared enthralled, nearly comatose. Justin continued to pray, sensing he was in a battle with Candace for the future of the world. *I must surrender as totally as Moses did*, he thought. *I give myself to you, God—all that I am, all that I have.*

His arms and legs felt limber again. He shook them and they responded. His prayers had been heard. He edged forward, crouching low and moving behind another amplifier before hiding behind a tower of lights.

Candace was twenty feet away.

He exploded toward her and lunged for the pendant.

Screams erupted across the stadium. The guards flew at him, sandwiching Candace between them and knocking her backward.

He yanked the pendant from her neck and crashed to the stage. When his hand hit the solid wood, the pendant jarred loose.

A thick plume of smoke flared up.

It billowed as if caused by a raging fire, but there were no flames.

He rolled away. Everyone on stage reeled back and covered their faces.

The crowd's screams became shrieks. The smoke grew thicker and whirled like a tornado, whooshing and howling.

Someone yelled, "It's a bomb! We're under attack!"

As quickly as it had appeared, the smoke dissipated . . .

And revealed a long black snake coiled in a striking position.

Shouts from the crowd intensified.

"What is that thing?"

"Could it be . . . a snake? Oh, my God! It's a snake!"

Justin had thrown down the pendant, and it had turned into a serpent. With a thick black body at least eight feet long, the snake rose up ready to strike. Its eyes flashed with cunning, its neck flattened out like a cobra's. It bobbed and weaved, hissed and parried.

Everyone on the stage hid behind amplifiers and speakers. Their faces were white with disbelief and panic. Justin sprang up . . .

And seized the snake by the neck.

As soon as he touched it, the creature turned into a staff.

He stared at the walking stick of twisted, mahogany-like wood. The breath went out of him and his heart stopped. Something like lightning flowed out of the staff and down his arm. Such tremendous power entered his body that he felt ready to explode.

He stumbled to the microphone and began to speak. "This is no trick or illusion. You saw a pendant turn into a serpent and a serpent turn into a staff. It was a display of divine power."

The crowd erupted into chaos.

He held up the staff. "This is no ordinary walking stick. It's the most miraculous artifact ever discovered. Behold the staff of Moses!"

The crowd let out a thunderous roar. Row upon row of spectators fell to their knees, their faces animated with wonder. Candace stayed back and massaged her neck. She regarded him with a dazed expression, her head cocked in a quizzical pose.

The energy that poured into his body through the staff filled him with ecstatic joy. His tongue grew thick but nimble.

"Some of what Candace said is true. Bad religion causes destruction and evil in the world and in our lives. We saw that on September 11th. It was a glorious late-summer morning in Manhattan, crisp and cloudless, drenched with sun, brimming with life and possibility. But the fanaticism of the hijackers turned that morning dark and toxic. The answer isn't to get rid of religion—that would be impossible, because worship is to the human spirit what oxygen is to the lungs. No, the answer is to take back the glory of that morning through transformed faith—faith that is a force for love and justice, goodness and peace. Religion is like rain. When its water is pure, it irrigates the earth and makes it teem with life. When the rain is polluted with ignorance, fear, and hatred, it brings death and disease."

More cheering broke out. "We need this message."

"How can we keep our religion pure?"

"Pure religion has love at its center. Only love can deliver us from terrorism and heartbreak, guilt and shame. I'm not talking about a feeling that comes and goes on a whim but an unshakable relationship with the source of love, which is God.

"When we're grounded in this relationship, it heals our lives. We get honest about our shortcomings and pour ourselves out for others. We focus less on the things of this world like fame and fortune, youth and beauty, and more on preparing our souls for eternity. Love is the truth that sets us free. When we live this truth, we think critically about our faith and engage others in dialogue because we're no longer afraid. Perfect love casts out fear, and when fear is banished, it takes ignorance with it. People who are being transformed by love create a critical mass of community that no hostility can penetrate or evil destroy. This is the way to end injustice, vengeance, and the suffering caused by strife. This is the way to maximize our creativity and unleash the unrealized potential of our humanity."

The crowd on the infield began to clap. The applause spread as the masses embraced one another with tears streaming down their cheeks. Justin allowed the power of their response to ripple through him. He held the staff higher.

"Surrender your hearts completely to love. Begin by believing in a personal God and trusting that we're not here by accident. We've been given our unique bodies and minds for a purpose. We only fulfill our destiny by recognizing how powerless we are over our flawed human nature. When we're at our worst, when we fail most miserably, we discover the miracle of God's grace. Then we find strength and wisdom greater than our own. This is the way to end our violence and attain the fulfillment we crave. This is the way to take back the morning of hope from every night of despair."

"Could this be for real?" someone shouted. "Could he actually be holding the staff of Moses?"

Justin waved the staff dramatically. "Absolutely. And Moses is a revered figure in Judaism, Christianity, and Islam. He's a hero for the ages, but he didn't make it to the promised land. He only glimpsed it from Mount Nebo before he died."

Justin raised the staff with both hands and shook it. "We can finish the journey! Moses used this staff to liberate his people from slavery. The staff can lead us to the promised land of spiritual freedom today. The freedom to act as compassionately toward ourselves as God does. The freedom to treat ourselves as we want others to treat us—with respect, understanding, and forgiveness.

"Problems begin when we lose our inner connection to love. We feel inadequate, alienated, angry. We get depressed. We become susceptible to all kinds of addictions and many other violent and destructive behaviors. It doesn't have to be this way! We're spiritual beings created in God's image. A limitless supply of love is available to us, but we have to learn to draw on it and stay connected to it when our dignity or our welfare comes under attack. Learning this skill breaks down the most insurmountable barriers. In the affirmation and security of God's love, we find the peace and joy we've always craved. We'll love even our enemies, including the inner ones that make us suffer most.

"This process is perfected in eternity, but it begins on earth. All our experiences, even the most painful ones, are part of our evolution. Don't lose heart in the face of your worst blunders and defeats! See them as part of your spiritual awakening. Rather than being ashamed of failures and imperfections, give thanks for them. God uses our suffering to accomplish more good than we could possibly imagine."

The crowd began to rush the stage. More applause and cheers broke out. Candace was leaving through the back. He tried to stop her with the power of the staff, but the applause drowned him out. She disappeared down the stairs. He turned back to the crowd and held the staff vertically in front of him.

"When we carry our wounds with dignity and use them to heal others, we grow closer to God and to the mystery of our own lives. I ruined my life, but I found Jesus in hell. More accurately, he found me. Rather than let me suffer forever, he gave me a second chance. I stand before you today to offer you the same forgiveness, healing, and freedom Jesus offered me. You can begin your journey of transformation here and now. Through you, the world will find new hope for peace!"

He waved the staff from side to side. The applause quieted into reverent silence. People all over the stadium wept and hugged one another. Many faces shone with brilliant radiance. The light reflected back and nearly blinded him. It was time to stop; he'd spoken his message and told his story as honestly as he could. The effect was out of his hands. The people would either discover transforming faith or not. He turned and headed out the back. A surging crowd met him at the stairs.

"Please, don't leave."

"We want to hear more!"

The rolling sea of humanity reminded him of the waves on Block Island Sound. This time he didn't think of being submerged or drowning but rather of swimming toward Sharon Jenkins and doing his best to save her. *This is the way to take back the morning of hope from every night of despair.* He'd tried something similar in the stadium. No matter how shamefully he'd failed in the past, he had begun to redeem himself.

He pushed through the crowd, gripping the staff with gratitude and joy, then fled the stadium.

48

THE GREATEST CHALLENGE

The frantic knocking on the door of Justin's room at the Salisbury Hotel jolted him awake. He glanced at the clock: 12:38 A.M. Who could have found him here? Only Tori and Paul knew where he was staying. He'd checked his voice mail in the taxi and heard Tori's messages, but his shame over the locket had prevented him from calling her back.

He threw off the covers and stepped into his jeans. The knocking turned into a feverish pounding. "Justin, it's Paul. We need to talk!"

He checked the peephole and hesitated. The tension between him and his former best friend sickened him. He didn't want to face it, but Paul sounded desperate. His hair was disheveled, his face contorted.

Justin opened the door.

Paul burst into the room. "Tori's missing. I need your help."

"What!" The doorknob turned cold in his hand. "For how long?"

"A couple hours."

"Where did you last see her?"

"I dropped her at Shea—"

"Shea Stadium?" He closed the door as his head pounded. "I was there too."

"I know. I heard you on the radio. I'm still stunned by how the crowd responded."

"Where were you?"

"I waited on the street in the Mustang. Tori had Amanda's backstage pass. She planned to confront Candace in her dressing room and snatch the pendant." Paul jabbed the air with a fist. "Rathbun must've abducted her. We've got to find her . . . and take guns with us."

"Where could we get them at this hour?"

"Legally? Nowhere. But Rathbun will have one."

"We don't have time to worry about that. We have to call the cops." Justin withdrew the staff from the closet. "At least we have this."

Paul threw up his hands. "I heard your claim about the staff of Moses. Even if what you said is true, how can the staff help us find Tori?"

"It probably can't, but I've got to keep it with me. This staff's going to make a big impact on the world." He pulled on his shoes and shirt, grabbed his wallet and phone, and led Paul out the door. "I'm calling 911."

When his phone powered up, a new message stopped him cold. The voice mail was from Rathbun. Justin put the phone on speaker so Paul could hear.

"We have Tori on Candace's yacht off North Cove. I left the dinghy at the dock for you. Come alone, only in the dinghy, and bring the staff. No cops, no guns. Come by 3 A.M. or Tori dies."

Justin raced down the hall. His vision blurred with rage and fear as his mind flashed gruesome images of Tori being tortured or killed. The entire situation was his fault. He deserved to suffer; she didn't. Paul caught up at the elevator. On the way down, he told Justin the only way he believed they could rescue Tori and keep the staff.

∽

Paul parked the Mustang at North Cove and told Justin he would meet him at the dinghy after he made a phone call. He dialed Linda's number and got her voice mail. No wonder, he thought; it's the middle of the night. He glanced at the Hudson and felt as if the hovering fog was engulfing him. He opened the door and reached beneath the seat to hide the phone.

It vibrated.

He answered and heard Linda's groggy voice. "Paul, what's going on? Did you just call me?"

Paul saw a light in the fog. "I wanted to set up our date for ice cream."

"At one-thirty in the morning?"

"I might not get another chance."

"Not if you don't tell me what's going on, you won't."

"I'm with Justin. There's a problem. It could be dangerous."

"Can't you let him handle it himself?"

"No. There's too much at stake."

She fell silent. "Is this about his performance at Shea Stadium? I saw him on TV."

"I'll explain later. Now, regarding our date . . . I want to talk to you about that business deal you've been working on."

She gave a laugh. "About selling my salons?"

"No, about putting a couple of lawyers out of business."

"Are you saying . . ."

Paul's chest ached from his heart thumping so hard. "I'm saying that if I make it back, the lawyers who've been working on our divorce are out of their jobs."

"*If* you make it? Paul, tell me—"

"That's all I can say right now." His voice grew hoarse. "I just want you to know that I'm done with lawyers for good. There's nothing standing between you and me getting back together." He willed himself not to let his voice break. "I love you, okay? I gotta go."

He hung up and rushed to meet Justin on the dock.

Tori felt like an alien in her own body. Her stomach roiled, her head throbbed, her muscles ached. She saw only darkness. She tried to scream, but her mouth had been taped shut. She wanted to move her arms, but they had been tied behind her back.

Where am I? What happened? She thrashed and rolled on some kind of mattress until she maneuvered herself upright against a couple of pillows. The darkness was impenetrable, as if she were locked in a cellar at night.

Then she remembered the confrontation outside Candace's dressing room, Rathbun's attack, the pinch of the needle. A cold shiver crept down her spine. Rathbun had drugged her.

She was being held in some seedy location. What would he do to her next?

She dragged her legs over the side of the bed and sat up. She needed a moment to stop her head from spinning. She stood and began to walk. Her bare feet stumbled across a thinly carpeted floor. What appeared to be an open door lay in front of her. Her heart surged. She entered a small room with a tile floor. Her hands explored behind her . . . a countertop . . . drawers . . . towels . . . a roll of toilet paper. A bathroom? She brushed against one wall and pushed up on a switch. A light and a fan came on. She stared into a cabin-like bedroom with rich wood paneling and a surveillance camera rotating on the ceiling. She ran to the bedroom door and shook the knob.

Locked.

She tried to flee into the bathroom.

It was too late.

The bedroom door burst open. Rathbun lunged and wrapped his arms around her. He wrestled her outside then down to the lowest level at the stern of the yacht and held her at the rail.

A full moon hung low over the misty Hudson as Justin motored out to the yacht in the pontoon-style dinghy. The last time he'd been on Candace's yacht, he'd tried to undermine her credibility with Manhattan's investment bankers and only narrowly escaped. Tonight his pulse sounded louder in his ears than the smack of the dinghy's bow against the water.

He steeled himself for a confrontation with Rathbun while hoping this matter was too sensitive to involve hired guards. Without a weapon, Justin was at a disadvantage, but he and Paul had formulated a plan. The staff was his bargaining chip. He also had Paul's skill as a swimmer and fighter . . . if he could survive while clinging to the dinghy's pontoon.

But Rathbun and Candace had Tori.

Justin would refuse to turn over the staff until they released her . . . and he would stall for time.

As he approached the yacht, he saw Rathbun holding Tori at the rail of the swim deck. Candace wasn't there, nor were the guards.

"Throw me the staff, Connelly!" He gestured with a handgun then pointed the barrel at Tori's temple.

Justin pulled the dinghy next to the yacht. "Not until you let her go."

Rage burned in his eyes. "All right, come on board. We'll make it an even exchange."

"Not until you remove the tape from her mouth."

"Why?"

"I want to hear her voice."

∼

Tori sensed Justin was stalling for time, but she wondered what staff Rathbun was talking about. When he took the tape off her mouth, she tried to break free. He jammed her against the rail and tightened his grip.

"He's serious, Justin!" She kept struggling. "Just do as he says . . . please."

Justin was jostling the line of the dinghy and having trouble tying it up. "You're going to be all right. Your hosts wouldn't harm one of their guests."

Rathbun dug his fingernails into the back of her neck. "Tell him to cooperate."

His breath was hot against her cheek. She felt nauseated but tightened her gut and fought to stay on her feet. Justin needed more time.

She heard footsteps. When she turned, her chest convulsed. Candace had come onto the deck . . .

And was holding baby Justin.

Tori screamed and flailed mightily but couldn't break Rathbun's grip. The baby began to cry.

"Now are you ready to give up the staff, Connelly?" Rathbun's voice oozed sarcasm.

The staff? What was he talking about? Justin continued to fumble with the rope. A walking stick of some kind was in his hand.

He caught her eye and gave a cryptic nod. "From the pendant," he whispered.

The comment shocked her. Then she remembered her research on the staff of Moses and felt her jaw drop. Could the pendant have become—

A thud sounded behind her and the deck shook. Rathbun tensed. She turned and squinted into the dark. A man had leaped down from the back stairs.

Paul!

He flew at Rathbun and knocked Tori free. She reeled back as Rathbun hit the rail, his face dark with surprise and fury.

Paul drove a fist into Rathbun's gut and reached for the gun. His legs and arms felt numb from the cold water; his fingers had been chafed bloody from holding on to the rope on the pontoon. But he gripped Rathbun's wrist. They fought for the gun, its barrel hoisted high.

A shot shattered the early morning quiet. The gun recoiled. Rathbun kneed Paul in the groin. His breath went out of him as a dagger-like pain shot through his abdomen. Rathbun hooked a foot around his ankle, and Paul fell backward. If he let go of the gun, he would be shot . . . as would Tori and Justin. He held on . . . tightening his grip . . . trying to twist the barrel free.

Rathbun drove him into the deck.

Paul's head slammed against the fiberglass. Flashes of light and grinding pain ripped through his skull. Rathbun jolted him with a knee. The last breath of air went out of his lungs.

Out of the corner of his eye, he saw Tori struggling with Candace for the baby. He was growing woozy, faint. His grip loosened. His last chance to gain the advantage was slipping away. He tightened his gut, levered himself against the deck, lurched upward . . .

And unleashed a desperate head butt.

He connected with Rathbun's nose. Watery liquid fell on his face. Blinded, he rolled right and tried to throw him off while hanging on to the gun. He only needed seconds; Justin was coming to help. He pulled one way, Rathbun the other. The gun left his fingers and skittered across the deck. Paul felt the crack of a fist against his jaw.

Everything went black.

∼

Justin catapulted onto the deck still holding the staff. He was aghast to see that Candace had his son. His instinct was to help Tori, but Rathbun was brutalizing Paul. He had to help him first. Rathbun abandoned the stricken Paul and lunged.

Justin caught a shoulder in the gut. He toppled backward, and his shoulder blades scraped against the deck, sending shards of pain across his back.

Rathbun pounced and went for the staff. Justin held on, but Rathbun forced the staff against his throat to choke him. Greater and greater pressure bore down. Justin felt as if his face were on fire and his skull ready to shatter. He couldn't breathe. He was desperate for air and retched.

"Drown in your own blood." Rathbun's voice dripped with hatred.

With his peripheral vision, Justin saw Tori fighting with Candace for the screaming baby. In desperation he released the staff with one hand and punched at Rathbun's face. The blow landed on his cheek but failed to slow him. Rathbun pulled the staff away and swung it at him. Justin parried and grabbed one end. Rathbun tried to wrench the staff loose, heaving and gasping. "You're done, Connelly."

Justin scrambled up and thrust with the staff as if it were a sword. The move surprised Rathbun and shook him loose.

Paul staggered to his feet and charged.

Rathbun dodged and hurtled over a jet ski. Justin joined the chase with the staff in hand.

Rathbun snatched up the gun and aimed at Paul.

Justin threw himself in front of him. "No!"

Rathbun fired.

The bullet hit Justin's shoulder and spun him sideways in a torrent of agony. He landed on his back but held on to the staff. In the chaos, Tori caught Candace off guard and wrestled the baby free. Rathbun still had the gun, but Paul was fighting him for it. Candace bolted toward them and tried to pull Paul off.

Justin gripped the staff. He raised his good arm, waved the staff over the Hudson, and prayed for deliverance.

An enormous wave rose up and hurled the dinghy over the stern.

The dinghy crushed Rathbun and Candace against the deck.

Paul was knocked free.

Everyone was swept overboard.

Tori clung to her son and descended into the cold, murky depths. She kicked and sculled with her free arm, swallowing water, engulfed in darkness. She needed air . . . couldn't get any . . . kept kicking . . . started to pass out.

Her head finally broke the surface. The baby wailed. She swallowed more water then spit and coughed. She wiped her eyes and glimpsed the dinghy. She scissor-kicked toward it while holding the baby out of the water. Finally she seized the rope that hung horizontally on the pontoon. She gasped and supported the baby with her other hand. The Hudson was silent under a brilliant moon.

"Paul! Justin!"

Her cries went unanswered. Then the backs of two heads broke the surface a short distance away. She braced herself to flee if the heads belonged to Rathbun and Candace.

One of them turned.

She recognized Paul and said a silent prayer of thanks.

He sculled toward her on his back using a lifeguard's carry to bring the other survivor.

She kept her gaze trained on him. "Are you all right?"

"I'll survive." He spoke through staccato breaths.

"What about him?"

"I'm not sure."

Tori could see the back of a man's head but couldn't tell if it belonged to Rathbun or Justin. The darkness closed in on her. When Paul drew closer, she saw blood in the water. The man in Paul's embrace was holding his shoulder.

Justin.

The darkness receded.

"I'll be all right too." Justin pulled away from Paul and eyed Tori. He raised the staff out of the water and grabbed the rope with the same hand. "If you'll forgive me and let me come home."

Tori pondered the request as Paul climbed on board. The anguish caused by Justin's treachery rose in her chest. It was more threatening to her heart than the water was to her body. At some level, that danger would be with her always, threatening to drown her future in hurt and blame.

But the messages he'd spoken under the power of the pendant came back to her along with the story of his life. His treacheries didn't define all of who he was. It was unfair to judge him only by those acts. After his near-death experience in hell, he'd grown into a very different man. He was dedicated to helping others experience a similar transformation. In the end, his heroism had saved them all. How could she not forgive him?

Paul hauled Justin into the dinghy then reached down for the baby. He handed Justin his son and pulled her in. They sprawled in the dinghy, wiping away water and heaving to catch their breath. She found Justin's eyes. "Yes . . . yes, I forgive you . . . but . . . we can't be a family."

He held his wounded shoulder with a vulnerable expression on his face. "Do you think we ever could?"

"I can't answer that right now." She took the baby. "I need time to heal, to listen to my heart and hear what it asks of me. But one thing I know . . . I'm strong enough to make it on my own if I have to."

She turned toward Paul. "What about you, my friend?"

He wrapped one arm around her. "I'm strong enough too, but thanks to Justin's challenges, I'm excited about building a new kind of marriage with Linda and giving my best to my daughter."

∽

Justin's throat constricted. He glanced across the water to study Manhattan's glimmering lights. His eyes found the empty space where the towers of the World Trade Center had stood. He pondered the experiences he'd had since the day the towers had fallen—running away to Providence, nearly drowning, going to hell, coming back.

The cold water grew warm. Each experience had involved powerful suffering . . . and even more powerful grace. Now he understood why this greatest of gifts was called amazing. He had more to give the world than ever before. His most important work lay ahead of him, not behind.

His gaze fell on the staff.

He picked it up and held it over Tori's head and then Paul's. Peace flooded him with the force of the rogue wave. "May we walk the path of love wherever it leads. May we take back the morning of hope from every night of despair."

Questions for Group Study & Personal Reflection

1 Justin Connelly is knocked unconscious in a sailing accident and, while in a coma, taken to the depths of hell itself. Do near-death experiences provide reliable information about the afterlife? Read I Peter 3:18–22 and reflect on Justin's encounter with Jesus Christ in hell. How does his encounter relate to this passage of scripture and to the statement in the Apostles' Creed that Jesus "descended into hell"?

2 The terrorist attacks on September 11th, the suffering Justin brings on himself and others, and the horror he endures while he is in his coma are all examples of the experience of hell. How do these examples either support or challenge your ideas about whether hell exists and/or what it might be like?

3 The title of the novel is a reference to September 11th, 2001. The day began with blue skies and brilliant sunshine in the East, but the terrorist attacks turned the morning dark and filled it with suffering. How does the "take back the morning" theme apply to Justin Connelly? To other characters? To the Seven Challenges of a Transformed Life? (See Genesis 1:1–5; John 1:1–5; 8:12).

4 The complications of romantic love is a major theme in the novel. Discuss the ways in which you empathize with and/or question the romantic choices that Justin, Tori, and Paul make. How might the predicaments faced by the men and women of the Bible inform this discussion? (See Genesis 21:1–21; 29:1–30; 2 Samuel 11:1–27; Matthew 1:18–25; 2:13–15).

5 Justin, Tori, and Paul each suffer heartbreak in their intimate relationships. How do they find healing and reconciliation, and what can we learn from their individual stories? (See 2 Corinthians 5:17–21).

6 Candace Donahue and Quentin Rathbun are entangled in an intricate web of deception, greed, and lust for power. What do their stories reveal about the problem of evil and how the problem plays out in everyday life? Are Candace and Quentin evil to the core or are they in any way sympathetic characters? (See Genesis 3–6; Matthew 4:1–11).

7 Reflect on the role of the pendant in the novel. In what ways does it drive the plot? If such an artifact were actually discovered today, do you think it would create a scenario similar to the one dramatized in the novel, or would you envision a different scenario? (See

Exodus 4:1–20; 7:6–24; 8:5–19; 9:22–26; 10:13–15; 14:15–22; 17:1–7).

8 When Justin encounters Reverend Robert Sherman in St. Paul's Chapel, he asks the priest, "Do you believe that a person can ever be so bad that God stops loving him?" Do you agree or disagree with Reverend Sherman's answer? Is Justin redeemed by the end of the novel? If not, why? If so, does he still have to suffer the consequences of his actions? (See Ephesians 1:3–10; Colossians 1:9–14; Hebrews 9:11–15).

9 Corporate greed, religious fanaticism, and cultural decadence are among the contemporary problems addressed in the novel. Is the spiritual vision it presents capable of solving these problems? Why or why not? (See Mark 3:20–30; Ephesians 6:10–20).

10 As Justin speaks under the power of the pendant, he reveals the Seven Challenges of a Transformed Life. Discuss each challenge and the scriptures that support it.

1. Accepted Acceptance: Luke 15:11–31; Matthew 20:1–16; Romans 5:1–11

2. Healed Emotions: John 4:1–30; Luke 5:27–32; Luke 7:36–50

3. Awakened Intimacy: Mark 12:28–34; Matthew 5:43–48; John 13:34–35

4. Reimagined Abundance: John 10:7–10; 2 Corinthians 9:8–9; Ephesians 3:14–21; Philippians 4:19

5. Liberated Service: Mark 10:35–45; Luke 22:24–27; Philippians 2:1–11

6. Inspired Creativity: Acts 2:1–47; I Corinthians 12:1–11; Ephesians 5:15–21

7. Transformed Faith: James 1:19–26; James 3:13–18; Romans 12:1–21

Acknowledgments

I am grateful beyond words to everyone whose encouragement, support, and professional guidance made the publication of this novel possible:

To my wife, Carol, and sons, Evanjohn and Peter, for your love, patience, and longsuffering spirit in enduring the stresses and annoyances of having a writer for a husband and a father.

To the best of all literary agents, Robert Gottlieb, chairman of Trident Media Group, for affirming the potential of this project and working with me to refine the manuscript; and to everyone at Trident who had a hand in this process, and especially to the eBook Operations Team for preparing the digital version.

To Paul Sanderson, exceptional spiritual mentor, for continuing to walk this journey with me and for contributing many stellar insights on the mountaintops, in the valleys, and at every bend in the road.

To Peter Gelfan, extraordinary editor and partner in the creative process, without whom this novel could not have been written. Thank you so much for taking all of my spontaneous phone calls, answering every e-mail, and persevering with me through the demanding days and sometimes exhausting nights of spirited consultation and rigorous critique.

To Lou Quetel, friend for the ages, for all of those inspiring, informative, and hilarious conversations, and for undying support and companionship every step of the way.

To David Howard, Jan Molinari, Victor Wildman, and Kathleen Tremblay, writing group partners, for reading many sections and offering suggestions that significantly improved the story. You are each outstanding writers, and I feel blessed to have benefited from your artistic expertise and even more so from your friendship.

To Marjorie Hanlon, insightful editor in the early stages; Laine Cunningham, transformative editor in the later stages; Amy Knupp, skillful copyeditor; and Beth Jusino, flap copy critique partner. Many, many thanks for greatly improving this novel at every stage of its development.

To Dave Burnham, master sailor and soulful friend, for teaching me so much about boats and even more about life and faith.

To Anne Burns, spiritual guide and reflective listener, for wisdom, understanding, prayers, and friendship.

To the people of the Community Church of Providence, wonderfully supportive congregation.

To attorney Eric Rayman for friendship and wise counsel.

To Vinny Plover, FDNY, for an informative tour of Staten Island and many helpful insights into the life of a firefighter; and to his sister Jean, wonderful supporter and friend.

To Kate Perry for her interest in the book and her enthusiasm and hard work as church secretary.

To Craig Bartow, Prosecutor, Warren County, NJ; and Sal Monteiro, Institute for the Study and Practice of Nonviolence, Providence, RI, for sharing your knowledge of the law and of the youth culture with me.

I owe all of you a profound debt of gratitude!

About the Author

Evan Howard writes novels of suspense that engage the heart and challenge the mind. He is the author of *The Galilean Secret* and the pastor of the Community Church of Providence, Rhode Island. He and his wife, Carol, have two young adult sons.

Share the Message

Please consider helping others to "take back the morning" by doing one or more of the following:

- Give the book as a gift to your family members, friends, coworkers, or others whom you believe would benefit from reading it. Discounts are available for the purchase of five or more copies.

- Involve your congregation in the "Read Across the Church Project." Contact the author for more information.

- Lead a book group that reads and discusses the novel or suggest it to such a group.

- Use the novel in a Bible Study group as a creative way to engage issues of life and faith. Questions for Group Study and Personal Reflection can be found at the end of the book.

- Invite the author to discuss the book with your group.

- Purchase a set of books to distribute at prisons, nursing homes, shelters, community centers, and the like. Bulk discounts are available.

- Write a positive review on Goodreads.com or Amazon.com.

- Write a Blog post about the book or mention it in other forums on the Internet such as Facebook.

- If you own a business, make the book available to your customers. Discounts are available for this purpose.

For more information or to order books:
www.wilcoxpublishinggroup.com
www.evanhowardauthor.com

CPSIA information can be obtained at www.ICGtesting.com
Printed in the USA
BVOW03s2026070514

352839BV00001B/70/P